The Greysons

Book 3 in the AMI Series
A Contemporary Romance Novel

Published by:
Southern Yellow Pine (SYP) Publishing
4351 Natural Bridge Rd.
Tallahassee, FL 32305

www.syppublishing.com

This is a work of fiction. Names, characters, places, and events that occur either are the products of the author's imagination or are used fictitiously. Any resemblance to actual persons, places, or events is purely coincidental.

The contents and opinions expressed in this book do not necessarily reflect the views and opinions of Southern Yellow Pine Publishing, nor does the mention of brands or trade names constitute endorsement.

ISBN-13: 978-1-59616-091-0
ISBN-10: 1-59616-091-8

Printed in the United States of America
First Edition
March 2019

Dedication

To Bob

The love of my life and the best friend I've ever had. Wherever you are is home.

The Greysons

Dana L. Brown

Books by Dana L. Brown

The AMI Series

Lottie Loser
Call Me Charlotte
The Greysons

Prologue

The Greysons

Nick helped me into the backseat of the cab without uttering a word. Once he was seated and buckled in, he gave the driver the go ahead, and we were on our way to his mother and stepfather's Park Avenue apartment. Before we left the airport, I could see that his eyes had turned stormy and dark, a sure sign that he was hurting but trying to hide it. I reached over and took his hand, and thankfully he didn't pull away, but his face was still turned toward the window.

"Nick," I said softly, "please look at me." I waited a moment for him to respond before gently rubbing my thumb over his fingers. He didn't look at me but did squeeze my hand. That little gesture helped me to breathe again, at least for the moment.

My name is Charlotte Luce and just four days ago the beautiful man sitting next to me, the one with his nose almost pressed against the glass, asked me to marry him. This whole summer has been one issue after another, but I really thought that it was all behind us now and that Nick and I could finally be happy. And did I mention that I'm pregnant? That's just one part of the drama I fondly call The Nick and Charlotte Show.

Nick finally turned his head and looked at me, and I could see the hurt and regret written all over his face. I thought my heart would break then, but it really shattered when he started to speak.

"He's still in love with you, you know," Nick said quietly.

I grabbed my locket and said another silent prayer to Gran. The way this day was going I was definitely in need of her help.

Chapter 1

Now

It's hard enough meeting your future mother-in-law for the first time, but the pressure of coming face-to-face with the man you gave your virginity to, and whose heart you had captured, on the same day that your new fiancé was taking you to meet his mom, well, hard doesn't even begin to describe it.

It's not like running into Ryan was planned, Charlotte thought. Of course, she knew he lived in New York City, but so did about nine million other people. Why would she expect to run into him at the airport of all places?

The dark spheres of Nick's eyes were more blue now than black, and Charlotte was still a little shaky over how he had reacted when he realized who the other man calling out her name in the airport was. Ryan had been very polite, even congratulating them on their engagement, but Nick's G-Man persona had shown through, and she was sure Ryan had noticed it.

Exiting the cab, Nick took Charlotte's hand and led her to the sidewalk outside of his mother's very grand, Park Avenue apartment. Needing a moment to get his emotions under control before facing the mom he had never known very well, Nick pulled Charlotte close to him.

"I'm sorry if I embarrassed you in front of your ex-boyfriend, and I'm sorry if I made you feel like running in to him was somehow your fault," Nick told her honestly, "but there's always going to be a piece of you that he has, and that's killing me."

"I thought we'd been through this," Charlotte replied. "What happened at the Senior Sendoff was a terrible mistake on both of our parts, and yes, it shaped the decisions we made, but Nick, it's you I love, and Ryan knows that."

Running her hand over his strong chest, Charlotte could feel the tension leaving Nick's body as he started to relax. "I know that Charlotte, I really do, but seeing Ryan up close and personal, in his expensive suit and shoes, and knowing the kind of life you could have had with him made it all too real. That and knowing I'm about to see my wheelchair-bound mother just took its toll, I guess. Forgive me?"

"There's nothing to forgive," she told him with a smile, "but I understand because I'm nervous about meeting your Mom, too." Then with a flip of her hair she added, "And when did you become an expert on men's fashion? I'm pretty impressed that a Florida boy like you would recognize a tailored designer suit."

Nick gave her a huge smile and a swat on her backside before leading her into the foyer of the apartment building. "I'm still officially an Agent in the FBI," he whispered in her ear. "You don't want to meet my Mom in handcuffs, do you?"

Charlotte's eyes got big as saucers, and she demurely shook her head. Life with Nick Greyson would never be dull, but that's exactly what she'd been waiting for.

Chapter 2
Now

Nick had been just ten years old when his mom had shipped her three children back to their father at Anna Maria Island, saying that her new husband wanted to travel, and they couldn't do that with school-age children. The truth of the matter was that she had been diagnosed with scleroderma not too long after leaving her husband and moving back to her home in New York, and her pride kept her from sharing her illness with her ex-husband. That and the fact that she was still in love with him.

Nick let out the huge breath he'd been holding and looked up at the beautiful apartment building standing before them. "I'll say this for my mom," he told Charlotte, "she always married up, way up."

The doorman allowed them access to the lobby, but that was as far as they could go without clearance. "Nick Greyson here to see Elizabeth Harris," he told the gentleman at the desk. Before a call was even made to the Harris apartment, both Nick and Charlotte had to show the man their IDs.

"Agent Greyson, your mother is expecting you. Please go right up," the concierge told them. "The elevator across from this desk will take you directly to the penthouse, and I'll have your bags brought right up."

Charlotte looked at Nick and mouthed "penthouse?" Nick thanked the concierge, and with Charlotte by his side, stepped into the elevator.

"Are you doing okay?" Charlotte asked him. "You look a little pale."

Nick shook his head as he answered. "I knew that Mom's husband Gus worked for the Governor of New York, but I had no idea they lived like this. Makes our home in the marina look like a dump, doesn't it?"

"Don't you ever talk about the marina like that again, Nick Greyson," Charlotte scolded. "Your home and our memories there are worth more than all of the luxury apartments in Manhattan, and I wouldn't trade them for anything."

Nick kissed her hand and smiled. "You're right, Charlotte," he said, "but all this glamour makes it easy to understand why my mom loves it here."

Just then the elevator stopped, and the door opened. Charlotte had been expecting a hallway and a door, but the elevator opened right into the foyer of the apartment, and there sat Nick's mom, in a wheelchair, her face soft and beautiful, her body completely covered by a caftan.

"Nicky!" she cried, as Nick leaned down to kiss her. "I'm so happy to have you here." Before Nick could get in a word, Elizabeth Harris reached for Charlotte's hand.

"And Charlotte," she said, "it's a pleasure to finally meet the girl who captured my Nicky's heart."

"Mrs. Harris," Charlotte said, reaching out to touch Nick's mother's hand, "it's lovely to meet you as well."

Elizabeth took hold of one of Nick's hands and one of Charlotte's hands and replied, "Having the two of you here is a dream come true, and I'm Elizabeth, not Mrs. Harris. We're going to be family, Charlotte, and I'm excited to finally be getting a daughter-in-law."

At that moment Gus Harris came into the room, and after handshakes and introductions, Charlotte took a minute to really appraise Nick's mom and her husband. Elizabeth looked like an older version of Nick's sister Maya, and she was still a beautiful woman. Her face was smooth and didn't seem to have been affected by her scleroderma, but the stiffness with which she moved let Charlotte know that her body had not been as fortunate.

Gus Harris was not at all what Charlotte would have pictured as a husband for Nick's mother. She knew that Elizabeth had been a model when she and Nick's dad met, and she had been closer to her own height

4

of five-ten. In the pictures Charlotte had seen of Pop in his youth, he had been a replica of Nick, tall, dark, and handsome, nothing like the short, portly Gus Harris standing before her. It wasn't that being shorter than Elizabeth was such a big deal. But when Gus looked at his wife, Charlotte could see the love in his eyes, and when he softly kissed her cheek, she saw Gus in a totally different light. He may not have looked like Adonis, but Elizabeth was his Aphrodite, and he was willing to do everything in his power to care for and protect her.

They had been so intent on introductions that both Nick and Charlotte had forgotten about their bags until the elevator door opened and a uniformed deliveryman asked where they should go. Nick was just about ready to answer when his mom spoke-up.

"Just leave them right there, Randall," she said. "I'll have Stuart take them to the guest room."

"Mom we have reservations at a hotel," Nick told her. "We couldn't check in until three o'clock, so if the bags aren't in your way, they can stay right there."

"Nonsense, Nicky," Elizabeth said. "I've hardly seen you in the last ten years, and I want you here with us. You understand Charlotte, don't you?"

Charlotte did not want to get in the middle of a disagreement between Nick and his mom. She could see the way Nick had his jaw set, but she could also see the hope in Elizabeth's eyes, which meant if she took sides someone was going to be unhappy. Looking at Gus for help, she finally decided to take matters into her own hands.

"Gus," Charlotte said sweetly, "I would love a tour of the apartment, if you're up to showing it to me." Relieved to also be out of the disagreement, Gus graciously agreed.

Chapter 3
Now

The Harris' apartment was spectacular, with floor to ceiling windows in every room and décor that Charlotte could only dream about. There were four guestrooms, each complete with their own ensuite bathroom, a master suite, and a powder room. A dining room, den, office for Gus, plus a chef's kitchen rounded out the tour, and Gus was just about to take Charlotte back to the formal living room when his phone rang.

"I need to take this, Charlotte," Gus explained. "Can you find your way back?"

Charlotte nodded and was about to enter the massive living room when she heard Nick still arguing with his mother.

"I understand, Mom, I really do, but Charlotte's a very private person, and she wouldn't be comfortable sharing a room with me in your home," Nick said forcefully.

"But I haven't seen you in so long," Elizabeth responded.

Charlotte took that moment to enter the room and, looking directly at Nick, said, "I think I would like to stay here, Nick. There are plenty of guestrooms, and if your mom doesn't mind, we can each have our own."

She didn't know if the look Nick was giving her said he wanted to kiss her or kill her, but he finally relented. "I guess I'm out numbered," he grumbled, "so yes, Mother, we'd love to stay here with you and Gus."

Elizabeth clapped her hands like a little girl and smiled up at them both when Charlotte added, "We can wake up looking at Central Park, Nick. Won't that be wonderful?"

Nick put a smile on his face, but Charlotte could tell it wasn't genuine. She could also read the look in his eyes that said, "It might be wonderful to wake up looking at Central Park, but you won't be in my bed or my arms, and there's nothing wonderful about that."

Looking away Charlotte addressed Elizabeth. "It was an early morning, so if you can tell me which room mine will be, I'd like to freshen up."

Nick growled but allowed his mother to show them to their perspective rooms. Charlotte gave him a sweet kiss on the cheek as she looked over the gorgeous bed where she would be sleeping. She would have loved for Nick to join here there, but not with his mother and stepfather just down the hall.

Stuart, the Harris' live-in helper, arranged Charlotte's bags in the walk-in closet and shut the door behind him. She was just about to take her toiletries to the attached bathroom when her cell phone rang. Seeing that it wasn't a number she recognized, she almost didn't answer, but at the last minute changed her mind.

"Hello," she said tentatively into the phone.

"Please don't be mad at Becca, Charlotte, but I just had to talk to you." Charlotte held her breath knowing that the only person who could have gotten her cell phone number from Becca was Ryan.

"Ryan," she began, "is something wrong?" Charlotte couldn't think of any other reason Ryan Noble would be calling unless there was an issue with Jared or the kids, and Becca asked him to call.

"Hell yes, something's wrong," Ryan said very emotionally. "When I saw you today, I knew I couldn't just let you walk out of my life again without at least trying to win you back. I love you, Charlotte. I still love you, and I can't stand the thought of you marrying another man."

Charlotte was dumbstruck and for a moment couldn't breathe, or even think of what to say. Finally, she opened her mouth and the words came out.

"Please don't say that, Ryan," she began. "You knew before I did that my heart belonged to someone else, and that someone is Nick. I don't want to hurt you again. I'm in love with Nick Greyson, and we're going to be married. You know that." Charlotte was tempted to tell him about her pregnancy but felt that might be rubbing salt in his wounds.

This time it was Ryan who held his breath, so Charlotte kept going. "You need to find a girl Ryan; someone who deserves the wonderful man that you are, but that girl isn't me."

Charlotte thought her heart would break in two when Ryan told her, "I have a girl, Charlotte, and actually we've been talking marriage, but when I saw you today it brought up all those unresolved feelings. Haven't you missed us at all?"

Charlotte sighed. "When you first left for New York I was scared and lonely, and I missed you terribly. Then Gran died and my whole world was turned upside down. But Ryan, once I moved back to the island and started my job with Olde Florida, I realized how I had allowed you and Gran to take care of me and that what I needed was to stand on my own two feet. You were a great friend to me, and I'll always cherish what we had, but I'm not the self-conscious young girl I was when you knew me."

Ryan laughed, but it was a harsh laugh, not a joyful one. "Friends, huh?" he asked her. "You thought of me as a friend? I guess that explains a lot."

"Stop it," Charlotte cried, "that isn't what I meant at all. You know I cared about you, and you were wonderful to me, but I couldn't love you the way you needed me to. Now you need to listen to me, Ryan Noble. Your girlfriend deserves a man who would walk through fire for her, one who is totally committed to their relationship, and if you're not, you need to tell her now. But don't make this about me. I let you walk away from me because we both knew I was never going to be who you wanted me to be, and now you need to decide if she's that woman or not."

Charlotte was shaking by the time she was finished, but Ryan must have listened, because by the time he replied his tone had softened. "You have grown-up, Charlotte," he told her, "and you're right about everything. I guess seeing you today just caught me off-guard, but I'm fine now. And, I do love Julie, but it seems I have a few things to work out before we think about walking down the aisle."

"Thank you, Ryan," Charlotte told him as she dried her eyes. "I want nothing for you but the best."

"I feel the same way," he answered, and then the line went dead.

Charlotte was trying to gain her composure when she heard a knock on her bedroom door as Nick asked if he could come in. *Shit! Shit! Shit!* she thought. How long had he been standing there? And what all did he hear?

Chapter 4

Now

Charlotte tried to dry her tears before telling Nick to come in, but the moment she looked at him they started all over again. Surprisingly, he opened his arms, and Charlotte melted into them, her tears falling freely on his shoulder.

"Ryan called," she told him meekly.

"I gathered that from what I heard. Are the tears for him, or for you?" Charlotte could hear the concern in his voice, and she knew she had to put it to rest.

"Maybe for him, but definitely not for me," she answered, a smile starting to form. "I have everything I've ever wanted right here."

Nick pulled her in tighter and only said two words, "Thank God."

From the dining room, they could hear Nick's mother calling that it was time for lunch They separated but held hands as they walked out of Charlotte's room. If Elizabeth or Gus could tell that she'd been crying, they didn't say a word.

Lunch was a magnificent feast of lobster salad, freshly baked rolls from the bakery down the street, and a fresh fruit compote for dessert. Charlotte was thankful to be past her morning sickness because lobster was a delicacy, and she wanted to enjoy every bite.

"Stuart will bring the car around and be ready whenever you want to leave," Gus said to Nick. "Your mother rests in the afternoon so take your time and enjoy the New York experience."

Charlotte looked at Nick for clarification. "Are we going somewhere?"

"As a matter of fact," he responded with a wink, "we're going shopping. Isn't a trip down Fifth Avenue one of the things you said you'd always wanted to do?"

Charlotte was giddy but trying to act like an adult. "I did say that, but I thought you would want to be here with your mom."

"That's so kind of you, Charlotte," Elizabeth chimed in. "But I'll sleep most of the afternoon. You and Nicky go out and enjoy yourselves, and we'll meet for cocktails around six." Her smile was so warm that Charlotte just nodded, excited about the shopping but sorry she couldn't have the cocktails.

Charlotte felt like a celebrity touring New York City in a limousine. All her adult life she had enjoyed high-end designer labels, but she had never been chauffeured around. Stuart showed them a few points of interest and then pulled-up in front of Tiffany & Co., the iconic jewelry store.

Charlotte was speechless as Stuart helped her out of the back of the limousine and gave Nick his cell phone number. "Call me when you're ready to leave, and I'll be back as quickly as possible."

"Do you know what you're doing taking me into Tiffany's?"she asked Nick. "Having one of those blue boxes has been on my bucket list since I was in college."

"Then a blue box you shall have, My Lady," Nick teased, bowing from his waist. Charlotte all but giggled as she reached up to kiss him smack on the lips.

"I like this New York persona of yours," she said as they walked into the store. "Maybe if I call you Nicky it will last."

And like that, G-man Nick was back. "Miss Luce," he said in the very controlled voice that both scared her and gave her chills, "My mother is the only person who has ever gotten away with calling me Nicky, and it's going to stay that way. Agreed?"

Charlotte saluted him, and then took his hand as they wandered together into a fantasy of diamonds and gold. Nick let her look around for a few minutes and then a tall, willowy brunette stepped up and shook his hand.

"Good afternoon Agent Greyson," the beauty said to Nick. "I'm Ella, and I'll be your personal shopper."

At first Charlotte thought the young woman was just flirting with a hot looking guy, but when she heard her call Nick, Agent Greyson, she was really confused. "You got a personal shopper, Nick?" Charlotte asked. "I doubt if what I buy to get my blue box is worthy of that."

Nick looked at the beautiful woman beside him, hardly seeing the very attractive personal shopper, and knew more than ever how thankful he was to have her back in his life. The summer had been a whirlwind, that's for sure, but he wanted this day to be just one more that Charlotte would never forget.

"We're here to buy our wedding rings, Charlotte," he told her. And as she started to open her mouth to protest, he kissed her. "Any questions?"

Holy crap! First, they had run into Ryan at the airport, and then he had called her! Nick just kissed her in Tiffany, and he wanted them to buy wedding rings? This day just kept getting crazier by the minute!

Chapter 5

Now

Charlotte looked at Nick, and then the personal shopper, trying to find the right words. She had told him she needed input on decisions that affected their life together, but hot damn! A wedding ring from Tiffany? And he had planned this on his own!

"I thought we were going to wait to talk about our wedding," Charlotte said guardedly. She didn't want to embarrass Nick, but she needed to make sure that he respected her feelings, too.

Nick smiled, and Charlotte was pretty sure she saw the personal shopper swoon, and when he looked Charlotte in the eye, she was pretty sure she did as well! "Well," he began, "I may be just a Florida boy, as you pointed out, but I do recognize the love of high-end design that you have, and what's more high-end than Tiffany? Besides, I thought if we actually bought our rings, it might entice you to set a wedding date."

The brunette standing next to them looked as if she was ready to do anything that Nick suggested, which made Charlotte batt her eyelashes and say to them both, "Well, I guess it can't hurt to look."

Looping her arm through Nick's, she allowed the personal shopper to lead them to a special area where couples could look at rings privately.

"Tell me what you're looking for," the brunette said to Nick, almost as if Charlotte wasn't present. "I'll bring in a selection based on that, and we can go from there."

"Something fancy," Nick told her, holding up Charlotte's left hand. "And something that will go well with her engagement ring."

"I think plain platinum bands for each of us would be perfect," Charlotte chimed in. "Don't you Nick?"

"For me yes, but for you, I want something special to show the world that you're mine."

Charlotte blushed, and the pretty brunette sighed. Obviously, the poor girl hadn't had a gorgeous FBI Agent as a client before!

"I love that you want to do that, Nick, I really do, but should we be spending that kind of money on a ring? You know, with everything else that's going on?" And by going on she meant her being fired, his recent brush with death, and him deciding to go back to school to become a teacher, and oh yes, the baby they were expecting.

"Charlotte," Nick said, running his hand through his thick, dark hair, "I didn't get to buy you an engagement ring, but I love that I was able to give you the ring of your gran's that you wanted. Please, let me do this for you, for us."

Reaching up to caress her locket, Charlotte spoke silently to her gran. *What did I ever do to deserve this man?* she thought. *And what can I do to show him how blessed I am to have him in my life?*

Charlotte smiled and nodded. "Bring 'em on!" she exclaimed, and then Nick kissed her again.

After looking over lots of bands, the personal shopper and her guard went back to the display case for more rings. All of the rings she had seen so far were beautiful but didn't grab Charlotte's heart. The shopper had just returned and opened a new box of rings when Nick spoke-up.

"That one," he said pointing to a platinum band with channel set diamonds encircling it.

Charlotte slipped the ring on her finger and then added the aquamarine ring that had been her gran's. "It's perfect, Nick," she said with tears in her eyes. "It's just as perfect as you've made this day."

Nick engulfed her in his arms, and for a moment they held on to each other. When they turned around the pretty brunette personal shopper had tears in her eyes too, but whether it was from the emotions in the room, making a sale, or realizing she didn't have a chance with Nick, Charlotte didn't know.

Charlotte held out her hand, admiring the ring, the sparkles in her eyes as bright as the diamonds on the band, and then looked directly at

Nick. "I want to get married now," she told him boldly. "I don't need to wait anymore."

Nick was dumbstruck! "You mean here in Tiffany?" he laughed. "I think there's a movie about that."

"I'm serious, Nick." Charlotte continued. I want to get married this week while we're in New York. Your mom has missed out on so much of your life, wouldn't this be a wonderful memory for her? Besides, I'm ready to be your wife."

Nick was stuck between a Hallelujah and an Amen, but realistically he knew he needed to get the conversation back on track. "Charlotte, think of what you're saying," he said, "you'll want your mom and Becca there when we get married, not to mention Pop and my family. I love that you want to do this but…."

"You don't want to marry me now?" Charlotte asked as her chin quivered. She had gone out on a limb, and now Nick was rejecting her?

"Oh, Honey, I want to marry you more than anything in the world, but I don't want you to rush into a wedding and then have regrets." Nick kissed her hand and looked into the glass-green eyes that were threatening to spill over with tears.

"I've never been as sure of anything as I am that this is the right thing to do," Charlotte told him. "My mom wants us to have a double wedding with her and Thomas this fall, which means she won't be coming back to the island anytime soon. And Becca will understand and be happy for us, no matter what, so the decision is yours, Nick Greyson. Are you going to marry me or not?"

Then the last thing in the world Charlotte would have expected happened. Nick got down on one knee, again, and said, "Charlotte Luce, will you please do me the honor of becoming my wife… just as soon as we can get a license?"

Charlotte threw her arms around him and laughed and cried all at the same time. "I thought you'd never ask," she squealed, and everyone in Tiffany applauded.

Chapter 6
Now

They looked around Tiffany, and bought gifts for a few special people, plus a pair of really cool sunglasses for Charlotte, before Nick called Stuart and planned for where they could meet. Charlotte was glowing with shopping endorphins, and Nick was smiling from ear to ear. They each had one of those precious blue bags in their hands, but their other hands were linked tightly together between them.

"What do you think your mom will say when we tell her the news?" Charlotte asked Nick. "This will just be a simple wedding, and she won't need to do a thing."

Nick chuckled. "I realize you just met my mom, but even with her illness, she's going to want to do things. Are you going to be okay with that?"

"I'll make sure she knows we just want her to be a part of the celebration, and I'm sure she'll understand." Charlotte looked so confident Nick didn't have the heart to tell her that when it came to a celebration, simple wasn't in his mom's vocabulary.

Stuart picked them up and delivered Nick and Charlotte back to his mother's apartment. It was shortly before five o'clock, but Elizabeth was sitting in the den with Gus, waiting for Nick and Charlotte to arrive.

"Well how did it go?" Elizabeth Harris beamed. "Were you surprised, Charlotte, and did you find the perfect ring?"

"You knew about this?" Charlotte asked her future mother-in-law.

"Nicky asked my opinion," Elizabeth answered. "He told me you weren't a fan of surprises, but I told him there wasn't a woman alive who wouldn't love a clandestine trip to Tiffany. You're not upset with me, are you?"

Charlotte took Elizabeth's hand and shook her head. "Not at all," she smiled down at Nick's mother, "and in fact, we have a surprise for you." Waiting a moment for effect, Charlotte continued. "We decided to get married while we're here in New York, and if you'll let us, we'd like to do it right here."

Nick could see the tears welling up in his mom's eyes, as he stepped beside them and took hold of her other hand. "You don't need to do a thing Mom," he told her, "but Gus, I need some help from you. We'll need a marriage license and someone to officiate, and I'm hoping you have some ideas on that?"

Gus shook Nick's hand and kissed Charlotte's cheek. "I can definitely help," he smiled, "and I can't think of anything we'd like more than to host your wedding, right Liz?"

Elizabeth was still trying to get herself under control when Charlotte added one more thing. "We'd be honored if you would be our attendants," she told Nick's mother and stepfather, and that's all it took for Elizabeth Harris to really let the waterworks go.

Chapter 7

Now

Thankfully for Charlotte all the excitement around them getting married made everyone forget about cocktails so that was one bullet she dodged. By the time Stuart announced that dinner was being served, calls had been made to Nick's family, as well as Charlotte's mom and Becca. Everyone seemed genuinely happy for the couple, instead of disappointed at missing the big day. Becca apologized for giving Ryan Charlotte's cell number, but Charlotte said it was a conversation for another day.

"Wow!" Charlotte exclaimed as Nick held her chair so she could sit down for dinner. "I can't believe how much the four of us accomplished in such a short time. Now we can just enjoy our time together tomorrow."

"This is just the beginning." Nick's mom exclaimed gleefully. "Tomorrow we need to order flowers and a cake, and of course you'll need to find a dress."

Charlotte took a drink of her water and glanced at Nick before answering. "Elizabeth, I, no we so appreciate your enthusiasm, but all Nick and I want is to get married in a nice simple ceremony in your den. We don't need all those frills, right Nick?"

Nick was pulling at the tie around his neck, obviously not wanting to get in the middle of the two strong women at the table. Finally, he spoke, afraid to look either of them in the eye.

"Mom, Charlotte's right, we just want to be married. You can understand that, can't you?" When he did look up at his mom, he could see the pout beginning.

"Nicky," Elizabeth said softly, "you know that your dad and I eloped, and at that moment it seemed very mysterious and romantic. But as time went on, I realized what we had missed by not having a traditional wedding, and when Maya got married, I longed to have a wedding dress to pass down to her, but of course I didn't."

Nick shook his head and looked at Charlotte, not sure what to say. "Mom, all that matters to us is getting married. We don't care about flowers or cake, just being here with you and Gus as we start our lives together."

Finally, Gus entered the conversation. "Charlotte, Nick, we'll do whatever it is you want to make your wedding the one of your dreams, but Elizabeth and I would really love to do something special for you. We never had a child of our own, and this will probably be our only chance to be a part of an occasion like this."

Charlotte smiled and looked at Nick. "Okay," she told them. "You can order flowers and a cake, and tomorrow I'll find a nice appropriate dress, but that's it, okay?"

Elizabeth clapped her hands like a school girl and blew her husband a kiss. "Of course, Charlotte, whatever you say!" Elizabeth told her. "But I may have forgotten to mention that one of my dearest friends is a buyer for the Kleinfeld Bridal Salon, and right after dinner, I'm going to call her and see if she can bring some dresses by in the morning.

Charlotte was speechless! "Kleinfeld, Elizabeth?" "I'm pretty sure a nice simple dress is not in their inventory or in my budget."

"Nonsense!" Nick's mother exclaimed. "The dress is my gift to you, and to be honest, Honey, you'll need a dress that won't show your baby bump in the pictures."

"You know?" Charlotte shot back, giving Nick the dirtiest look, she could.

"Hey, don't look at me," he said, lifting his arms up in surrender.

"I'm a woman, Charlotte." Elizabeth tried to soothe her. "We just know these things."

Charlotte put her head in her hands and then started to laugh. "It's probably a good thing you and my mom never knew each other," she said. "I'm pretty sure that Anna Maria Island wouldn't have been big enough for the two of you!"

By the time the plates had been cleared, and coffee and dessert were served in the den, the wedding plans were set, and Charlotte was exhausted. "Can you imagine what it's like for people who plan a wedding a year in advance?" she whispered to Nick. "Becca's idea of becoming a nun is starting to make more sense to me now."

"I think that ship has sailed," he chuckled, "but I know what you're saying. Let my mom have her fun and keep your eye on the prize. In two days, we'll be legally married, and our honeymoon can begin." He gave her a look that made her mouth dry and other body parts wet, and Charlotte knew that sleep was going to be the last thing on her mind when she climbed into bed tonight.

Chapter 8

Now

Charlotte was right. Sleep was elusive, and after tossing and turning for a while, she decided a glass of milk might help her relax. Elizabeth had urged her to make herself at home, and Charlotte was hopeful that included a late-night visit to the fridge.

Quietly she slipped out of her room and headed down the hall to the kitchen when she heard Nick's voice coming from the den. She had every intention of going in to make sure he was okay, but when she got closer, she could hear he was talking with his mother, and about her.

Yes, it was wrong to eavesdrop, and yes, she felt guilty about it, but not enough to turn around or to make her presence known! Standing as still as she could, Charlotte listened to the private conversation between her fiancé and his mom.

"I like your Charlotte very much," Elizabeth Harris told her son. "In many ways, she reminds me of how I was when I was young."

Nick coughed, trying to keep from telling his mother he hoped Charlotte wasn't like her, but he said instead, "Charlotte's a special woman, and I'm glad that you like her because I love her more than I ever thought possible."

Elizabeth smiled. "I remember that kind of love," she told him. "I had it with your father, but as much as I loved him, I married him without really knowing him, and that's where our troubles began."

Nick bristled a little, not wanting to hear his estranged mother talk badly about the man who had loved and raised him and his siblings, but thankfully she didn't.

"Your dad and I only knew each other for a few weeks before we eloped, and all we really knew was that we were crazy about each other, and we thought that was enough. When he told me he was going to purchase a marina in Florida, I saw white sand and Mai Tais. When I told him I was an orphan, he thought that meant I wanted a big family." Elizabeth stopped then and took her son's hand. "Please don't ever think that I didn't love you and Maya and Noah, because I did, and I do, very much, but I thought I was heading into a life of tropical passion...."

"And that's not what you got." Nick finished the sentence for her.

Her head bowed, Elizabeth softly answered, "No."

"I'm sure it wasn't easy for you, Mom," Nick tried to assure her, "and Pop did a great job of being both mother and father to us, but we missed you. All four of us missed you."

"I know," she answered him, "and I missed all of you. Did you know that your dad and I spoke several times a week after I moved back here? It started on the pretense of checking-up on the three of you, but he never ended a call without telling me he loved me, and he was waiting for me to come home. Even after I sent you kids back, he continued to call me, and those were the hardest and best calls of my life. I made a huge mistake Nicky, and it's one I'll always regret."

Charlotte could hardly contain the tears that were starting to fall on her cheeks, so as quietly as possible, she backed away from the den. When she was close to her room, she wiped her eyes on her robe, and purposely made enough noise for Nick to know she was up.

"Hey, why aren't you asleep?" he asked, following her into the kitchen.

"It's been a surprising day," she told him honestly, "and my nerves are on overtime. I'm hoping a glass of milk will help me calm down."

Nick took her in his arms and held her tight. "There has been a lot going on today, and I'm sorry that you're having trouble sleeping. Would a massage help?"

A massage would help all right, but Charlotte was afraid of her response if she allowed Nick to get his hands on her while she was in bed. Instead she smiled sweetly and said, "I think the milk will be enough."

With the glass in hand, Nick walked her back to her room and gave her a chaste kiss at the door, knowing, too, it was better if he stayed outside of the room. "I love you," he told her, "and I can't wait to make you my wife."

Charlotte took the glass of milk from his hand and set it down on a table in the hall. Then, wrapping her arms around him she said, "I love you too, Nick Greyson, and you're still my best friend. Well, you and Becca."

Nick held her closely as he laughed. "Our marriage will be anything but boring," he told her, and then he turned her around and gave her a gentle nudge toward her waiting bed.

Chapter 9
Now

Charlotte woke up the next morning, both excited and apprehensive about the day to come. Not knowing Nick's mom well enough to have an idea of her expectations had her stomach in knots. She did love designer fashion and having a buyer from Kleinfeld bring dresses to her was darn amazing, but still, it didn't make a lot of sense to have a formal wedding gown when only four people were going to be looking at it.

After a hot shower, Charlotte picked a simple Jones New York black and white striped knit dress that was slightly fitted, but without an actual waist. If Nick's mom had realized she was pregnant after just meeting her, she cringed to think what people back on Anna Maria Island were saying. She wasn't sure about whether she would step into the gowns she would be trying on, or putting them over her head, so a swipe of IT Vitality Cheek Flush in peony, and a little Je Ne Sais Quoi clear gloss on her lips, and she was done. Her curly, strawberry-blonde locks secured in a high ponytail and a pair of black sandals, and Charlotte was ready to face the day.

Nick and his mom were just sitting down to breakfast when Charlotte walked in. Nick stood and gave her a soft kiss before pulling out a chair and helping her sit down. "You look beautiful," he told her across the table, and for some reason that made her blush.

"Nick's right, Charlotte," his mother added. "You look lovely and perfect for our day ahead."

Charlotte smiled, but the butterflies inside her stomach were definitely swarming. "Thank you, Elizabeth," she answered demurely. "I wasn't quite sure what to wear… I've never tried on wedding dresses before."

Nick could see the discomfort on Charlotte's face, but he didn't know how to help her. "You always look wonderful," he told her, his eyes filled with love. "I want you to enjoy today and not stress about anything, okay?"

Charlotte nodded and looked down at her plate. Chocolate croissants? She felt as if she'd died and gone to heaven. There had been a bakery in Indianapolis that made them, and every Saturday morning she and her roommate Ellen would get there when they opened the door to get the warm, flaky confections. Cristi would be back at the apartment making coffee and setting the table, and it was a ritual she had loved so much. Looking at the pastry on her plate she gave silent thanks for friendship and put a big piece in her mouth.

"This is so good," she said, her mouth still filled with the chocolatey croissant. "I really shouldn't be eating it when I'm going to be trying on clothes, but I can't resist."

Nick chuckled as he reached for a second pastry. "They are good," he told his mother, "but it's probably best for both of us if this is a one-time treat. Charlotte's already told me that she likes her men lean, and many more of these and I'll need to go for a run."

Charlotte could feel her cheeks heat as Elizabeth Harris looked right at her. "I feel the same way, my dear," Nick's mother told her, "but Nicky has his dad's metabolism, so you won't ever need to worry about him getting fat."

Charlotte was thankful that Gus hadn't joined them because she felt certain his wife's words would have hurt him. Gus was more roly-poly than lean, and compared to Pop, he was just down right fat, but he was Elizabeth's husband, and Charlotte couldn't believe she had been so thoughtless. Nick must have felt the same way because he gave his mother a look that scared even her.

Before anymore could be said, Stuart arrived to clear off the table, and Elizabeth told Charlotte they would set-up the gown fitting in the den, where they could have privacy.

"Nicky," Elizabeth smiled to her son, almost as if the awkward conversation hadn't happened, "Gus will be back soon to take you away from the apartment, so you don't get a glimpse of Charlotte in her wedding dress. We don't want any bad luck now do we?"

Nick looked at Charlotte and replied to his mom, "We've already had enough bad-luck for one lifetime, but if Charlotte wants me to go, I'll go."

Once again, she felt as if she was caught between Nick and his mother, but she did manage to get out, "I would like to surprise you tomorrow," and that was all it took to make Nick smile.

"You've been one surprise after another, Sweetheart," he told her, coming around to kiss her goodbye, "but there's always room for one more." And with that he left the ladies to do whatever it is ladies do to prepare for a wedding.

"Now, Charlotte," Elizabeth began, as she rolled her wheelchair away from the table, "have you given any thought to the style of dress that you'd like?"

Chapter 10
Then

Lottie loved the nights she slept over at Becca's house. Becca's mom was warm and loving, and her dad was really nice to her, too, even though he spent most of his time watching sports or playing ball with Becca's brother, Brad. Dinners were always a family sit-down at the table, and Lottie told herself when she had a family, they would do the same thing. It's not that she and her mom didn't eat together, but it was usually on trays in front of the TV, and while most kids would have liked that, Lottie wanted the whole family experience.

With the dishes cleared, the girls went to Becca's room and started a game of Monopoly. When Charlotte drew the card that said she had to pay a $75.00 luxury tax, she looked at the graphic of the diamond ring and asked Becca what kind of wedding she wanted when she grew up. Becca hadn't started talking about becoming a nun yet, but she hadn't thought about marriage yet, either.

"Gosh, I don't know," she told her friend. "I've never really thought about it. I suppose you have your entire wedding planned, don't you, right down to the groom?"

They had only known the Greyson family for a few months at this point, but as much as she wanted to deny it, Lottie was smitten with Nick. Blushing over Becca's comment, she got up from the bed and walked over to the window where she draped a flowy white curtain panel over her head like a veil.

"I know just what I want," she told Becca. "I saw an old movie the other night with an actress named Rita Hayworth, and she was so beautiful. She had long red hair and was wearing a slinky dress that almost looked like a long slip. I want to look just like her, elegant and chic."

Becca almost choked on her Dr. Pepper. "I don't think we're supposed to think about a wedding dress being chic," she cringed. "They're supposed to be poufy with lots of lace."

"It doesn't matter anyway," Lottie told her. "I'll never be thin like Rita was, and I'll probably never get married anyway. Boys just don't like me."

"Nick and Noah like you," Becca answered. "Besides, we have a lot of growing-up to do before we get married."

Lottie agreed and looked from her friend to her shelf of books. "Hey, let's pretend that we're Trixie Belden and Honey Wheeler, and go spy on Brad. Maybe we can discover who his new girlfriend is."

The Monopoly board was put away and Lottie and Becca plotted how they could solve the mystery of Brad's new girlfriend, just as Trixie and Honey would have. And for now, all thoughts of marriage and wedding dresses were put aside.

Chapter 11
Now

Just as the ladies were ready to get settled in the den and discuss wedding plans in earnest, Gus called Nick's mother. Charlotte could tell from the conversation that she wasn't thrilled with whatever he was telling her, so after a curt good-bye to Gus, she turned to Charlotte.

"Apparently even Gus's position with the Governor isn't enough to bend the rules. It seems that you and Nick are going to have to go to the courthouse this morning to get your marriage license if you're going to get married tomorrow afternoon. There's some silly twenty-four-hour rule, I guess. Anyway, Nick is on his way back up to get you, and Gus is waiting downstairs. I'll see if Gloria can come a little later, so you have plenty of time. What size dresses should I tell her to bring?"

What size? Charlotte said to herself. As far as she was concerned that was privileged information, but she knew they needed something to start with. "Well," she finally answered, "normally a size six or eight works fine, but with my, you know, condition, it may depend on the dress."

Elizabeth smiled and said she and Gloria would work it out, but she thought Charlotte would look lovely in a ballgown with lots of tulle! *Shit! Shit! Shit!* Charlotte thought. *I may end up looking like a marshmallow instead of my dream of a glamour girl*, but there was no time for more conversation because just then the elevator dinged, and Nick walked in.

"I'm really sorry about this," Nick told her as he ushered her into the elevator. "Gus thought he might be able to get a waiver, but the governor is out of town, and the city clerk won't budge. Hopefully, this won't take too long."

Charlotte tried to smile but instead asked, "Any chance we could just sneak away tomorrow and get married at the court house? I know your mom means well, but I'm feeling like she's trying to Shanghai our wedding."

"Is that what you really want?" Nick asked, taking her hands in his. "Because if it is, I'll go right upstairs and tell my mom to back-off. Or we can stop all of this now and wait until we get back to the island. It's up to you."

Charlotte sighed. "No, it's not what I want at all. I want to be married and sleep in the same bed as you. I want to be held and wake up looking at your beautiful face, and I want to go to sleep feeling limp and satisfied after you've done all that stuff to me that you do so well." Charlotte was trying not to blush when she realized that Gus and Stuart were right there and had probably heard every word.

Nick stifled his grin and changed tactics. "How about this?" he said gently. "We'll go get our marriage license, and that will give you some time to calm down and think about everything. If this afternoon isn't better, or if you start to feel uneasy, you just tell me, and I'll take care of it. Okay? We've waited half our lives for this Charlotte, and if this isn't what you want, or what you've dreamed about, then we'll wait until it's right."

How could she not feel like the luckiest girl alive? Nick was caring and loving, gorgeous and sexy, and he was willing to do whatever it took to make her happy. Looking up at his deep blue eyes, she answered, "Okay." But that was all he needed.

Chapter 12

Now

Marriage license in hand, Nick and Charlotte arrived back at his mother's Park Avenue apartment to a cyclone of activity. Racks of wedding dresses were lined up in the den, and an attractive woman with a short silver bob was looking at shoes and accessories with Nick's mom.

"Oh, Nicky and Charlotte, come in and meet my dear friend, Gloria London. I've known her since my modeling days at Macy's." Elizabeth Harris was perched in her wheelchair, looking like a queen on her throne, and Charlotte could see that her cheeks were flushed, and she looked more alive than she had since they'd arrived.

Both Nick and Charlotte shook hands with Elizabeth's friend, and before she knew what had hit her, Charlotte had been told to go "strip down" to her undies and meet the ladies back in the den. Trying not to panic, she grabbed Nick's hand and started to pull him into her bedroom. But his mom had other ideas.

"Now Nicky," she called after them, "this is all private girl stuff, so you leave Charlotte to us, and you go with Gus and have lunch at his club."

Nick ran his hands through his hair and sighed. Why had he thought bringing Charlotte to meet his mom was such a good idea? Trying to gage her reaction, he cautiously asked, "What do you want to do? I can put a stop to this right now or...."

Charlotte put a finger to his lips and shushed him. "I'll be fine, Nick," she told him honestly. "Just look at how happy your mother is. I wouldn't take this away from her now for anything, even if it does mean looking like the Michelin Man tomorrow."

"You're pretty darn amazing, do you know that, Charlotte Luce?" he told her. "I'm not sure what I ever did to deserve you, but I promise I'll never let you forget how special you are or how much I love you."

Leaving her with a kiss that had her thinking clean undies might be in order, Nick walked away, and Charlotte went in to change. With her dress off, Charlotte ran her fingers gingerly over her swollen belly and talked softly to her unborn child.

"Well, what do you think of your grandma so far, Babycakes? She's definitely a force to be reckoned with, but she means well, and she is your daddy's mother." Caressing the little bump that was just protruding over the top of her bikini panties, Charlotte continued. "It's a good thing we have Pop and your Auntie Becca in our lives, because from my viewpoint, this being a mom stuff must be harder than it looks."

After securing her curls on top of her head, Charlotte donned her robe and stepped out into the hall. "Okay," she told herself. "Wedding mania here I come!"

Chapter 13
Now

"Oh Charlotte, come look!" Nick's mother squealed, "Have you ever seen anything more beautiful?" Charlotte looked at her future mother-in-law and fought for the right words to say. She had meant what she said about looking like the Michelin Man if it made Elizabeth happy, but that didn't mean she was giving in without at least making her feelings known.

"It's beautiful, Elizabeth," Charlotte began, "but would it really be wise for me to wear such a voluminous dress inside your apartment? With that full skirt, I'd be afraid every minute of knocking one of your lovely things off on the floor." With a wistful smile Charlotte thought, *there, that should get her seeing things my way.*

"Well, I guess you do have a point," Elizabeth said with a small pout, "but I do so love a ballgown."

Gloria intervened, seeing from Charlotte's reaction to the dress that it wasn't really her cup of tea. "What style of dress do you have in mind Charlotte?" she asked her. "Most girls plan their weddings a little farther out than this one, but surely you have some vision of how you want to look."

Charlotte felt a little reproach coming from Elizabeth's friend, but she tried not to let it phase her. "Well, as a matter of fact, I've always wanted a long slinky gown like the kind Rita Hayworth wore in Gilda. I really love that sexy, elegant look. I'm not sure there's even a style made like that anymore though," she sighed.

"I think what you're referring to is a slip dress, and they're very popular in wedding gowns, but they're also very snug and form fitting,"

Gloria told her. "Um, Elizabeth shared your condition, and even if I could find one your size, you might not be happy with the way it looks."

Shit! Shit! Shit! Charlotte was mortified! *I might as well wear a sign that reads "knocked-up", since everyone seems to know about my pregnancy.* Turning her head to hide her heated cheeks from Elizabeth and her friend, Charlotte tried to calm down before asking, "What do you suggest, Gloria?"

Gloria pulled a dress from the rack, looked at Elizabeth and Charlotte, and smiled. "Personally, I think this dress would be perfect." Giving both women a chance to look over the gown, she continued. "For an afternoon wedding, especially one here in the apartment, I feel that tea length would be the most appropriate. This is a David Fielden strapless dress that incorporates the tulle that you love so much, Elizabeth, but has the sleek sexy top that Charlotte admires. And," she said clearing her throat, "it has a small embroidered peplum at the waist that will help cover your tummy."

Charlotte looked at the dress and saw the possibilities immediately. Her only real concerns were that the dress was strapless, and her usually large chest was now increased by pregnancy.

"Why don't you try it on and see what you think," Gloria encouraged. "A dress on a hanger never looks the same as on a body."

Charlotte slipped off her robe and allowed Gloria to help her into the dress. Turning to look in the full-length mirror that Gloria had brought with her, Charlotte was amazed to see how much she not only liked the dress, but how much like a bride she felt in it. But it was when she looked into the face of Nick's mom, who had tears running down her cheeks, and heard her say, "It's perfect," that Charlotte knew for sure.

"This is the one," she said. "This is the dress that I'm going to wear to marry your son." Trying to keep from wrinkling the dress, or worse yet, getting mascara and tear stains on it, Charlotte and Elizabeth hugged and then picked out a veil.

The whole process had been painless and even left Charlotte with some time to do some honeymoon shopping! The three ladies had a quick lunch of chicken salad, along with another one of the divine chocolate croissants. While Gloria was packing things up Charlotte asked her where the closest lingerie shop was.

"You'll want to go to Pinkies, just a few blocks down the street. They have everything from classy to raunchy, and all the good stuff in between. Why don't you give me a few minutes to pack things up, and I'll take you there myself? I can even give you the best advice of what to wear to keep those girls in place tomorrow." Gloria laughed, and Charlotte looked over at Elizabeth, seeing the hurt written all over her face.

"I'd love it if you could go with us, Elizabeth, I mean if you're up to leaving the apartment." Elizabeth reached out to take the hand of her son's bride-to-be and shook her head.

"I truly appreciate that you asked, Charlotte," Elizabeth said, "but my shopping days are behind me. As much as I would love to go with you, I need a nap, but I'm grateful that Gloria can stand in for me."

Charlotte thought her heart would break, and she gently hugged Elizabeth and nodded. "I'll show you everything I buy after your rest, okay?"

Right then Stuart came to escort Elizabeth to her bedroom, and the currier from Kleinfeld came to pick up the extra dresses. "That was a nice thing you did, offering for Elizabeth to come along," Gloria told Charlotte. "It breaks my heart to see her deteriorating like she is, but today was good for her, and I hope it was good for you, too."

Charlotte nodded, determined to keep the tears at bay. "It was," she said truthfully, "and I'm thankful we'll have this memory together." Walking out the door, she was thinking of how precious life was and of sexy, light blue lingerie to wear under her wedding dress. Now if that wasn't hormones messing with her mind, what was?

Chapter 14

Now

Pinkies was fantastic, and Charlotte returned with two bags filled with sexy honeymoon lingerie. She knew she'd only be able to wear some of it for a short time longer, but what the heck, a girl doesn't get married every day.

Gloria had been a great help and even helped Charlotte find a long white, slip-style negligee to wear on her wedding night to offset some of the disappointment of not being able to have her dream wedding gown. She was also able to find Charlotte the perfect, light blue corset to wear under her dress to hold her ample breasts in place without being too tight against her belly.

When she entered the apartment, Charlotte was aware of the silence around her and figured Elizabeth was still resting, but she wondered where Nick had gotten off to. Trying to move as quietly as possible, she was almost to her room when she heard Elizabeth calling her name.

"I've been waiting for you, Charlotte," Elizabeth called out. "Come show me all the wonderful things you bought to entice my son."

Charlotte blushed at the realization that some of the items she had purchased were down right risqué, so she quickly grabbed the nightgown and the corset, and threw the other bags in her room. It wasn't like Nick's mom didn't know they were having sex, but Charlotte still wasn't comfortable parading things like crotchless panties in front of her.

Elizabeth was sitting up in bed when Charlotte entered, and it broke her heart to see Nick's mother look so frail. But when she saw Charlotte, her eyes lit up, and she opened her arms for a hug. It was a gentle one, as Charlotte didn't know how much pressure Elizabeth could take, but it was a hug all the same.

After showing off her purchases, or at least the ones she was willing for Elizabeth to see, Charlotte asked, "Where's that son of yours? I thought he'd be here when I got back."

"Stuart told me he and Gus went on an outing, whatever that means, but they'll be back by five," Elizabeth told her. "Now Charlotte, come sit beside me, I have something for you."

Tentatively, Charlotte sat down and took Elizabeth's out stretched hand. "You have your grandmother's ring as your something old, and your wedding dress is something new, you even have blue lingerie to wear on your wedding day, but you still need something borrowed."

Reaching under her pillow Elizabeth brought out a small box and handed it to Charlotte. "Nicholas bought these for me when Maya was born," she said. "We couldn't afford them, but he knew that I'd always wanted a pair, and he was trying so hard to make me content. I would love it if you would wear them tomorrow at your wedding."

Charlotte opened the box and inside were a pair of Mikimoto pearl and diamond stud earrings. She carefully ran her finger over the exquisite white spheres, and trying her best not to cry, replied, "I'd be honored to."

Her purchases and Elizabeth's earrings in hand, Charlotte headed to her room, deciding that a bath would help with the emotions and the fatigue she was feeling. She turned on the tap of the huge garden tub and added a big handful of the lavender bath salts that were sitting on the ledge. Then, stripping down, she grabbed her phone and eased herself down into the soothing water. As soon as she was comfortable, she found the contact number she was looking for and placed a call to her mom. Even though Maggie had said she understood Charlotte's decision to get married in New York, Charlotte actually missed having her mother there and hoped that a phone call would ease the ache in her heart.

As soon as she heard her mom's voice on the other end Charlotte said, "Hey Mom, it's me. Your pregnant, bride-to-be daughter."

Chapter 15
Now

Thirty minutes and a long talk with her mother later, Charlotte sank down into the now tepid bath water. Had they only been in New York for two days? They had come here for Charlotte to meet Nick's mom, and she had, but from there things had gotten crazy! Looking down at her sparkling aquamarine and diamond engagement ring, Charlotte wondered what Gran would think about her spur of the moment decision to get married the next day.

Mindlessly, Charlotte reached up to touch her locket, forgetting that she had removed it when she got in the tub. "Well Gran," she said, lightly touching the spot on her neck where the locket always lay, "what do you think? I'm getting married tomorrow; can you believe it? You always knew that Nick and I would find our way back to each other, and I'm so glad we did. I really love him Gran, and I love wearing your ring."

Before she had a chance to go on there was a knock on her door. "Charlotte," Nick called out, "are you okay?"

She wanted to ask him where he'd been all afternoon, but instead she answered sweetly, "I'm fine, and I'm just getting out of the tub. I'll meet you in the den in thirty minutes."

With the luxurious, Egyptian cotton towels that had been draped over a towel warmer wrapped around her, Charlotte anointed herself from head to toe with Jose Maran whipped Argan oil in fresh peach. The smell took her back to the time when she and Becca used to buy a Georgia peach from the gas station fruit stand and slurp the sweet, juicy goodness as they walked home from the beach.

Putting her hair in a high ponytail, Charlotte donned the thick terrycloth robe that appeared freshly laundered in her bathroom each morning and headed out of the ensuite to pick out something appropriate to wear for dinner. Expecting that she was alone in the room it startled her when she heard, "Hey there, sexy lady."

Charlotte gasped as she looked at Nick lying comfortably on her bed, his hands behind his head. Dressed in dark chinos and a gray button-up shirt, he was the most gorgeous thing she had seen all day, and she'd spent her morning looking at wedding gowns.

"I thought I told you I'd meet you in the den in thirty minutes," she scolded, walking closer to the bed. "What are you doing in here?"

As soon as she was in arms reach, Nick grabbed her around the waist and pulled her down next to him. "We've hardly had a minute alone in the last twenty-four hours," he said nuzzling her neck, "and this may be the only time we have until after the wedding." Gently trying to ease his hand inside her robe, Nick growled when Charlotte caught it and held on tight.

"Nice try," she smiled, "but you're going to have to wait a few more hours."

Nick sulked. "You're killing me Charlotte Luce." In his deep FBI voice, added, "You better sleep well tonight, my love, because tomorrow night, you're going to make up for all these weeks of torture you've put me through."

Charlotte felt her whole body get hot, and all of a sudden it hit her. Were they going to spend their wedding night in a guest room at Nick's mother's apartment?

Almost as if he could read her mind, Nick eased her fears. "And don't worry, I've booked us a hotel room for the next two nights," he told her with a twinkle in his eye. "Once you say, "I Do," I don't plan to ever feel this desperate again."

Charlotte wrapped her arms around him and drew him in for a kiss. "That makes two of us, Mr. Greyson," she teased, "and thank you for getting the hotel room."

With one more kiss and a moan from each of them, Nick got up and left Charlotte to get ready for dinner.

Chapter 16

Now

Charlotte always loved to dress up, and since this was the night before her wedding, she chose her ensemble carefully. Finally deciding on the one really nice outfit she had brought, she fingered the rose silk-georgette Michael Kors dress and knew it would be perfect. Black and white always looked good with her strawberry blonde hair, and pared with her black, Manolo Blahnik ankle-strap sandals, she was feeling very bride-to-be.

She gave her hair a spritz of coconut-mango hair refresh and decided to leave her soft curls down for the evening. In the morning, she would wash her hair and maybe put it in some type of updo, but tonight it hung long and luscious. Makeup was always pretty basic for Charlotte, but she did add some bronzer to her cheeks and eyelids, before adding two coats of Mally black mascara and a healthy swipe of Josie Maran natural volume lip gloss in Dyani.

The flowy, soft material of her dress slipping over her head made Charlotte start to feel excited about her upcoming nuptials. It wasn't until she tried to pull the dress down over her hips that her worst fear was realized. What had once been a small waist and flat stomach was now an actual belly, and it hadn't come from eating too many chocolate croissants! Sucking it in for all she was worth, Charlotte was finally able to get the dress in place and the belt fastened, but she was pretty sure there wouldn't be room for dinner without loosening it a notch or two.

"Oh Babycakes," she sighed, "I love you and your daddy so much, but fashion is my kind of my thing, you know? Couldn't you have waited just a few more weeks before making such an appearance?"

Not expecting a response, Charlotte gave herself a spritz of the Joy Perfume that Elizabeth had left on her dresser, fastened her locket around her neck, said a silent prayer to her gran, and headed out to meet the others. A little concerned that she might have overdressed, Charlotte was pleasantly surprised when she saw that she hadn't. The men were both in suits and ties, and even Elizabeth had donned something other than her usual caftan.

As soon as she walked into the den her eyes met Nick's, and he took her in his arms. "You look amazing," he told her with a soft kiss to her lips and then without warning kissed her, really kissed her in front of his mom and Gus! Charlotte was blushing like a schoolgirl, but Nick had a huge smile on his face, and she realized that both Elizabeth and Gus were clapping.

Gus handed Nick and Charlotte a champagne flute, lifting his up in the air. "To love," he said, "and to Nick and Charlotte."

Everyone took a drink, and Charlotte put the glass to her lips, not wanting to offend, but knowing she couldn't drink alcohol, when Gus smiled and said to her, "It's sparkling grape juice Charlotte, I wouldn't compromise our grandchild by giving you real champagne."

Charlotte blew Gus a kiss and, taking Nick's hand, walked with him into dinner.

Dinner was a delicious meal of Beef Wellington, roasted vegetables, and a golden beet and goat cheese salad, and Charlotte felt like she was going to explode! Trying very casually to loosen her belt she had just about succeeded when Elizabeth looked her way.

"You poor dear," she said sympathetically. "No one understands more than I do what it's like to be carrying a Greyson baby. Every one of them was big, even Maya." Elizabeth smiled, and Nick cleared his throat, not sure where the conversation might lead. Deciding that talking about their wedding was safer, he had just opened his mouth when Elizabeth interrupted.

"Our good friends the Ramsey's are out of town for the rest of the week, so I made arrangements for you to stay there tonight, Nicky." "We don't want to take any chances with you seeing the bride before the wedding, do we? Their apartment is just next door, so you'll still be close. And while you're gone, Stuart will be moving your things into Charlotte's room, because it's bigger than the one you're using now."

Shit! Shit! Shit! Charlotte thought. *I cannot spend my wedding night in this apartment knowing that Nick's mom and Gus are just down the hall!*

"Um, Mom," Nick began. "I'll be happy to sleep at your friend's apartment tonight, if you think it's necessary, but Charlotte and I will be leaving after the wedding celebration tomorrow."

"What do you mean you're leaving?" Elizabeth cried. "You were supposed to be here until Friday morning Nicky, you can't just leave."

Nick let out a sigh and ran his hand through his thick, dark hair. "We'll come over for dinner on Thursday," he told his mother, "and we'll be back early on Friday before our flight, but this is the only honeymoon we get right now, and we're not spending it here."

Elizabeth was just about to protest again when Gus stepped in. "We understand completely," he said to Nick, while looking directly at his wife. "We're just thrilled to have you here at all and to be able to share in your special day."

Elizabeth was speechless and sobbing quietly into her napkin when Nick got up and went to her. "I love you, Mom," he told her, "and Charlotte and I appreciate everything that you've done, but in your heart, you have to know that our going to a hotel is the right thing for all of us."

Elizabeth reached up and stroked the cheek of the man her son had become and smiled. "I love you too Nicky, I love both of you and you're right of course. Just promise me we won't ever lose each other again."

Nick kissed her head and gave his promise, and Charlotte joined him by his mother's side. "You'll always be a part of our lives Elizabeth," she said, trying to hold in her own tears. And with those small words, Elizabeth smiled and held out her hand to Gus. "I really have been blessed," she told them, and she meant every word.

Chapter 17

Now

Dessert and coffee were served in the den, and Elizabeth shared with Nick and Charlotte the other arrangements she had made while they were out that afternoon. "The wonderful bakery that made the divine croissants is making the cake, and I went with chocolate, Charlotte, because Nicky said that's your favorite."

Charlotte smiled but before she could even say thank you, Elizabeth continued chattering away. "We didn't have a chance to discuss what kind of flowers you like, so I hope you'll approve of what I ordered." Elizabeth paused a moment for effect and continued.

"Claire de Lune Peonies are in season right now, and they're so feminine, so I paired them with some Jasmine, Hellebores, and some beautiful greenery. If I do say so myself, the combination is fabulous!" Elizabeth smiled at Charlotte again, waiting for her reply, but all Charlotte could think of was, *What in the hell are Hellebores?* But instead she said, "I'm sure whatever you picked out will be beautiful Elizabeth. Thank you for taking care of this for me."

It was all Nick could do to keep a straight face as he listened to his mom and Charlotte's exchange. If there was one thing he knew about Charlotte Luce, it was that she didn't like to have decisions made for her, but he also knew that she would never cross his mom. "We both appreciate everything that you've done, Mom," he said, and then added, "What you both have done." Looking at Charlotte he lifted his glass and said, "To Mom and Gus. Thank you for your love and hospitality."

The rest of the evening was uneventful, with Nick sharing his plans to leave the FBI to become a teacher and coach like he had always planned. Charlotte talked a little about her small accounting business and her own mother's upcoming marriage, and before she knew it, Elizabeth was nodding off, and they realized it was time to say goodnight.

Nick kissed his mother goodnight and nodded to Gus, who was wheeling Elizabeth into the master bedroom, and then turned to Charlotte. Taking both of her hands in his, he pulled her close and whispered in her ear. "This time tomorrow you'll finally be my wife," he told her. "You're not having any regrets about getting married here without our family and friends, are you?"

Charlotte's stomach had felt a little queasy all evening, but she'd hoped it was from the rich food at dinner. "This is the right thing for us to do," she answered him, "but I do admit that I wish everyone could be here. I was Becca's maid of honor, and she was always supposed to be there for me, but being your wife is the most important thing."

Nick tipped her head and kissed her softly on the lips. "As disappointed as I would be for the plans to change, I'll totally understand if you want to call tomorrow off," Nick told her. "Your happiness is everything to me, you know that don't you?"

As she brushed a tear from her cheek, Charlotte smiled up at the face she had been in love with for almost twenty years. "I do know that, Nick, and I want that for you, too. All brides have a case of nerves the night before their wedding. Please don't worry; I'll be fine."

For a few minutes they just held on to each other, and then Nick carefully pulled away. "We have a big day tomorrow," he said with a smile, "and I meant what I said about you needing your rest. Stuart will pack your things up in the morning. All you need to do now is have sweet dreams and wake-up ready to become Mrs. Greyson."

Charlotte nodded as she shivered at the thought. After all these years, was she really going to marry the boy who had stolen her heart and turned into the man of her dreams? "I'll be ready," she assured him, and letting go of his hands, she walked into her bedroom and her last night as Charlotte Luce.

After brushing her teeth and washing her face, Charlotte slipped into a night shirt and climbed into bed. She was laying there wondering how in the world she would sleep when her phone rang. Looking at the caller ID brought a huge smile to her face as she answered, "Rebecca Rose, you are an answer to prayer."

Chapter 18
Then

Charlotte looked at her childhood friend, the person she trusted above all others, except for Gran of course, and smiled. Tomorrow was Becca's wedding day, and she was so excited for her. After years of believing she was going to be a nun and devote her life to the church, Becca had met Doctor Jared Tyler, and had fallen in love.

They spent the night before her wedding in Becca's childhood room, which was as emotional for Charlotte as it was for Becca. This room had been their haven for so many years as they played with dolls and read the Trixie Belden books they had found stashed in the attic, while talking about their future, and of course, about Nick Greyson.

Becca looked at Charlotte, her face aglow with love and apprehension, and Charlotte knew without asking what her friend was thinking. "You're thinking about tomorrow night, aren't you?" Charlotte asked her friend.

Becca blushed and nodded. "It's not that I don't know about sex," Becca told her. "My mom has always been very open about intimacy and relationships, but since I didn't think it was going to apply to me, I probably didn't listen like I should have."

Charlotte smiled at her friend's admission. "Have you and Jared talked about your wedding night, Bec? I know that he respected your decision not to have sex until you were married, but I'm sure he's a little nervous, too."

"We've talked a little bit, but I want to know more. Asking him things about how it will feel, and will it hurt, just seemed a little personal. I know Jared has been with other women, and I don't want to hear about how it was for them. But," she said with a gleam in her eye, "I wouldn't mind hearing about how it was for you."

Now it was Charlotte's turn to blush. She had told Becca about the night she had lost her virginity to Ryan Noble, but only that it had happened, not the details. After all, at that point, Becca was still planning to enter the church after she graduated.

"Please, Lottie," Becca pleaded, "I don't want to disappoint Jared, and I'm so afraid that I will."

Charlotte smiled again at her friend. "Oh Honey, there isn't anything in the world you could do to disappoint Jared. You two are perfect together, and I know that when you finally make love, it will be perfect, too."

Becca had a dreamy look on her face when she answered. "When he kisses me, I feel as if I'm burning up, but I don't know how to quench the fire." Looking at Charlotte, her face the color of crimson, Becca added, "And I feel throbbing and achy, you know, down there."

It was all Charlotte could do not to laugh at Becca's innocence, but she reined it in. "I think everything is going to work out just fine, Becca," Charlotte encouraged. "If Jared's kisses make you that hot, he'll know exactly how to cool you off. It may not happen the first time, but trust me, Jared will know how to make it happen."

Becca squeezed Charlotte's hand and thanked her friend for her honesty. The trouble was that Charlotte knew what was supposed to happen; it just didn't happen for her quite like she knew it would for Becca. She loved kissing Ryan, and he definitely was skilled at making love, but that throbbing achy feeling that Becca had described, rarely happened to her.

This wasn't a subject that Charlotte was comfortable talking to anyone about, so she touched her locket and wondered if she was ever going to feel the love and passion that her friend was feeling. As she turned over in the twin bed, Charlotte closed her eyes and a picture of Nick Greyson popped in her head. *What would sex with Nick be like?* she thought. And she let that thought take her right into her dreams.

Chapter 19

Now

Charlotte stretched and let out a big yawn! Today was her wedding day, and after a long talk with Becca last night, she was certain she was doing the right thing. Weddings are fun, Becca had pointed out, but it's the marriage that counts, and Charlotte knew that more than anything she wanted to be married to Nick. *Mrs. Nicholas Greyson*, she thought. *It had a nice ring to it!*

Just as she swung her legs over the side of the bed, there was a knock on the door. Charlotte smiled, thinking that Elizabeth was probably having Stuart bring her breakfast in bed, so even though she needed to pee badly, she crawled back under the covers and called out, "Come in."

"Good morning, Sweetie," came the voice entering the room.

Charlotte's tears were flowing as she cried out, "Becca! What are you doing here?" The two women hugged like they hadn't seen each other in years, instead of just a few days, and it was only the call of nature that forced Charlotte to break away.

Hands washed, and tears dried, Charlotte walked back into the bedroom to find Becca snuggled up in her big comfy bed. "Get in here, Lottie," Becca teased, pulling back the covers. "We have your wedding night to discuss, and you owe me the chance to tell you all about what to expect from your new husband."

Charlotte climbed into the bed, both of them near hysterics at the thought of Becca telling Charlotte about the birds and the bees. It wasn't that she couldn't have told some sexy stories, but after all, Charlotte was pregnant with Nick's baby, and Becca had shared with

Charlotte years ago that she had been right, things with Jared had worked out very well in that department.

Getting herself under control, Charlotte looked at her friend and asked, "Seriously Bec, what are you doing here? We just talked last night; you couldn't have gotten here that quickly."

With an impish grin Becca answered, "I was in New York when I called you, Lottie. In fact, I was right next door."

"I don't understand," Charlotte said shaking her head. "Nick is staying next door in his mother's friend's apartment, why were you there?"

"For such a smart lady, you sure can be dense," Becca laughed. "I stayed in the apartment with Nick last night, Jared and I both did. Don't you get it yet? Nick flew us in so I could be here for your wedding."

Charlotte couldn't stop the tears from falling again. She didn't even try. "Oh Becca, even after our talk last night I thought I would be okay without you being here, but to be honest, my soul was hurting at the thought. I can't believe Nick did this for me."

"I'm pretty sure he'd do anything to keep you happy and willing to marry him today. The last man I saw this in love was my husband, so I guess you're going to have to put this one out of his misery."

Just then there was another knock on the door, and this time it was Elizabeth, followed by Stuart and a delicious looking tray of food for Charlotte and Becca to share. "So, what do you think of my son's surprise?" Elizabeth asked as Stuart passed glasses of chilled orange juice to Charlotte and Becca.

"It's the most amazing thing anyone has ever done for me," Charlotte said. "Well maybe the second most amazing thing," she added, considering her gran had deeded her a cottage on the beach and a hefty savings account to go with it. "Anyway, I can't get over Nick doing this, and I need to tell him how much it means to me."

Charlotte reached for her phone, but Becca stopped her. "No talking to the groom before the ceremony, Lottie," Becca reminded her. "It's bad luck."

Charlotte was awfully close to pouting when Elizabeth handed her an envelope. "Becca's right, Charlotte. You'll be seeing Nick soon enough, but he did ask me to give you this."

Her hands shaking, Charlotte took the envelope from Nick's mother and carefully opened it. Just reading the first line had the waterworks staring again.

"Charlotte,"

> *Ever since the day I walked into your office this summer and saw the beautiful, confident woman you had become, I've thought of nothing but how to make you mine. It took my breath away to see you sitting there, trying hard to be the Market President, and keeping your feelings at bay, but they were there, and that just made me want you more.*
>
> *I know how important Becca is to you, and how special she is in your life. I also know how you were struggling with the thought of getting married without her by your side.*
>
> *So, Becca is my wedding present to you. She isn't a piece of jewelry that you can wear and then keep in a box, but she's part of your heart, and I hope that I'm part of it, too.*
>
> *You are the most amazing, gorgeous, sexy woman that I've ever met, and I want nothing more than to be your husband, your friend, your lover, and the father to your children for the rest of our lives.*

Forever....
Nick

Even though Charlotte read the letter to herself, both Becca and Elizabeth cried right along with her, knowing how moving it must be. Finally, Stuart stepped in and told the women, "If you let this breakfast go to waste after all my hard work, I'm going to be very unhappy with you. And besides, if you don't stop crying, Miss Charlotte, no amount of makeup in the world will cover up your puffy eyes." Then with a wink he proceeded to lovingly dish up plates of fruit and quiche, and at least for the moment, the tears were dried, and smiles were on all three women's faces.

Chapter 20
Now

"Okay Lottie," Becca said after both women had eaten every bite of Stuart's delicious breakfast. "It's time to start making you wedding ready." Becca knew more than most people how long it took for Charlotte to get ready for an event, and this was no ordinary event. Today was Charlotte's wedding day, and Becca wanted it to be perfect for her friend.

Charlotte nodded and tentatively got out of the big bed. Looking back at Becca snuggled in the soft sheets, her very pregnant belly rising like a highland out of the moors, she couldn't keep the smile off her face. "I love you Bec," Charlotte told her, "and I'll remember this day for the rest of my life. Now you lay there and relax while I do my shower thing because, when I get out, you're going to make me look like a bride."

Thirty minutes later Charlotte emerged from the shower squeaky clean and smooth as silk. Her long strawberry blonde locks had been washed and deep conditioned. Her body had been scrubbed and polished with a new loofa that Elizabeth had given her and then slathered with the Pure Fiji coconut body butter that her soon to be mother-in-law said would make her skin, "Smoother than a fresh jar of Skippy." Charlotte smiled, remembering the quirky phrase Elizabeth had used, but hey, she loved peanut butter so why not?

Becca was out of bed and on her phone when Charlotte stepped back into the bedroom. Seeing Charlotte, she said, "I love you, too," to the person on the other end, and hung-up.

"Why is it you get to talk to Jared, but I can't talk to Nick?" Charlotte pouted.

"Because you're the bride and I'm just the matron of honor," Becca giggled her reply. "But Jared did say to tell you that Nick is going crazy next door, and he can't wait to see you. Apparently, he wanted to call you too, but Jared put his foot down. I love it when that man takes control."

Charlotte rolled her eyes, not sure what kind of control Becca was referring to, but then sighed, hoping that her relationship with Nick would be what Becca had with Jared. Giving her friend a big hug, Charlotte moved the focus back on the wedding.

"What do you think?" Charlotte asked her friend. "Should I wear my hair up or down?"

Becca looked at Charlotte's mane of damp curls and replied, "I know that Nick loves your hair down, but I'm thinking up for the ceremony, and then you can let him take it down for the wedding night. What do you think?"

Charlotte almost choked, she was laughing so hard. "Wow!" she exclaimed. "Whoever knew my friend, Sister Rebecca Rose, could have such a sexy side to her? Honestly though, I love it! I'm going to make up to Nick for all these weeks of celibacy I've put him through, and you're going to help me."

Chapter 21

Now

Charlotte looked in the mirror and could hardly believe the woman staring back was her! Becca had skillfully arranged her strawberry blonde locks into a crown of curls that perfectly held the thin tiara she had chosen to hold her veil. The shear foundation Becca had applied was flawless and even covered the few freckles on Charlotte's nose. With a dusting of IT Pretty in Peony cheek flush, Mallygirl Champagne eyeshadow, and a double-coat of mascara, Charlotte was ready for everything but her lipstick and perfume.

"Wow!" Charlotte exclaimed. "I'm starting to feel like a bride. You do good work, Bec; maybe you should have gone into cosmetology instead of nursing."

Becca laughed as she answered her friend. "Probably not a big call for makeup in a convent, Lottie, and if you'll remember, that's where I thought I was headed when I left for college."

"You don't have to remind me, girlfriend. I wasn't sure what I was going to do if you ended up cloistered somewhere, but it all worked out the way it was meant to be. You and Jared have medicine in common, among a few other things, and when your kids get older, you can probably help him more at the free clinic. And speaking of the Tyler Tykes, where are they?" Charlotte asked.

"Since we were just at my parents last week, Jared's mom is doing grandma duty. With her living in New Smyrna Beach, she was able to come over right away. They're all at our house just waiting by the iPad for pictures."

"I would so have loved to have Anna and Lolly be my flower girls, and Nikki and Steffi as bridesmaids, but I had to do this for Nick's mom. You understand that, don't you?" Charlotte could feel the emotions welling up in her throat, and the last thing she needed was to cry again.

"Sweetie we've been through this before. Of course, I understand, we all understand. The important thing is to get you and Nick married before your bump becomes a belly or one of you does something stupid again."

Charlotte's eyes were as big as saucers as she looked at her friend. "What?" Becca asked innocently. "I just call 'em as I see 'em." And then they both burst out laughing.

Chapter 22
Now

Charlotte slipped her short robe off her shoulders and looked at the light blue silk and lace corset hanging in her closet. As much as she would have liked to have kept it just between her and Nick, she knew she would need Becca's help getting it fastened. Pulling on the matching thong, Charlotte wiggled her hips into the corset and then called for Becca's help.

"Uh, Bec, could you come here a minute?" Charlotte called out to her friend. Becca's hand flew to her mouth when she saw her friend standing there, all but naked, a tiny blue piece of silk covering her bottom, and another awkwardly twisted around her hips.

Doing her best not to laugh at her friend's predicament, Becca asked, "How can I help?"

"I probably should have put this thing on before you did my hair and makeup but since that's not an option now, tug! This little piece of material is part of my wedding present to Nick, so I have to get it on."

After a few minutes of pulling and tugging, the little piece of material was firmly in place, and Charlotte was blushing and smiling all at the same time. "Thanks, Becca," she said to her friend. "That isn't something I could have asked anyone else in the world for help with. Now you go get outfitted while I fasten my stockings to the garters, and then you can help me with my gown and veil."

A short time later Becca retuned, outfitted in a gorgeous, lilac Infinity Maternity dress with a V-neckline that crisscrossed just under the bodice. "Oh Becca, you look so beautiful," Charlotte exclaimed when she saw her friend. "I couldn't have picked out something more perfect if I'd have done it myself."

"Nick's mom had a hand in this," Becca replied. "When he told her I was coming, she called her friend at Kleinfeld and had this sent over. I don't look half bad, if I do say so myself." Becca twirled in front of the mirror like a girl getting ready to attend her first dance.

"You look amazing," Charlotte said honestly. "Now help me finish getting ready, so you don't show me up!"

With her wedding dress finally on, Charlotte sat down so Becca could attach her veil. But instead of that happening, Becca opened the bedroom door and Elizabeth wheeled in. "I know this is the job for the mother of the bride," Elizabeth said softly, "but since your mom can't be here, I was hoping you'd let me stand in?"

With a genuine smile Charlotte replied, "I would love that."

The veil attached, shoes and lipstick on, Charlotte sprayed herself lightly with Nick's favorite perfume, and with excitement in her voice said, "Let's go get me married."

She was just about to open the door when Elizabeth dropped one more bombshell. "Um, Charlotte, Gus and I have a special wedding present for you and Nicky, and it's in the hallway," she stammered. "I know that this wedding is happening today so I can be a part of it, and I decided that if you could do this for me, I needed to do something just as wonderful for you."

Without waiting for Charlotte to reply, Elizabeth opened the door and there stood Pop.

"I heard you needed a dad to walk you down the aisle, Lottie" he told her gently. "I hope that I'll do."

Makeup be damned, the water works were in full force as Charlotte threw herself into the arms of Nick's dad.

"I can't believe this," she cried. "First Becca and now you?" Reaching down to grab Elizabeth's hand, Charlotte whispered, "Thank you," as she looked with love on the two people who had made her dreams come true. Not only was their son the love of her life, and an amazing man, but they too held special places in her heart, and she knew that she now had the family she had always wanted.

Chapter 23
Then

"Am I ever going to have a brother or sister?" Lottie asked her mommy. She had just started school and understood that she didn't have a daddy, but neither did Katy Wagner, and she had two brothers.

Shaking her head, Maggie Luce tried to answer as honestly as possible. "You know that your daddy is in heaven, Lottie. We've talked about that before, but you are my special gift from him, and you're the only little girl that I want."

Lottie thought for a moment and then replied, "Okay, so how about a brother then? I can be your little girl, and he can be your little boy." Lottie beamed, deciding she had come up with the solution for them both.

With a sigh Maggie put her arms around her daughter. "You're it for me kiddo," she told Lottie, "and with your gran in our lives, we have all the family that we need." Lottie was about to push the issue even more, but when her mommy left the room, she knew that the conversation was over.

Grabbing her box of crayons and some drawing paper, Lottie sat down and drew a picture of the family of her dreams. It had a mommy and a daddy, a baby brother and of course, Gran. Becca had a brother and Katy Wagner had two, and it just wasn't fair that Lottie couldn't even have one. She put a sun in the corner, because this was her Happily Ever After, but in her head was a picture of her with Mommy and Gran, and there were dark skies all around them. Even at age five, Lottie knew she was missing out on something, and that something was hanging over her like a big, dark rain cloud.

Chapter 24

Now

Pop pulled a handkerchief from his pocket and did his best to pat the tears from Charlotte's face without doing any more damage to her makeup. He looked over the lovely young woman who was about to become his daughter-in-law and smiled. As far as he was concerned, Charlotte Luce had been his daughter since the day they met.

"Does Nick know?" Charlotte asked between gulps of air. Trying to get herself composed was taking a little longer than she was comfortable with, so she focused on her breathing in hopes it would calm her down.

"He does," Pop answered. "I stopped in to see him first, but the surprise doesn't end there, Lottie. The whole family is here." Knowing that more tears were going to be shed, Pop handed Charlotte his hanky, and gently put his arms around her.

Stepping out of his embrace, Charlotte stooped down next to Elizabeth's wheelchair and put her arms around the frail woman. "I know what a sacrifice it was for you to invite Pop here, and to allow him to see you this way after all these years, but I want you to know that I will never forget what you've done for us. Your children are three of the most decent and loving people I've ever known, and you're a big part of why that is. I am blessed to be marrying into this family, and I'm thrilled that you will be my child's grandmother."

Charlotte and Elizabeth hugged for several more minutes before Gus came in to tell them it was time. Lovingly, he took hold of his wife's wheelchair, and with just a nod to Pop, he pushed her in where her children and Becca's husband were waiting.

"This is it, Sweetie," Becca smiled. "Are you ready to go make your fairytale come true?"

Pop put out his arm, and Charlotte linked them together. Her bouquet of flowers, with names she couldn't remember, was laying on the etagere, and in true Elizabeth fashion, there was a smaller bouquet for Becca as well. Smiling up at Pop she said, "Let's do this!"

Unlike the aisle of a church, the hallway in the Harris' apartment was short, and before she knew it, Charlotte was face-to-face with Nick, Noah standing close beside him, Kenney Chesney's, "You Had Me From Hello," playing softly in the background. Maya, Dimitri, and the twins were on either side of Elizabeth, and Jared stood to the side of Gus. The only person missing, besides her gran of course, was her mom. Just then a light caught her eye from above, and she realized that a computer monitor was facing them with her mom, Thomas, and Carol, Skyping the ceremony. She blew a kiss to her mom, and then thought, *Shit! Shit! Shit! this is really happening!*

Pop kissed her cheek and joined Charlotte's hand with Nick's. She could tell from looking at him that he had shed a few tears as well, and that just made her love him more.

As they stood there, listening to the words coming from the minister about marriage being a celebration and a sacred trust and not to be entered-into lightly, Nick rubbed his thumb over her fingers, and she could tell he was shaking. When he caught her looking at him Nick winked, and just like that a peace swept over her that she had never felt before. *This is my forever,* she thought, and the next thing she knew, she was saying, "I do."

Chapter 25

Now

When the minister said, "You may now kiss your bride," Charlotte was aware of Nick cupping her face in his hands and lowering his head toward hers, but when their lips touched, the awareness became like fireworks, scorching all the way through to her soul. She could hear applause around her, but all she wanted to do was to sink into the kiss and never come back to the surface.

"Congratulations, Big Brother," Noah said, slapping Nick on the back hard enough to get him to come up for air. "It's been a long time in coming but you finally got the girl, and no one deserves it more." Noah kept the smile on his face, and Charlotte could only hope that he was sincere. Not that long ago he had confessed his love for her, knowing that she'd always thought of him as the brother she'd never had.

Charlotte blushed at Noah's words, but when he pulled her in for a hug and said, "I really am happy for you, Lottie," she relaxed and hugged him back. After that, she and Nick were pulled apart as everyone else in the room surrounded them with hugs and best wishes.

It was only then that Charlotte remembered the people watching the celebration from afar. Stepping closer to the monitor she looked at her mom and was relieved to see nothing but love and pride on her face. "Mom," she said, "I hope you understand about all of this. I really just wanted to have a simple ceremony here for Nick's mother, and things just kind of snowballed."

"Oh Charlotte," her mom replied, "we've never been much of a conventional family, so why start now? Nick and Gus both invited us, even offered to foot the bill, but we just couldn't be gone again right now. I hope that you can understand that?"

Charlotte nodded just as Nick found her. "We'll be there for your wedding, Maggie," he told Charlotte's mom. "I promise I'll take good care of your daughter."

"I wouldn't expect any less of you, Nick Greyson, but be warned, my daughter does a pretty good job of taking care of herself." Nick put his arms around Charlotte and held her close while they finished the conversation with her mom. With a promise to call her when they got back to Anna Maria Island, Charlotte told her mother how much she loved her, and they said their goodbyes.

Nick didn't leave Charlotte's side as the cake was cut, toasts were made, and pictures were taken, but finally he bent down and whispered in her ear. "Are you ready to get out of here, Mrs. Greyson, because I can't wait another minute to get you alone."

Charlotte could feel the blush start in her toes and work all the way up to her face, but she didn't care. After all the years of friendship, and all the years of hurt, she was exactly where she'd always hoped she'd be, Nick Greyson's wife. Linking her fingers in his, Charlotte gave him a look that both delighted and ignited him, and said, "I have never been more ready."

Chapter 26

Now

"Put me down, Nick!" Charlotte squealed when Nick picked her up and carried her into their hotel suite. "I weigh a ton, and you're recovering from a gunshot wound, remember?"

Nick carried her to the massive white bed before carefully laying her down. "There are two things I'm only going to do one time in my life," he growled. "The first is carry my bride over the threshold on our wedding day, and the other is getting shot." Just as Charlotte opened her mouth to answer, he covered it with his own, and anything she had to say was forgotten.

After a few minutes of kissing that had Charlotte squirming on the bed, she held up her hand to stop him. "Wait," she said breathlessly. "I haven't thanked you for my wonderful wedding present, and I need to give you mine."

Nick's face softened, but he grabbed her hand and tried to pull her back down beside him. "Can we talk about this later?" he asked her. "I knew how much you needed Becca with you, but now I need you with me, so focus."

Charlotte smiled and shook her head. "But I want to give you your present," she said with a pout. Nick flopped back on the bed and with a sigh asked, "Okay, where is it?"

"Right here," she answered coyly. Pulling him into a sitting position Charlotte put his hands around her waist and continued. "I'm your present," she told him, "and now you get to unwrap me."

"Yeah?" Nick questioned with a seductive grin on his face. "This may be the best present I've ever gotten." He pulled Charlotte down so that she was sitting on his lap and started a slow assault of kisses down her throat and almost to the top of her dress. Just when she thought he would go further, he stopped and nibbled on her lips. He could see the effect he was having on her, but Nick continued to tease and torment.

Charlotte felt as if she were dying! Her skin was on fire and her beautiful wedding dress felt prickly and rough, and all she could think about was getting it off.

"Please Nick," she begged, but he was oblivious to her protests.

"I want to enjoy unwrapping my present, Charlotte," he said with a smile. "I've never opened a present from my wife before."

Shit! Shit! Shit! She thought. *Why did I think this was a good idea?* Nick was obviously more experienced than she was at the art of seduction, and she was ready to be done with the hors d'oeuvres and move on to the main course! Finally, he put his hand on the back of her dress, hoping to unzip it, only to find a cascade of buttons, each one needing to be unfastened.

Lifting Charlotte off his lap, Nick turned her around and began down the slow descent of buttons. He was still dressed in his tux, so even though she was tingling from head to toe, she got some satisfaction when she turned to look at him and at the very large tent in his pants. With a giggle, she moved back and forth on her toes, hardly able to contain her excitement. When he finally got to the last button and slipped the dress off her shoulders, his response made the wait worth it.

No words came out of his mouth, but his face was filled with love and his eyes dark with need. It was exactly the response Charlotte had hoped for.

Chapter 27

Now

Nick ran his hands up her sides, slowly and thoughtfully, stopping to caress her breasts. When the caresses became more urgent, Charlotte cried out. Startled, Nick stopped. "Did I hurt you?"

"Oh, no," Charlotte told him, taking his hands and returning them to her throbbing chest. "It feels amazing, like little bolts of electricity running through me. Please don't stop."

This was the most Charlotte had ever said about what she needed from him as a lover, and damn if it wasn't arousing. Slipping his hands inside the bodice of the corset, he found flesh… warm, taut, wonderful flesh, and when he gently tugged on a swollen nipple with his teeth, Charlotte cried out in pleasure. "I love the sounds you make, Charlotte," Nick said, his voice husky with desire. "You have no idea what they do to me."

Smiling Charlotte replied. "You have on way too many clothes, Mr. Greyson," she told him. "Why don't you let me help you with that?" Never taking her eyes from him, Charlotte slipped off Nick's tie and jacket and began slowly unbuttoning his shirt. When his shirt was unbuttoned Charlotte pushed it aside and laid a trail of small, wet kisses from his collarbone to his waist, paying particular attention to the pink scar on his chest. When she rubbed his length through his tuxedo trousers, Nick thought he had died and gone to heaven.

But when she unbuckled his belt, and put her soft fingers around him, he almost came undone. Realizing she needed to give him a moment to get things back under control, Charlotte took Nick's hand and guided it to the crown of curls on top of her head. "I wore my hair up for the wedding, but I thought you might enjoy taking it down."

As the pins fell to the ground, and Charlotte's mane of strawberry blonde curls fell around her shoulders, Nick used one hand to pull her in for one of his earth-shattering kisses, and the other he slipped inside her very wet panties. All it took was one touch to her slick, swollen flesh, and Charlotte went over the edge. *This marriage thing might be alright*, she thought, as her sated body fell against his.

"I guess the past few weeks have been just as hard on you as they have been on me," Nick said with a big grin on his face. "Or is it the outfit? Because I'm thinking it's something you need to wear every day."

"Enjoy it while you can," she answered saucily. "It won't be long until my sexy lingerie is too small, and I'll be wearing granny panties and a nursing bra."

"You'll always be sexy as far as I'm concerned, but since it's our wedding night, let's leave the imagery for another time." Nick told her. "Now, where were we?"

It didn't take long to get Nick's pants and boxer briefs off, and all of a sudden, Charlotte was looking at the anaconda dead on. When her eyes got big, Nick took her face in his hands and covered it with butterfly kisses. As her concern started to ease, he began telling her all the things he loved about her body, while moving the kisses with his words.

"I love your silky soft hair, and how it smells like coconuts and mangos. I love your bewitching green eyes that always give away what you're feeling. I love your creamy smooth skin, and how it tastes like peaches. I love your big heart, and the way you take care of your friends, and I love your...."

"Please Nick," Charlotte moaned, "I can't take anymore, I need you now."

In an instant, the lacy panties were gone, and Nick was between her shaky thighs. He kissed her and found her core, trying to be gentle, but Charlotte wanted more.

"Nick," she begged.

To which he responded, "I'm right here, Baby," and with just one thrust, Charlotte came undone. Again.

Chapter 28

Now

Charlotte was deep in sleep, exhausted from the events of the past few days, not to mention the last few hours! She was aware of a gentle touch brushing the hair from her face, so she forced her eyes open and came face to face with the most beautiful sight she had ever seen. The friend of her childhood, the boy she had fallen in love with, the man she had married was sitting beside her wearing black silk pajama pants, his chest bare and his hair still damp from a shower, eyes overflowing with love.

"Hey," Nick said as he leaned down to give her a soft kiss. "I've ordered room service. I hope you're hungry."

"I'm starving," Charlotte said truthfully, realizing that she hadn't really eaten since breakfast. "Do I have time to shower first?"

Nick nodded and kissed her again, this time with a lot more passion. "I love you Charlotte," he said as he nuzzled her neck. "I love you more than I ever thought possible."

"How long do we have before the food comes?" she asked him with a smile, and pulling him down beside her, she showed him just how much she loved him, too.

Charlotte had just stepped out of the shower when she heard the knock on the door and the requisite, "room service." Rushing so the food wouldn't get cold, she quickly lathered her body with Jose Maran Whipped Peach Butter Argan Oil, brushed out her tangled hair, and slipped on her long white slip-style nightgown. She ran her fingers over the very visible bump that was showing in the formfitting gown and talked softly to her unborn child.

"This is about me and your daddy tonight," she said, running her hands over her stomach, "but we both love you, don't ever forget that."

Peeking her head out of the bathroom door to make sure Nick was alone, Charlotte watched him light the candles and arrange the covered dishes of food on the coffee table. She knew she had taken her locket off when she showered, but instinctively she reached up for it as she talked to her gran.

"I never allowed myself to see Nick as my forever, Gran," she whispered. "But I truly believe he's my gift from God." Then, seeing that Nick was looking her way, she stepped into the room.

"You look good enough to eat," Nick told her, as she walked into his arms.

"That's what I'm counting on," she replied with a smirk.

"The things that come out of your mouth, Charlotte," Nick laughed as he kissed her lips.

"But how about what goes in it?" she asked him, nipping and licking his jaw.

Nick's voice was deep and gravelly when he was able to respond, and all he said was, "Charlotte."

Charlotte pulled away, because she truly was hungry, and sat down on the couch, lifting the lids from the serving dishes. "Bacon cheeseburgers, Nick!" she squealed. "I couldn't have asked for a more perfect meal."

"Well it was what we had the first time we ever had dinner alone together. I thought it was fitting that we have it tonight, for our first dinner together as a married couple."

Charlotte patted the couch, and he sat down beside her. Taking a fry from her plate, she seductively fed it to him before putting one in her own mouth. "I was scared to death walking into Duffy's with you," she laughed. "My mom had always told me it was a bar, which is why I steered clear of it. I remember thinking I was sure the police were going to come after us even though we were taking our food to go."

"Then we took the food to the beach and sat at the playground they had for kids because we hadn't thought to bring a blanket. We were just awkward teenagers, but I thought you were the prettiest girl I'd ever seen," Nick said, with a slight blush. "I'll admit I wasn't thinking marriage that night, but I sure was thinking about other things."

Charlotte had just started to reach for her burger, but when Nick said that, she reached for him instead. "We were way too young for other things back then," she said, "but we're not now."

"Then eat your dinner quickly, Charlotte Greyson," Nick said with a wink, "because we need to make up for lost time."

Chapter 29
Now

Every inch of her body had turned to mush, Charlotte realized as she tried to open her eyes. After dinner they had teased, touched, and tasted each other for hours until they both were content and exhausted. She didn't remember falling asleep, but she must have because now a strong arm was laying protectively over her stomach and a battering ram was nestled up against her butt. Making her eyes focus enough to see the clock, she saw that it was three o'clock in the morning, and her wedding day was officially over.

Trying to gently dislodge Nick's arm so she could exit the bed, Charlotte almost jumped when he kissed the back of her neck. Turning over she saw that he was very much awake, and so was the anaconda! *Shit! Shit! Shit!* she thought. *I need to pee before I explode, and he's got lust in his eyes again. Men!*

"Uh, Nick," she said, trying hard to wiggle herself out of his embrace. "I think your son or daughter has been sleeping on my bladder, and I really need to go. Plus, I don't remember what I put in my mouth last, but I feel like I need to brush my teeth, too."

Looking at Nick's face reminded Charlotte of what she had put in her mouth last, and she blushed a nice shade of crimson. "And you need to brush your teeth as well," she told him as she rushed to the bathroom, replaying the last hours before sleep in her mind.

She wasn't sure that she liked the way Nick was laughing, but she really didn't like it when he walked into the bathroom while she was sitting on the toilet.

"Hey!" she said with force. "A little privacy, please."

Nick shrugged his shoulders and closed the bathroom door but said loud enough for her to hear, "You're the one who told me to brush my teeth. I was just trying to be a dutiful husband."

Hurriedly, Charlotte finished her business, washed her hands, brushed her teeth, and splashed cold water on her face. When she came out Nick was patiently waiting his turn, but she didn't acknowledge him when she walked by. Instead she walked straight to the bed, climbed in and pulled the covers up, as if she intended to go back to sleep.

A few agonizing minutes later Nick came back into the bedroom and sat down next to her on the bed. "Are you really mad at me?" he asked tentatively. Charlotte pretended to be contemplating her response when she pulled back the covers and invited him in. The sexy white nightgown that she had donned before leaving the bed was gone, and her warm, naked body welcomed him.

"If this was our first fight, I'm pretty sure I'm going to like making up," he chuckled, and when Charlotte touched him, all the laughter turned to love.

Chapter 30

Now

"Breakfast in bed makes me feel so pampered," Charlotte said, popping a strawberry in her mouth. Before her was a brandy snifter filled with strawberries, a perfectly cooked cheese omelet, and a basket of assorted muffins. "But if I even eat a third of this food, I'll be waddling by the time we get to your mom's apartment for dinner. I'll bet I've gained ten pounds this week as it is," she told Nick. "So, you'd better chow down big boy."

Putting another strawberry on a fork, Nick dangled it before her lips and then watched her suck on the juicy fruit. "We won't make it to my mom's for dinner if you keep that up," he said. Eat what you can and then decide what you want to do today. And for the record, your body is perfect. You're perfect."

Charlotte gave him a soft, slow kiss that tasted like strawberries and yearning before asking, "Is it like this for everyone, Nick?"

"Is what like this for everyone?" he teased her. "Breakfast in bed?"

"You know what I'm talking about," Charlotte replied, running her hand over his very visible five o'clock shadow. "Is making love like we do normal?"

Nick was trying hard not to laugh at her because she looked so innocent and unsure. "I can't speak for everyone," he proceeded cautiously, "but I know that what we have is rare, and I hope it never ends. I can't promise you what happened yesterday, and last night, and early this morning will happen every day, but I can promise you that every time it happens it will be just as wonderful."

Charlotte looked up at him and smiled because he had given her just the answer she had hoped for. All of her adult life she had wanted the kind of relationship that Nick offered her so freely, and she never wanted to take it for granted. Her body was sore in places she didn't know could hurt, but if Nick were to reach out for her again at that moment, she'd gladly move into his embrace.

Pleased that Charlotte was satisfied with his answer Nick asked, "What do you want to do for our last day in New York? More shopping, sightseeing, stay in bed all day, your wish is my command."

"Well," she said honestly. "What I'd really like to do is stay in bed for a while and then go to Ground Zero. I know it's not really a festive place to visit, but it's important to me. What do you think?"

"I think you're about the most amazing woman I've ever met, and I like the sound of your plan. Why don't we finish eating, I'll give you a massage, and then we can shower and get dressed," Nick told her.

"And what exactly does a massage entail?" she asked, raising her eyebrows.

"That's entirely up to you," Nick answered with a wink. "I'll rub your soft shoulders and strong back, your long sexy legs, and even those feet that you torture with ridiculously high heels. And if you feel the need to reward me afterwards, I won't embarrass you by saying "no."

Charlotte was laughing so hard by the end of his speech that her sides hurt. Laughing right along with her, Nick rubbed his scruffy face over hers and gave her forehead a gentle kiss. "Good thing I'm so confident in my masculinity," he told her. "Laughing at your husband less than twenty-four hours into the marriage could really be an ego crusher."

"Your masculinity will never be called into doubt, my love," Charlotte answered with a sly smile. "Now get over here and start my massage. I can't reward you unless the service is exemplary!"

Chapter 31

Now

Finally, squeaky clean from head to toe, Charlotte stepped out of the shower and stared at her reflection in the mirror. *That's the look of a woman who's had a lot of sex*, she thought to herself with a smile, *a lot of really amazing sex.* Her face and neck had a pink rash from where Nick's five o'clock shadow had rubbed over them, and as her eyes moved down her body, she saw the rash did as well. Her lips were swollen from kisses so raw she wouldn't have believed they were possible if she hadn't experienced them herself, but she had, and boy did her husband knew how to kiss.

With a soft, thick towel around her body, and another one around her head, Charlotte applied some Josie Maran Whipped Argan Oil Face Butter to her chaffed skin, adding extra to her cheeks and neck. That was followed by the Whipped Argan Oil Body Butter in peach like she had used the night before, and soon her skin was feeling refreshed and silky again.

Not wanting to take the time needed to dry her long, thick hair, Charlotte opted instead for pulling it into a high ponytail and wrapping it into a tight bun. Normally she would have just used a little mascara and blush, but with her face still showing the telltale signs of love making, she added a little concealer to the affected areas and followed with bronzer on her cheeks and a double coat of mascara on her lashes.

Deciding what to wear was a whole other problem. She had already worn everything she had brought with her, but she decided the black and white knit Jones New York dress that she had worn to her wedding gown fitting would have to do. That and a pair of black ballet flats and she'd be dressed fine for an afternoon in New York. Adding a pair of silver hoop earrings and her locket, Charlotte closed her eyes and said a quick prayer to Gran, followed by a spritz of perfume and a swipe of coconut lip gloss.

When Charlotte stepped out of the dressing area, she saw that Nick was on his cell, and it gave her time to look him up and down. *My husband is gorgeous!* she thought, seeing Nick in a pair of tan linen trousers and a dark green boatneck shirt. Maybe walking him through the streets of New York wasn't such a great idea after all.

Nick looked up and caught her staring at him, and the look he gave her just about took her breath away. It was love and lust all wrapped up as one, and it was almost more than Charlotte could do not to strip down and take him back to bed.

Instead she took a deep breath and asked, "Who were you talking to?"

"Pop," Nick replied, putting his phone in his pocket. "He and Dimi are going to take the twins and head back to Tampa today, but Noah and Maya are going to stay with Mom and Gus through the weekend. I wish we could stay the weekend too, not to be with my family, but just so we could have more time here together."

Nick was moving her way, and Charlotte knew they would never leave the room if she didn't do something fast. "I'm ready to go if you are," she said innocently, holding out her hand.

Nick took it in his and kissed her palm before moving toward the door. "And you look delectable," he told her with a grin, and he led her out into the beautiful New York sunshine.

Chapter 32
Now

Nick and Charlotte stood in front of the 9/11 Memorial, her back to his front, his arms wrapped protectively around her. For a few moments they just stood there, reading names of those lost on that terrible date so many years before and looking over the beautiful design of the memorial. When Charlotte finally spoke, it was in a hushed, reverent tone.

"We were just kids when this happened Nick, but standing here today, I feel as if it were yesterday. We're so blessed to have each other and our families, but just think, every one of these people left behind someone who loved them and someone they loved."

Nick pulled her in tighter as he heard the emotion in her voice. "I was raised to believe that there's good in everyone," he told her, "but I struggle to find the good in anyone who uses terrorism to further their own agenda."

"I know what you're saying, and it's not that I don't agree, but I can't help but wonder what causes an ordinary person to become so evil. Gran used to tell me that the Bible says to pray for your enemies, but that's hard to do. Especially when you see up close and personal the devastation they've caused." Charlotte tried to blink back the tears, but she was fighting a losing battle.

"I'll keep you and Babycakes safe, Charlotte," Nick told her, the emotion in his own voice coming through. "I promise."

"But you can't protect us from hate, can you?" she asked him.

Nick had tears in his eyes as well but choked them back as he answered with just one word, "No."

They held hands all the way back to the hotel. While others talked and laughed on the subway, Nick and Charlotte were quiet and subdued. As soon as they entered their room they were in each other's arms. The lovemaking was an affirmation of their love and devotion to each other and was more about being close than having sex. It was meaningful and significant and one of the most beautiful things Charlotte had ever experienced.

"I love you so much, Nick," she told him as she lay breathless in his arms. "I can't even put into words how I feel right now, but I know this is a moment in time that I'll never forget."

Kissing the top of her head and gently caressing her cheek, Nick answered, "I won't forget it either. I can't imagine my life ever again without you, Lottie. You and our child are my everything."

Charlotte smiled and closed her eyes. With little sleep the night before, and a very emotional afternoon, she was ready for a nap, snuggled safely in the arms of her very own FBI agent.

Chapter 33

Now

Charlotte looked over Nick's sleeping form. *This man is my husband!* Who would have ever thought that chubby, geeky, red-haired Lottie Luce would end up with the hottest boy in school? Charlotte smiled to herself wondering what Ashley Marshall would think if she saw them now. She had done everything in her power to break the bond between Charlotte and Nick, and even though it had for twelve years, they were together now, right where they belonged. At that moment, Nick turned over and the sheet fell away from his naked body, putting all thoughts of those years, and Ashley Marshall, aside.

Oh, he was one magnificent hunk of man. The time spent at the marina this summer had bronzed his skin, and the years of competitive swimming had sculpted his arms, shoulders, and legs with strong, defined muscles, but it was his butt that had her mouth watering. The saying about being able to bounce a quarter off it came to mind, and Charlotte giggled at the thought.

Just then Nick turned over, and wouldn't you know, the anaconda was looking right at her! "Hey," Nick said, trying to pull her back into bed. "What are you doing up?"

"I got a text from Maya that Stuart will be here in an hour, so we need to get ready, or we'll be late," Charlotte told him. "I need to shower so you can lie there a few minutes more, but then you need to get moving, too."

"Or," Nick said with a gleam in his eye, "we could shower together."

"Do you really mean shower or is that a euphemism for having sex?" she teased. "Because I'm not walking into your mom's apartment looking anymore *recently laid* than I already do. So, I'll shower with you and even wash your back, and maybe even your front, but my body is off limits, understand?"

Nick just winked and said, "We'll see."

Forty-five minutes later they were rushing to get dressed when Nick got a text that Stuart was downstairs. "I knew this was going to happen," Charlotte grumbled, to which Nick laughed.

Holding hands on the ride to Nick's mother's apartment, Nick and Charlotte were quiet, realizing their honeymoon was pretty much over, and they were making their first appearance as a newly married couple. Nick gave her knee a squeeze as they pulled up in front of the beautiful Park Avenue apartment building and said, "Are you ready, Mrs. Greyson?"

Charlotte took a deep breath and nodded. She wasn't sure why this seemed like such a big deal, but for some reason it did. It wasn't like these people didn't know she and Nick had slept together before they were married, she was pregnant for heaven's sakes, but being the private person she was, it just felt like too much too soon.

Everyone was there waiting for them when the elevator door opened, and while Nick stooped to kiss his mom, Noah pulled Charlotte into a big bear hug. "Marriage looks good on you, Lottie," he teased her, looking directly at her whisker rash. Charlotte blushed somewhere between pink and rose and thought, *Shit! Shit! Shit! This was exactly what I didn't want to happen.*

Nick saw the look on his new wife's face as he broke away from his mom and rescued her. "You okay?" he whispered. Charlotte smiled weakly and then turned to Maya for a hug. After hugs all around, and the news that Pop, Dimitri, and the twins had made it home safely, the family headed into the den for cocktails before dinner.

All in all, it was a lovely evening and both Nick and Charlotte were thrilled to hear how well the visit was going with Elizabeth and her two other children. It broke Charlotte's heart a little bit to think of all the time they had wasted not being a family, but they were together now, and that's what mattered. She only wished she knew for sure that Pop was alright and truly over the woman he thought was the love of his life.

Around nine o'clock Nick said they needed to go, and when Elizabeth started to protest, Maya stepped in. "Why don't you fuss over Noah tonight, Mom?" she said. "After all, Nick and I each have a spouse to keep us warm at night, but little Noah is all alone." She gave Noah a snarky grin, and he retaliated by sticking out his tongue, but it was all in fun, and it helped Charlotte and Nick to make their exit.

"Our flight leaves at eleven in the morning," Nick reminded them, which means we'll need to be here at seven if you still want us to stop by."

"Of course, we do, Nicky," Elizabeth said, grabbing his hand. "Breakfast will be ready, and we can say our goodbyes." Seeing a tear start to roll down his mother's cheek, Nick looked up at Maya and Noah, who immediately were by their mother's side.

With hands clasped, they stepped into the elevator and headed to their last night in New York.

Chapter 34

Now

It was an early morning, following a late night, when Nick and Charlotte met Stuart in front of their hotel at six-thirty a.m. Their luggage was carefully put in the trunk, and when the lid slammed, reality sunk in.

"Will you be glad to get home, Charlotte?" Nick questioned. "I know how much the beach house means to you."

"I do love the beach house Nick, but we're heading home to so many changes that a part of me just wants to stay here and pretend that real life doesn't exist."

Nick brushed her hair off her face and looked straight into her glass green eyes. "It does sound tempting, but don't you think you'd get tired of breakfast in bed and hot sex marathons?"

Charlotte smiled, but replied, "I'm willing to give it a try."

That brought a smile to Nick's face as well, and he pulled her back against him in the limo. "I'll do my best to keep the honeymoon alive," he said and gave her one of his signature kisses that Charlotte felt all the way down to her toes, just to prove his point.

Nick's family was gathered in the dining room drinking coffee when he and Charlotte arrived. They all enjoyed some of the chocolate croissants Charlotte had come to love, and they shared stories of the Greyson kid's childhood antics, as well as their memories of when Lottie came into their lives. It was a happy occasion for all of them, and just before it had to end, Charlotte asked Nick's mom if she could see her alone.

Elizabeth wheeled herself into her bedroom with Charlotte following close behind. Reaching into her pocket, Charlotte pulled out the small box Elizabeth had given her a few days earlier. Handing the box back to her mother-in-law, she spoke.

"I want you to know how much it meant to me to wear your special earrings on my wedding day. I know the meaning they have for you, and wearing them made me feel not only loved, but accepted as part of your family." Wiping a tear from her eye, Charlotte added, "Thank you for everything, Elizabeth. For the earrings, your hospitality, and mostly for the wonderful man you helped create. I will never forget this week or the bond that we formed."

With tears in her own eyes Elizabeth took the box from Charlotte's hand and turned it over in her own. "These earrings represent a different time in my life, and I treasure them. You agreeing to wear them on your wedding day meant so much to me, and I'm thankful it did to you, too. I even noticed Nicholas admiring them on you, so I know that he remembers them, just as I do. Someday I hope to pass them on, but for now, they're one little piece of my past that I like to keep close to my heart."

Just then Nick knocked on the door and asked if he could come in. "Stuart says we need to be going if we're going to get to the airport as early as we need to," he said. Then looking at his mom and his bride, he asked, "Is everything alright?"

Elizabeth reached up for Charlotte's hand and answered her son, "Everything is perfect."

Goodbyes were said again. Hugs and kisses and promises to FaceTime and call regularly were made, but just before Nick and Charlotte stepped into the elevator, Noah called out.

"Uh, could I talk with you for a minute, Nick?" Noah asked.

Stepping away from his bride, Nick answered, "What's up?"

"Right before we left for New York Stella came to the marina looking for you." Noah said running is hand through his dirty blond hair.

"What in the world was Stella doing at the marina? The only time she came there was right after I got out of the hospital."

Noah took a deep breath and let it out slowly. "It appears that Adam Jennings was badly beaten at the prison, but for now, he's still alive. The guard found him when he did his night rounds. He's on life support, but the outcome doesn't look good."

"Charlotte can't find out about this, Noah. At least not right now. Our honeymoon is short as it is, I can't have her worrying about this." Nick looked his brother in the eye, and Noah just nodded.

"I just felt like you needed to know," he responded guardedly. "I guess after the years of Adam stalking her, and then his attempt on your life, Stella is pretty broken up about it. Anyway, I promised I'd stay in touch with her, you know, since you obviously can't."

"Stella's a good kid, Noah, and as innocent as they come. All those years of being dragged around to modeling gigs and Adam stalking her have really done a number on her head. Maybe someone else would be better to be her comforter?" Nick was using his deep FBI voice, but it wasn't working on his brother.

"Don't worry about Stella, Big Brother, you just take care of your wife." Noah patted Nick's back and said, "I'm serious, Nick. Take good care of Lottie."

Understanding his brother's meaning, Nick nodded and gave his brother a hug. "I will Noah, you can count on that."

Stuart picked them up for the ride to the airport, and Nick and Charlotte got settled in the back seat.

"What are you thinking Mrs. Greyson?" Nick asked her, pulling her close.

"I'm thinking I'm ready to go home, Mr. Greyson," she replied. "And maybe for a little bit more of that hot marathon sex."

Chapter 35

Now

Charlotte kissed the fingers on her right hand, reached out and touched the airline's symbol on the side of the plane, and softly said, "Arrive alive." Nick followed suit, not because he believed in Charlotte's superstitions, but because he believed in her.

They found their seat and buckled their seatbelts, and Charlotte leaned her head against Nick's shoulder and closed her eyes. "I'm so tired that I think I might fall asleep before the plane even takes off," she said with a yawn. "You'll probably be just as happy anyway," she laughed. "If I'm asleep, I won't be able to hold your hand in a death grip."

"You fall asleep if you can, Charlotte," Nick said taking her hand, "but you gave me this hand in marriage just two days ago, and I intend to hold on to it forever."

Charlotte smiled and gave his cheek a gentle kiss and then true to her word, she fell asleep.

The flight to Tampa was uneventful, and before Nick knew it, the flight crew was telling the passengers to prepare for landing. Gently rubbing Charlotte's arm, he whispered in her ear, "Dream time is over, my love, time to wake-up and face the world."

They had just stepped into the boarding area when Nick heard his phone ding. Pulling it from his pocket, he frowned at the message as he guided his wife to the baggage claim carousel. "The last time I left you to get our luggage, you met up with an old boyfriend," he teased her. "This time we're going together."

Charlotte smiled and, looking at the worry on Nick's face, asked, "Is everything okay?"

"As far as I know it is, but I just got a message from Director James asking if I could meet with him in the next day or two. It's probably just more paperwork to fill out, but since we're here, would you mind if we just go over there now? We're going to need to rent a car to get home anyway now that Noah is staying in New York, and Pop is alone at the marina, so I'd just as soon get it over with."

Charlotte could tell that Nick was trying to look nonchalant about the message, but she knew him well enough to know that he was concerned. "I think it makes perfect sense Nick," she said, trying to be supportive. "Let's get Director James out of the way so we can head home to the island."

With a nod, Nick grabbed their luggage, and guided her outside to the sweltering Florida afternoon and the rental car booth. Thirty minutes later they pulled away in a fancy looking mocha brown Buick Enclave, ready to face the FBI, or at least its director.

Just like their last visit to see Director James, Charlotte suggested she stay in the car, but once again, Nick vetoed it. "If what the director has to say to me is confidential, he'll ask you to wait outside of his office, but I can't imagine it will be. Like I said, probably more paperwork to fill out."

Charlotte agreed, but only because she knew Nick was more worried about this visit than he was letting on, and she wanted to be with him if there was a problem. Traffic was lighter than normal so the drive to the FBI Field Office was short and quiet. When they arrived, Nick helped Charlotte out of the SUV and pulled her in close to him.

"I love you more than anything; you know that, right?" he told her.

"I *do* know that Nick, but you're scaring me. What's bothering you?"

Nick kissed her gently on the lips and answered. "I just know that I have to tell Director James today that I'm not returning to the FBI, and even though it's what I want, it's going to be hard. He's been my mentor ever since Quantico, and I really respect him." Nick scrubbed his hands over his face and continued, "Are you ready Mrs. Greyson? I can't wait to see everyone's face when I introduce you as my bride."

Charlotte took his hand but still had her doubts about what was going on. Did Nick really want to leave the FBI, or was he doing it for her? *Shit! Shit! Shit!* she thought, this was not what she wanted for this day.

Chapter 36

Now

Director James escorted them into his office and asked them both to sit. He was just getting ready to speak when Nick interrupted him. "Charlotte and I got married," he blurted out. Seeing the pink start to rise on Charlotte's face, Nick took her hand and held on.

"Congratulations to you both," the director smiled. "I was there for the engagement of course, but I didn't realize you had plans to marry so soon. But," he said his voice softening, "I can see how much in love you are, and I wouldn't have wanted to wait either."

Nick sighed, blew out the breath he had been holding, and squeezed Charlotte's hand. "It's kind of a long story," he told the director, "but you didn't ask me here to talk about my personal life, so what's going on?"

"You're right, Nick, I didn't," Director James told him. "I asked you here because I have a special case that needs a topnotch agent, and you're the best one I have. What I need to know is when you'll be cleared to come back to work, and is being away from Charlotte going to be a problem?"

Every emotion possible was running through Charlotte's head as she sat there waiting for Nick to answer. She thought her heart would burst right out of her chest, and then she heard Nick answer the director.

"I don't see my doctors again until next week," he said cautiously, "although I do expect them to release me at that time. The thing is, Sir, I'm not returning to the FBI." Nick looked up at his boss, trying to get a read on his face, but the director was stoic.

"I see," Director James said, looking right at Charlotte. "May I ask why you're turning your back on a career that you seemed to love and are so good at?"

Nick's eyes were turning that deep navy, which happened when he was hurting, and Charlotte wished she could do something to help him. She continued to hold his hand, even giving little reassuring squeezes to let him know she was there, but to be honest, she was hurting too because she wasn't sure how he would answer.

Finally, Nick began to speak. "When I was sixteen, I had my life all figured out. I was going to teach, coach the swim team, and live on Anna Maria Island with the people I loved most in the world. It's not the kind of thing most men will admit to, but I'm not ashamed by it. After I was shot, and I realized I had a chance to live out my dream, I've thought of nothing else." Nick stopped for a moment, but you could have heard a pin drop while they waited for him to continue.

"Anyway, a couple of weeks ago my old coach came to see me and told me that he's going to be retiring. He's already spoken with the School Board, and his teaching and coaching job are mine if I want them. Don't you see, Sir," Nick said to the director, "everything I've ever wanted has been dropped in my lap, and I feel like the luckiest man alive."

Director James stood up and gave Nick a pat on the back. "I do see that, Nick," he told him, "and I'd probably do the same thing in your shoes."

They only stayed a few more minutes, but Director James told Nick that he wouldn't accept his resignation until he was released by his doctors. That way he could continue to be paid and have his insurance benefits. They shook hands, and Nick started to lead Charlotte away when she turned back to the director.

"You're a good man," she said as she gave him a quick hug, "a really good man."

Chapter 37

Now

As soon as they were out of the building, Nick grabbed Charlotte and spun her around. "That went so much better than I expected," he beamed. "Let's go home!"

"Why were you so concerned about the meeting, Nick?" Charlotte asked him. "Did you think there was going to be a problem?"

Nick sighed and knew he had to come clean. "Right before we left, Noah told me that Stella Harper had come to the marina looking for me." Nick stopped long enough to gage her reaction. "She told him that Adam Jennings had been badly beaten but was still alive. While you were asleep on the plane, I got an email from one of the guys that Senator Harper thinks Adam was attacked because of his association to Stella, and he overheard Director James say I was the agent he wanted on the job. I guess I was afraid he would try to change my mind about resigning, and while that wasn't going to happen, I didn't want to let him down either."

"I understand, Nick, honestly I do," Charlotte told him, "but I meant what I told the director. He's a good man, and after all you've been through, I don't believe he would want you to stay if your heart wasn't in it. I hate that Stella has to go through something like this again, but you can't be her safe haven forever." Then with a sly smile she added, "I have a thought, Special Agent. Why don't we make use of this big old SUV and spend the rest of the weekend packing up your condo and taking your things to the beach where they belong?"

Nick looked at his wife and smiled. "Two things," he told her. "First, I won't be a special agent much longer, and second, if we spend the weekend at the condo it means staying overnight and sleeping in my big bed, and I'm pretty sure you made that a hard limit."

"Let me ask you this," she said, trying to look serious. "Have you ever made love to a married woman in that bed?"

"Hell no, Charlotte," Nick growled. "What do you take me for?"

"Calm down, big boy," she whispered. "If I'm the first married woman you've had in that bed, it will be something new and just between us. And Nick, while you're still a special agent, don't you think we need to put your handcuffs to good use?" She batted her eyelashes at him enough to make him laugh.

"What am I going to do with you, woman?" he laughed.

"I have a few ideas," Charlotte purred, "so let's get out of here and see if you really are the best special agent Director James has."

Without giving her time for any more banter, Nick put her in the car, buckled her up, and replied, "I'm the only special agent you're ever going to have, but you can review my performance later today. Much later today."

Charlotte smiled all the way to the condo. She couldn't wait for a rerun of their lust filled afternoon in New York, and she was ready to put to rest her feelings about Nick's big bed of bad dreams.

Chapter 38

Now

Relaxed after making long, slow love on Nick's big California king bed, Charlotte turned toward him and said, "Babycakes and I are hungry. What's the chance you have any food in this place?"

Nick stroked Charlotte's cheek and softly ran his fingers down her throat and over her breasts, before landing on her belly. "You haven't mentioned the baby since we got married," he answered. "I wasn't sure why, so I just kept quiet."

Charlotte leaned over and kissed him gently on the lips. "I wanted the past few days to just be about us," she told him, "and I didn't want to feel like you only married me because you knocked me up." She smiled, and Nick burst out laughing.

"I've said it before, and I know I'll say it again, but the things that come out of your mouth, Charlotte!" Then with a swat to her backside Nick said, "Let's go look over my take-out menus. They're as close to a stocked pantry as I have."

Over moo shu shrimp and Asian slaw, Charlotte and Nick put a plan in place for packing up his condo. "Other than my clothes and personal items," he said, "there isn't anything here I'm going to need on the island, so what do you say if we list the place as fully furnished? Even though we've exercised the ghosts from my bed, I think it would be easier to leave it here, too, and just buy a new one."

Charlotte nodded and reached for the last piece of shrimp from Nick's plate. "It's your condo, Nick," she told him, "but if you're asking for my opinion, then I agree." Looking at the empty take out containers she added, "Did you eat the last of the vegetables?"

"Everything I have is yours," he told her sternly, "but I'm glad we're on the same page. And as for the vegetables, you grabbed the last piece of broccoli right before you stole my shrimp. I may still have a box of Thin Mints in the freezer though if you're still hungry."

Charlotte squealed and clapped her hands in front of her. "Yes, please," she answered. "I love Girl Scout cookies!"

The food crisis avoided, Nick looked at the beautiful woman sitting in front of him and asked her another question. "Do you want to go back and see if my bed is still as comfortable as it was earlier, or should we really do some work?"

Charlotte puffed out her cheeks and laid her hand over her stomach. "As tempting as the bed sounds, I doubt if you're talking about sleeping, and that's exactly what will happen if I get in it again. I'm stuffed and if you move me just right, I'll probably hurl."

"While that's a pleasant thought," Nick teased her, "I think going through my drawers and closet is the best plan of action. I'm pretty sure there are some boxes down in the storage room. Why don't you start pulling things out of the drawers while I go down and get the boxes." Nodding, Charlotte gingerly moved off the couch and headed to Nick's room. Unfortunately, as soon as she saw his big comfy bed, she felt obligated to lie down in it, and oh did it feel good. Smiling at how easily she had gotten over her insecurities about other women, Charlotte closed her eyes and was just drifting off to sleep when her cell phone rang.

"Hello," she answered without bothering to look at the Caller ID, but when she heard the voice on the other end, all thoughts of napping were gone.

"Shelly!" Charlotte exclaimed. "Oh my gosh, I have so much to tell you."

"Like how you're an old married woman now?" Shelly teased her.

Charlotte's heart sank. Shelly had become a great friend, while Nick was under her care after the attempt on his life by Adam Jennings. But in all the commotion, Charlotte realized she hadn't even tried to call her when they had planned their impromptu wedding. Somehow though, her kind, new friend had found out. "Oh Shelly, I'm really sorry," Charlotte moaned.

"What are you sorry for Charlotte?" Shelly questioned. "I can't tell you how thrilled I am for you and Nick… talk about a fairytale coming true."

"Everything happened so quickly, and then Nick flew in Becca to surprise me, and his mom and her husband flew in Pop and Noah and Maya and… wait a minute. How did you find out?"

If they had been FaceTiming, Charlotte would have seen the pink creeping up on Shelly's face when she answered, "Nicholas told me."

"Nicholas, huh?" asked Charlotte. "He just got home yesterday; what did he do, call you from the airport?"

"Well actually," Shelly stammered, "he picked me up."

"And you went to dinner? Come on girlfriend, spill," Charlotte prodded.

"He brought me back to the island, Charlotte. I've been here at the marina since last night."

"OMG!" Charlotte yelled. "Just wait until Nick finds out about this."

"Find out about what?" Nick asked, walking into the bedroom, his hands filled with boxes.

Charlotte was stuck between wanting details from Shelly and knowing she had promised to start going through Nick's clothes, and all she could think to say to either one of them was *Shit! Shit! Shit!*

Chapter 39

Now

Nick sat the boxes on the floor and looked at his bride under the covers, snuggling in his bed. He was pretty certain she hadn't tried to go through his clothes, but he couldn't help but smile. Lottie Luce, correction Charlotte Greyson, was in his bed, and damned if it didn't make him want her all over again.

"So, listen Shelly," Charlotte stammered, "Nick and I are actually in Tampa trying to get his condo ready to sell. Would it be okay if I called you back tomorrow when my supervisor lets me have a break?"

But instead of hanging up, Charlotte continued to talk. "That's too bad," Nick heard her say, and then, "Wow! That sounds like a great offer," followed by, "I don't know, why don't I let you talk with him yourself."

Charlotte handed her phone to Nick but crawled up on his lap so she could hear the conversation. "I'm going to put you on speaker, Shelly," Nick laughed. "It appears my wife is a Nosey Parker!"

Charlotte gave him a swat but settled in so she didn't miss a word. She was beaming ear to ear when Nick told Shelly, "We don't have any plans to be gone on Sunday. Just give us a call when you're on your way."

"What do you think, Nick?" Charlotte quizzed. "Are you open to leasing your condo to Shelly for six-months while she figures out a plan? I can't believe she's really interested in selling her childhood home to a development company, but with the money they're offering, I don't blame her."

"Again, Mrs. Greyson," Nick scolded, "this is a decision for us to make together, but truthfully I think it's a perfect solution. Shelly can live here while she decides on her future, and we can get comfy in your beach house while I finish school."

"My beach house?" Charlotte asked raising her eyebrows. "If the condo is ours then the beach house is, too. But my real question is, what do you think is going on between Shelly and your dad?"

"Seriously Charlotte, that's what you're getting from all this?" Nick chuckled, "It feels a little high school to me."

A little high school? Charlotte thought, *I'll show him high school!* And with that, she flipped her hair, stuck out her chest, and walked away. Truthfully, she wanted to flip him the bird, but as a mother to be, she didn't feel it was something she should advocate.

"Charlotte, come back here," Nick growled, but she kept walking. When she got to the kitchen, she slowly poured herself a Diet Coke and then went into the living room and turned on the television. Nick followed her every step and stopped only when she did.

"So, the honeymoon is over?" he asked in the deep G-Man voice she loved so much.

"Maybe not over," she answered while flipping through the stations, "but definitely on hiatus."

Chapter 40

Now

After Charlotte's declaration about their honeymoon, Nick headed back to the bedroom, leaving her alone to pout. She took a sip of Diet Coke, wishing it was Beach House white instead. There was nothing interesting on TV, and she didn't really want to watch it anyway. It didn't take long for her thoughts to get the better of her.

A few minutes later, Charlotte realized how silly she had been and crept back to the bedroom to apologize. There were clothes laid out, and a few drawers were open, but what caught her attention was Nick sitting on the edge of the bed, staring at a picture.

"Whatcha looking at?" she asked cautiously.

Nick lifted his beautiful face up and looked her in the eye. "A picture of a girl I used to know," he answered.

Charlotte could feel her heart racing, but she couldn't stop herself from asking, "Was she pretty?"

Nick gave her a soft smile before answering. "Very pretty."

Shit! Shit! Shit! Charlotte thought. *We haven't even been married a week and already I'm driving him away.*

Charlotte reached up to stroke her locket, but before going further, silently asked Gran for strength. "Did... did you love her?" she asked, trying to keep her legs from shaking.

"I did," Nick replied, "very much," and then he turned the picture for Charlotte to see.

She could hardly get into his arms fast enough when she realized the picture he was looking at was of her in their senior year of high school. "I'm so sorry, Nick," Charlotte sobbed into his shoulder. "I know I overreacted again, but hearing you say the words high school pushed my buttons."

Nick stroked her back and pushed her mass of curls away from her face. "I'm sorry, too," he said. "I didn't mean to upset you. I was surprised that's all."

Charlotte kissed his nose and grinned. "It's the difference between men and women, I guess. Shelly and your dad are terrific people, and they've both been alone a long time. I want them to find the happiness that we have."

Nick nuzzled her neck and said, "I can't argue with that."

For a few moments they held each other and made out like kids, and just when Charlotte thought things were going to really get good, Nick stood up, pulling her with him and declared, "We need to get to work."

She decided that pouting again wasn't such a good idea, so Charlotte nodded and looked over the piles of clothes. But before starting any packing, she had to ask, "What do you think is going on with Shelly and Pop?"

Nick began to laugh and shook his head. "I seriously have no idea but I'm pretty certain that Shelly is the first woman Pop has had at the marina since Mom. I'm not sure what that means, but I love my dad, and I know how much you think of Shelly, so if they can find some happiness together, I hope they go for it."

Charlotte grinned ear to ear because that's exactly how she felt. "In that case," she added, "do you think Shelly is only looking for a place for six months because she's hoping to get a better offer?"

Nick grabbed her around the waist and gave her one of his heart stopping kisses. "Is it going to take me getting you back in bed to get off the subject of Shelly and my dad?" he asked her.

Charlotte just smiled and shrugged her shoulders, and once again, the packing was put off.

Chapter 41

Now

Charlotte stretched like a feline lying in a sunbeam, and with a smile reached over for Nick. Finding his side of the bed empty she was just thinking of getting up, when he walked into the bedroom. Showered and shaved, and smelling like spicy citrus, Nick sat down on the bed beside her.

"Sleep well?" he asked, gently massaging her shoulders.

"Umm," she replied, "I slept great, and that feels so good. Why don't you get naked and come back to bed?"

"No dice, Princess," Nick responded with a swat to her backside, "it's almost ten o'clock, and I've brought breakfast."

Charlotte jumped up and looked at the clock. "Ten o'clock, why didn't you wake me?"

"Because you had quite a workout last night, and I thought you needed the rest. But now you need to get up and eat before the food gets cold."

Swinging her legs over the side of the bed, Charlotte grabbed Nick's T-shirt she had been wearing before their spur of the moment love fest and slipped it over her head. *Who knew that a guy's T-shirt could be just as sexy as a black teddy?*

"So, what's for breakfast? I don't remember seeing anything edible in your refrigerator."

"I said I brought breakfast, not that I fixed it," Nick told her. "There's a coffee shop close by, so I called in an order, and they brought it by. It's pretty much the way I've lived since I moved here."

Charlotte followed Nick into the kitchen and watched him dish out spoonsful of fluffy scrambled eggs and arrange them beside pieces of crisp, thick-cut bacon. There were also two little cartons of orange juice, plus lots of dark, rich-looking coffee that he had apparently brewed himself.

"I'm impressed," Charlotte said, taking a sip of her coffee. "I would have gotten married a long time ago if I'd known I would be this well taken care of."

"It's all in finding the right man, Baby," Nick said with swagger in his voice, "and luckily for you, you did. Now eat because we have a big day ahead of us."

After breakfast Nick told Charlotte to shower and dress while he cleaned up. Grabbing a refill on her coffee, she kissed him, thanked him for the delicious meal, and wiggled her hips all the way to the bathroom.

"You'll pay for that later," Nick called after her.

To which Charlotte replied, "Promises, promises."

Chapter 42

Now

Charlotte felt the tears welling up in her eyes when they pulled up to her little pink cottage on the beach late Sunday afternoon. Correction, she told herself, their little pink cottage on the beach. The home that Gran had given her when she graduated from Indiana University, the place where she'd always felt safe and secure.

Nick reached over and took her hand. "Why the tears, Charlotte? I thought you'd be happy to be home."

As she wiped her eyes with the back of their hands, Charlotte smiled. "I am happy, Nick," she told him. "This cottage has been my refuge for so many years, and I want it to be our refuge now, yours, mine, and Babycakes. But I left here a newly engaged lady, and I'm returning a married one. I've met your mom, Shelly is going to lease your condo, and for someone like me, who likes to plan every step, there's been a lot of changes in a short amount of time."

Nick looked at the woman he would give his life for and nodded. "There have been a lot of changes, and there's going to be more. Are you going to be able to deal with that? You've lived alone in this cottage ever since you moved back from Indiana. How is it going to feel sharing it with me?"

Charlotte could see the worry showing on his face and gave him a saucy smile to alleviate his fears. "We're never going to know if we don't go inside, now are we?" Getting her keys from her purse, she opened the door of the SUV, but before she could even step out, Nick had her in his arms and was carrying her up the path.

"This is the last time I'm carrying you over a threshold Mrs. Greyson," he teased. "Hurry and unlock the door before we both end up on the ground!"

After several trips, the Enclave was unloaded, and all the boxes were safely stored in the guestroom. "I can't believe you own so many clothes, Nick," Charlotte exclaimed. "You're even putting me to shame."

Nick stepped up behind her and grabbed her around the waist. "Guys like to look nice, too, you know," he answered. "But I do have a feeling I have a lot of suits I'll be able to donate to the Salvation Army. Now, how about we get cleaned up, because I want to take my bride out to dinner."

"We don't have to go out, Nick," Charlotte tried to protest. "Let's just order in a pizza."

"Nope, we're going out. This is our first night on the island as a married couple, and I want to show off my wife." Nick turned her toward the master bathroom and gave her a nudge. "You can shower while I find something out of one of those boxes to wear, and then we'll switch places."

Charlotte grinned and headed to the bathroom. "I can see now that our water bill is going to go up because we sure do take a lot of showers," she called out to him.

"Then from now on we'll just have to shower together," he answered. "Good thing there's lots of room in that fancy shower!"

Chapter 43

Now

Charlotte stepped into her fancy shower, thinking about the day she had graduated from IU and her gran had given her the gift of this cottage. "What do you think about Nick and I being married and living together in the cottage, Gran?" she asked, absentmindedly reaching for the spot where her locket always hung. "I think that you'd be happy for us, just like I think you always knew we'd end up together, even though I would never have agreed." Charlotte let the hot water run over her back and shoulders and thanked her gran again for the amazing gift she had given her. "I love you Gran, always and forever."

As much as she had loved their mini-honeymoon, Charlotte was glad to be home. She wrapped herself in one of her thick, fluffy towels and headed into the dressing room so Nick could shower. She was just about to drop her towel and put on a robe when she glanced in the mirror and saw him lying on the bed looking right at her.

Even as intimate as they had been the past few days, the way Nick was looking made Charlotte blush. "What's going on behind those beautiful blue eyes of yours?" she asked him.

Nick sat up and started toward her. "Just thinking what a lucky bastard I am," he told her, his voice gravelly and low. "You are my every dream come true, and I promise never to let you forget it."

Charlotte put her arms around his neck and kissed him with all the desire she was feeling inside, and as she did, her towel fell to the floor. Nick cupped her breast, causing her to moan. Dinner? Well, dinner was a little later than they had expected.

Once she could catch her breath, Charlotte ran her hand over Nick's chest, letting her fingers play with the soft dark hair that covered it. She even ventured a little lower to where the hair became coarser and led like an arrow to the anaconda, but just as she was about to wrap her hands around it, Nick caught her wrist and pulled her back.

"It's not that I don't like where this is headed, but I need sustenance before I can go another round," he told her. "And now, I don't have the energy to dress and go out, so you win. Pizza it is."

Charlotte smiled but didn't pull her hand back. "Wouldn't it have been easier if you would have just seen things my way from the beginning?" she teased.

"Easier, yes," Nick answered, "but not nearly as much fun. Now be a good wife and go order pizza while I get my turn at the big fancy shower."

Chapter 44

Now

"It's been so long since I've had Oma's pizza," Charlotte said, tomato sauce dripping from her fingers. "Don't you just love it?"

Nick looked at the pizza on his plate and shook his head. "Where's the meat?" he questioned.

Struggling to chew up the spicy goodness in her mouth, Charlotte answered, "I asked them to leave off the sausage and pepperoni, but it still has ham." She gave him her sweetest smile, but he still looked grumpy.

"Men like meat, Charlotte," he told her, "lots and lots of meat." Nick picked up the slice of pizza and looked it over before taking a bite. Deciding that it wasn't so bad after all, he quickly devoured it and reached for more.

Charlotte giggled as she watched him wolf down the pie. "If I'd have left the meat on, chances are, I wouldn't have gotten any," she said, "but I shouldn't have any more anyway, so you enjoy."

"What do you mean you shouldn't have any more?" Nick questioned. "You haven't even finished one piece."

Charlotte pushed her plate away and sighed. "I've eaten more in the last week than I probably did the whole month before, and I have a doctor's appointment on Thursday. One look at my weight gain, and Dr. Stanley is probably going to sign me up for Weight Watchers!"

"Hey," Nick said, stroking her leg. "I know you don't want me involved in your eating habits, but you have more than your rockin' hot body to think about now. Our baby needs real food, and I'm sure your doctor would tell you the same thing. Besides, I like you having a little more junk in your trunk these days." Nick smiled, hoping she would see how sincere he was, and he was rewarded with a throw pillow to the face!

"Junk in my trunk!" Charlotte yelled. "Why don't you just come out and say that I have a big ass? From rockin' hot body to bubble butt all in one sentence. Unbelievable! Un-fucking believable."

Nick definitely had the deer in the headlights look when he finally answered. "Can we start this conversation over, please? Like, I can tell you how great the pizza is and how I really love vegetables, and how I really love you?"

Charlotte wanted to stay mad, but he looked so contrite that she just couldn't. "Only because I'm such a nice person will I agree to your terms. But never, I repeat never, refer to my butt or thighs or hips as anything other than svelte, got it?"

"Yes dear," Nick said trying to keep a straight face. "Anything you say, dear."

And then they both burst out laughing.

Chapter 45

Now

Crisis averted, Nick leaned back on the couch and pulled Charlotte between his legs. "So, what are your plans for tomorrow?" he asked.

Charlotte let out a deep breath before answering. "I need to touch base with my small business owners and pick up my mail from the post office. I'm sure I have bills to pay, but what I'd rather do is stay home and snuggle with you."

"I'd like that too," Nick told her, "but if that's all we had to do all day, what would we have to look forward to at night?"

"I know, I'm just being wishful, but I hate for our time alone to end." Charlotte laid her head on his chest, and he gently ruffled her hair.

"How about you?" she questioned. "Is there anything you need to do to get ready for class on Wednesday?"

"That's all taken care of, so I thought I'd check with Pop to find out what time Noah and Maya are flying in. If it works out, I could return the SUV and ride back to the island with him and Noah. And hey," Nick added, "while you're at the post office will you pick me up a change of address form? I guess I need to talk with Shelly about changing the utilities at the condo, too."

Charlotte smiled to herself, thinking about Nick having his mail coming to the cottage. She knew they were married of course, but somehow that made it all seem more real. And her next thought was, I need a long talk with Becca!

For a few minutes they just lay there, enjoying each other's company and the closeness between them. Finally, Charlotte spoke.

"Tell me the truth, Nick. Did you ever really think we'd end up like this?"

Nick pulled her closer before answering. "I thought about you all the time," he said softly. "I even prayed that you would forgive me and that we would be friends again, but this? No, I never allowed myself to think this far ahead. What about you? Did you ever see us married and with a baby on the way?"

"I don't know," Charlotte told him honestly. "One minute I'd be thinking about how humiliated I was at the Send-Off, and another you'd be creeping into my what-if thoughts. But I never expected any of this, not with you or any man."

"Any man, huh?" Nick teased her. "I'm glad to know that pretty boy Peter was never a husband candidate, and I won't even discuss Mr. New York. I think everything worked out the way it was supposed to, and for that, I'm forever thankful."

Charlotte decided to ignore the comments about Peter and Ryan because she understood what Nick was saying, and she agreed with him. Everything had worked out just the way it was meant to. In fact, it was better than even her dreams had been.

"My stomach is full, and my heart is even fuller, so what do you say we call it a night, and you can continue with the exploration you started earlier?" Nick suggested.

Charlotte turned herself over and laid soft, wet kisses down the exploration trail. She could feel the effect she was having on him, so she smiled sweetly and blew a raspberry on his belly button!

"Is that your idea of foreplay?" Nick asked her. "Because let me show you mine." With that he picked her up, threw her over his shoulder, and carried her into the bedroom.

Chapter 46
Then

Charlotte tossed and turned all night. Being back on Anna Maria Island after her years in Indiana was great, but everyplace she went she was reminded of Nick, and some of those memories weren't so good. She had called Becca the evening before, and that had helped some, but what she really needed was to talk with Gran. But Gran was gone and talking to her while she clutched her locket was all that Charlotte had left.

When morning came, the same nagging thoughts were twirling around in her head, but despite the throbbing in her temples, Charlotte knew she needed to get up and get ready for work. If only she hadn't seen Nick's dad in the bank yesterday.

Pop had been like the father Charlotte never had, and he was one of the few people in town who hadn't judged her mom for her easy loving lifestyle. In fact, Pop was so nice to her mother that at one time Charlotte had hoped they would get together. Of course, the problem there was what it would have done to her own relationship with Nick, but that was all water under the bridge now anyway.

With a sigh and a huge yawn, Charlotte slipped out of bed and into the shower. Oh, how she loved the feel of the water coming from the big, rainforest showerhead. Turning the small bedroom next to hers into a big master ensuite had been one of her first splurges when she moved into the beach house, and it had been worth every penny.

Between her income as a commercial banker at Olde Florida Bank and the nest egg Gran had given her, Charlotte was doing fine financially, and she intended to keep it that way. Her only real obsession was the designer fashions she had come to love, but hey, she needed to look professional, right?

Looking through her closet for the right outfit to wear, Charlotte came across an Ann Taylor light-blue sheath dress with three-quarter length sleeves and a boat neck. She had loved the dress when she bought it, but now looking at the soft blue color, all she could think about was Nick.

Nick's favorite color was blue, and he liked light blue the best. As kids she had teased him that he liked blue because it brought out the color of his eyes, but he had just laughed and shrugged it off. Now, looking at the dress she had once liked so much, all she could think about was getting it out of her closet.

"What are you doing to my mind, Nick Greyson?" she said out loud. "You humiliated me in front of our whole class, so please, just go away!"

Deciding on a lavender Banana Republic pantsuit, Charlotte put Bath and Body Works Vanilla lotion all over her body, pulled her curls into a messy bun, and got dressed. With a swipe of Bert's Bees lip-gloss, and a coat of Maybelline mascara, she looked as good as possible, considering.

After pulling on her favorite black heels, Charlotte gingerly stroked her locket and talked with her gran. "Hi Gran," she started. "I saw Pop yesterday in the bank, and it brought back so many memories. Why can't I get Nick out of my thoughts? Is it because I wouldn't forgive him like you said I should? I love this cottage that you gave me, and I love this island, but I can't keep letting Nick mess with my head. I need him out once and for all, Gran. High school and Ashley Marshall were a long time ago, so please, help me find a way to move on."

Charlotte kissed her fingers and touched the locket once more before heading out the door. "I'm leaving my memories right here," she told the trash can in the garage. And just to make the message clear, she opened the lid, pulled imaginary memories from her heart, and slammed the can shut.

"There," Charlotte exclaimed, "you're history, Nick Greyson, just like you were before I came back to AMI."

Chapter 47

Now

It had been weeks since she'd had a real schedule, but Charlotte woke up before six o'clock the next morning. Nick was still sound asleep, sprawled on his stomach, his hard-as-rocks glutes deliciously on display. Turns out she had liked his idea of foreplay a lot, and while she felt invigorated, Nick was apparently exhausted.

Carefully slipping from the bed, she crept silently to the kitchen to make a cup of coffee. Her bouts of morning sickness had halted her coffee addiction, and the week in New York meant she hadn't been to the grocery, so the Keurig supply was running low. But after rummaging around in the basket of pods, she found just what she was looking for.

Emeril's Big Easy Dark Roast was her all-time favorite, and the smell of the rich, fragrant brew almost had her drooling. There was no creamer in the fridge of course, but that didn't matter. Putting the cup up to her lips and cautiously taking a sip, Charlotte felt like she was in, heaven. Mornings were her favorite time of day, and she loved having her first cup while everything was still, and the sun was just coming up.

"Where's mine?" Nick questioned, coming up behind her. His hair was rumpled, and his glorious body was unashamedly naked, causing Charlotte to giggle nervously.

"Do you not know it's bad manners to laugh at your husband first thing in the morning?" he asked her. "A guy could get a complex."

A complex? she thought. *Nick Greyson's body was like a walking ad for Hercules, and even with the anaconda at less than half mast, it was still impressive.*

"And do you not know that it's bad manners to interrupt my coffee time by parading around without any clothes on? What if in my excitement I accidentally spilled on you?" Charlotte asked. "The last thing I want to do is add another scar to that sexy chest of yours."

"Noted," Nick responded, "now move aside or fix me a cup, it's your choice."

Charlotte put her finger to her chin like she was thinking, but then flashed him a saucy smile and put a fresh pod in the machine. "We're going to need to get groceries," she told him, handing him the steaming mug. "We're out of everything, including creamer, and you know how much I enjoy a sweet treat in the morning."

Nick cocked his eyebrow and questioned, "Sweet treat?".

"You kind of have a one-track mind, you know that don't you, Greyson?" Charlotte teased him. "I can't stop and have sex every time you feel like it."

"Now who has a one-track mind, Charlotte? I didn't say anything about sex, I was referring to your statement last night that you needed to slow down on your eating." Nick had a smug look on his face, which caused Charlotte's to turn red.

"Okay," she stammered, "my mistake. Now if you'll excuse me, I need to shower and get dressed."

She tried to get past him, but Nick had long arms, and he wrapped them around her. The anaconda was definitely on the move when Nick said, "Now I'm thinking about sex."

Chapter 48
Now

"I'll really miss you today," Charlotte told Nick as she reached up to put her arms around his neck. "What time are you and Pop leaving to pick up Noah and Maya?"

"I'll miss you, too," he said, stroking her back. "Their flight gets in at eleven so I'm going to swing by the marina about nine thirty and Pop will follow me to the rental agency. We'll have to drop off Maya, so my hope is we can have lunch at Stavros and then head for home."

"You'll be really careful, won't you?" Charlotte asked him, trying not to sound too mother-hennish.

"I was just going to say the same thing to you," Nick smiled. "Pop mentioned us coming over for dinner, but I told him I needed to ask you first. He's grilling grouper."

"Nicely played," she laughed. "You both know I have no will power when it comes to Pop's grouper. Now I've got to run or I'll be late for my nine o'clock appointment with Clay Stevens. Call me when you're headed home, and I'll meet you at the marina."

Nick held on to her for a few seconds longer and then gave her a parting kiss that made her toes curl. "That was so not fair," she said with indignation. "How am I supposed to concentrate on Clay's books when I'm thinking about you?"

"That's the point, Mrs. Greyson," Nick whispered in her ear. "I want you always to be thinking about me."

Nick watched her walk away, not seeing the tears that were forming in Charlotte's eyes. When he yelled out, "I love you," she kissed her fingers and lifted them up without turning around. *Shit! Shit! Shit!* she thought. *When did I become such a girl?*

Right away Clay noticed the rings on Charlotte's left hand. "I guess you and Nick Greyson were able to define your relationship after all," he said to her.

Trying not to blush, or offend her new client, she quietly told him, "Things moved a little quicker than I expected. There's no problem is there?"

Shaking his head, Clay gave her a weak smile. "Your husband's a lucky man. I'm just sorry that I didn't ask you out when you first came back to the island."

Charlotte's mind was going in all different directions, so to diffuse the uneasiness between them she asked, "How about we look over your books?"

After visits to two of her clients, Charlotte decided to take a break and run past the post office and Publix. She remembered to get Nick a change of address card, and looking through her stack of mail, she realized they were either bills or requests for a charitable donation. Knowing they could all wait until she got home, she shoved them in her big Michael Kors satchel and headed to the store.

The bad thing about overeating, Charlotte realized, is that once you get used to it, it's hard to cut back. She hadn't worked hard all of these years to allow herself to go back to her former shape, so she grabbed a carton of low-fat Greek yogurt and a banana for her lunch and then started filling her cart.

Skim milk, grapefruit juice, whole wheat bread, eggs, fruit, vegetables, two kinds of coffee creamer, a big box of coffee pods, plus a package of chicken breasts, and she was done. Feeling very domestic, she headed to the checkout line and ran right into her second old flame! Literally.

Chapter 49

Now

"Peter!" Charlotte exclaimed when she recognized the person attached to the cart she had just hit. "What a nice surprise." *Okay,* she thought, *it isn't really nice. It's awkward as hell, but what am I supposed to say?* "Sorry about running into you like that. I'm just really hungry and was rushing to get home to lunch."

Peter gave her cart the once over and said, "I'm glad to see that you're still eating healthy, Charlotte. I know how hard it is for you to eat right when you're stressed." He gave her a sincere smile, but Charlotte wanted to shove his pearly whites down his throat!

Trying to count to ten before responding, Charlotte could almost feel her blood boiling. Peter was looking at her like she was a kale smoothie, so she decided to do what she should have done previously when he discussed her eating habits, and that was put him in his place.

"I'm shopping for two now, Peter," she said brightly. "Nick and I got married last week so I finally got him into my bed after all." She had turned his taunt from the night of their break-up back on him, but the words were no sooner out of her mouth than she regretted saying them. *Shit! Shit! Shit!* she thought. *What's wrong with me?*

The look on Peter's face was breaking her heart, but like Gran always told her, once you let words out of your mouth you can never put them back, and now she didn't know how to fix things.

"Well, then I guess congratulations are in order," Peter said meekly. He reached out like he was going to take Charlotte's hand but at the last minute pulled back.

"I made a big mistake thinking you would wait while I tried to achieve the perfect life," he told her, "and that's on me. I hope you and

Nick will be happy, Charlotte, I truly do." And then Peter did the strangest thing. He gave her a platonic hug but whispered in her ear, "I did love you, Charlotte, I still do." And he walked out of the grocery store, leaving his cart full of groceries standing in the aisle.

Charlotte was mortified as she looked around to see if anyone had just seen the odd exchange between them. Feeling comfortable that no one she knew had been listening in, she did the only thing that she could. She headed to the cookie aisle for a big bag of Double Stuf Oreos.

Chapter 50

Now

Charlotte could not pay for her groceries and get home fast enough. She even peeled out of the Publix parking lot, garnering her some respect from the carryout boy. The cottage wasn't more than ten minutes from town, but it felt like hours as she tried to drive the speed limit and look inconspicuous. She had never been one who wanted to call attention to herself, but now, she felt as if she had a big red A on her shirt. Not for Adulteress of course, but for Abhorrent, because that's how she felt.

Safely inside the cottage, Charlotte was able to calm down long enough to get the food put away. She looked at the carton of yogurt and the banana sitting on the counter and did the most logical thing she could think of. She put the yogurt in the refrigerator, poured herself a tall glass of milk, grabbed the bag of cookies and sat down to call Becca.

"Well hello, Mrs. Greyson," Becca cheerfully answered the phone. "How is my friend-the-bride?"

"I'm terrible, that's how I am," Charlotte spat out. "I'm a horrible, awful person, and I think I have some kind of man attracting pregnancy pheromone coming out of my skin, and I don't know how to fix it!"

Charlotte was not amused at the way her friend was laughing at her. "This is serious, Bec," Charlotte whined. "Since Nick and I got engaged, I've had three men make a play for me, plus I'm pretty sure I just crushed Peter's heart. What am I going to do?"

"First of all," Becca told her, "you're going to take a deep breath and tell me what's got you so upset. Everything okay between you and Nick?"

"What? No, this doesn't have anything to do with Nick except we do make love a lot. Maybe the pheromones are affecting him, too?"

"Sweetie, I don't know what pheromones you're talking about, but it is pretty normal for a newly married couple to have a lot of sex. And yes, being pregnant might make you more horny than usual, but I don't think it's rubbing off on Nick."

"Did you just say horny, Becca?" Charlotte gasped. "OMG, what's the world coming to?"

"Listen girlfriend," Becca snapped, "you called me for help, so what's really going on?"

"I don't know what's going on," Charlotte cried. "First there was the incident with Ryan in New York. Then this morning my client Clay Stevens told me he wished that he would have asked me out when I first came back to the island, and a few minutes ago at Publix, Peter told me that he loved me! Guys don't like me, Becca! There has to be an explanation for this."

"Oh Sweetie," Becca sighed. "Guys have always liked you, but you were so into Nick that you never even noticed. My goodness Charlotte. You're stunning, you always have been, but you hid behind your self-imposed imperfections and never let anyone get near you."

Charlotte was sobbing at this point, caught between what her friend told her and the image of herself she had carried around for so long. When Becca spoke again it took Charlotte a minute to compose herself long enough to really hear what her friend was saying.

"I can't tell you how many of the boys in our school asked me to hook you up with them, but you never were interested. I know they say love is blind, but you were blind to what was going on right under your nose." Becca waited, letting her friend have her cry and her pity party, and then said, "What happened to cause this reaction with you?"

"I was so mean to Peter today, "Charlotte said between hiccups. "I didn't mean to hurt him Becca. I didn't mean to hurt Ryan either, but I did, and it's not a good feeling."

"Ryan and Peter are two totally different scenarios," Becca assured her. "What happened with Ryan isn't your fault, and he knows that. But what did you do to Peter that you feel was so mean?"

And so, Charlotte told her about the grocery store episode and how she had been cruel to Peter because he brought up her food issues. Before long, she was rational again.

"What would I ever do without you, Becca?" Charlotte asked her friend. "You are always my anchor in a storm."

"I love you, Charlotte Greyson, and I'm always here for you, just like you're there for me. I'm so excited that your happily-ever-after has come true, and that you and Nick are together. And since you are, I have to know… how did he like unwrapping his wedding present?"

Chapter 51

Now

By the time Nick called to say that he and his dad and brother were leaving Tarpon Springs, Charlotte had visited with two more of her clients and had her emotions under control. Talking with Becca had certainly helped, but she still wasn't sure she wasn't oozing some type of pregnancy voodoo. For the time being though, she was just looking forward to spending her evening with the three most important men in her life.

When she pulled up to the marina the memories of coming here just a couple of months ago played in her mind, and she smiled, grateful for how different things were now. Who would have guessed that evening in June would be the beginning of a renewed friendship between her and Nick? A friendship that had turned into all she had ever dreamed of. She would never have believed it then, that's for sure, but oh how happy she was that it had.

"Hey, Shortcake!" Noah yelled at her from the doorway. "Are you coming in to greet your favorite brother-in-law or are you going to sit out there and day dream?"

Charlotte gave him a saucy smile and replied, "I didn't know Dimi was going to be here." Batting her eyelashes at him in fun, she was just about to give Noah a hug, when a big strong body stepped between them."

"Hands off my woman, little brother," Nick told him. "Those days are over."

Noah raised his hands in surrender, and Charlotte blushed. Had something happened today to cause Nick to act so possessive, or was it those damn pheromones again? As much as she didn't want to, she knew she had to ask Nick.

Pop was in the kitchen, getting ready to put some kind of seasoning on the fish, when Charlotte walked in. As soon as he saw her, he stopped what he was doing and pulled her in for a big hug.

"You're glowing, Lottie," he told her, looking her over from head to toe. "I knew marrying my son would be good for you." He gave her a wink and a soft kiss on the cheek and turned back to the fish.

"When do I get my turn?" Nick questioned with a frown. "I guess I thought you would have missed me so much that you'd come running into my arms. Instead I have to fight my brother off and play second fiddle to my old man."

Looking over the big, strong body of her husband, the soon to be former FBI Agent, she couldn't help but see the boy she had known and loved for so long. Becca was right, it had always been Nick in her mind and in her heart, and that would never change.

"Come here handsome," she told him, crooking her finger in his direction. When Nick got close, she pulled his head toward hers and gave him a kiss that let him know just how much she had missed him. Then realizing she had just done that in front of Pop and Noah, Charlotte blushed and tried to pull away.

"Nothing doing, my love," Nick told her, holding on possessively, and he kissed her, and her knees went weak. Pop and Noah were both smiling once Nick let her up for air, and Charlotte did her best not to blush or lose her composure.

But when Pop teased, "Now I know where the glow comes from," Charlotte could feel her face turn as red as the paprika on the counter so she turned away and tried to change the subject.

"So, what can I do to help?" she asked her new father-in-law.

"How about if you put together the salad? My sons wanted fried potatoes, but I thought a salad and baked potatoes made more sense. I hope that's okay with you?" Pop asked her.

If they hadn't just had the whole, "Who's the most important," debacle a minute ago, Charlotte would have given Pop a big kiss! He knew how hard she worked to eat right, but instead of making a production out of it and embarrassing her, he had made a calm statement and gone back to preparing the fish.

Nick and Noah grabbed beers from the cooler, but before heading out to the deck Nick told them, "We'll be on clean-up duty, okay?" Pop and Charlotte nodded, but Noah broke out in a big grin.

"What the fuck? You're pussy-whipped already, Big Brother, just admit it," he laughed at Nick, but Nick wasn't having any of it.

"We don't talk that way in front of the twins, so I'd appreciate it if you didn't talk like that in front of my wife and baby, either." Nick told his brother.

Charlotte's eyes were big as saucers while she waited for a response from Noah. But he just held up his beer in a salute and repeated, "Pussy-whipped," and walked away. But under his breath Charlotte heard him say, "lucky bastard."

Chapter 52

Now

At dinner they talked about their visit to New York, and each shared their own perspective of Elizabeth; her illness, her life, and even her choices during her children's childhoods. Even Pop weighed in on the woman he had loved for so long, thankful to at least understand better why she had stayed away.

True to his word, Nick and Noah cleaned up the dishes and the kitchen, leaving their dad and Charlotte alone to talk. "So, what's going on with you and Shelly?" Charlotte quizzed.

Pop put his arm around his new daughter-in-law and smiled. "That's girl talk, Lottie, so I suggest you ask Shelly if you want a real answer."

Charlotte smiled and kissed his check. "Trust me, I will," she teased him and headed to the kitchen to find Nick.

When it was time to go, Nick and Charlotte walked out to her car holding hands. "You want to drive us home?" she asked, holding out her keys.

"What do you say to stopping by Two Scoops first?" Nick asked her. "I haven't had a Java Crunch cone in ages."

Trying to find a way to get out of a trip to her favorite ice cream shop without dampening Nick's enthusiasm, she said brightly, "I had a really big lunch, so no ice cream for me, but if you want to go…."

"A big lunch, huh," Nick chuckled. "What did you have? I know we didn't have any food in the refrigerator, and since we don't have fast food on the island, I can't imagine what you might have eaten. But it's no fun going to Two Scoops unless we both indulge so it can wait for another time."

Shit! Shit! Shit! Charlotte thought, *do I lie or tell him the truth?* Deciding the truth was always best she opened her mouth, but something else came out.

"How do I smell to you?" she asked, looking at Nick with a very serious expression on her face.

"What? What do you mean how do you smell? Like do you stink or something?"

Charlotte put her hands up to her face like she was praying and started over. "I need for you to smell me and tell me what I smell like," she said with frustration. "It really isn't that hard to do, is it?"

"If you weren't pregnant, I'd say you got in to Pop's liquor cabinet, but I know you wouldn't do that to the baby. Anyway, I'll smell you when we get home," he told her. "That's the oddest request I've ever gotten from you, and you've had some odd ones over the years."

Charlotte got in her car and slammed the door. She knew Nick must be thinking she was certifiable about now, but she was determined to figure out this whole attraction men had to her.

When they walked into the cottage, Charlotte saw the opened package of cookies lying on the couch and announced, "I got groceries!"

Nick picked up the bag and, noticing that there were more than a couple cookies missing, said, "I take it this was your big lunch?"

She was mortified that Nick had uncovered her secret, so Charlotte hung her head in shame. The look on her face was more than he could bear, and Nick took her in his arms and just held her.

"You smell like mangos and coconuts with a big dose of hot sexy woman thrown in," he told her, wanting to move past the cookie issue. "You smell like sunshine and promises and my forever. Is that what you're asking?"

Shaking her head, Charlotte told him about the run in with Peter and her pregnancy pheromone theory. "I think maybe you've been affected by it too since you know, you want to make love a lot."

"I'm not sure what in the hell a pheromone even is, Charlotte," Nick said, cupping her face in his hands, "but I guarantee you that my desire for you has nothing to do with some mysterious chemical you think you're emitting now that you're pregnant."

Letting out a deep breath, she asked, "Then, how do you account for the way Ryan acted in New York, or what Clay Stevens said, or even Peter? Peter never really told me he loved me when we were together, why would he do it now?"

Nick was afraid that she was on the verge of hyper-ventilating, so he told her what was in his heart. "Because my beautiful wife, he's an ass, that's why. And as for Ryan and Clay Stevens, and every other man on the planet, they want you because you're warm and loving, sweet and sassy, smart and generous, and so gorgeous that you take our breaths away. And to top it off, you're totally oblivious to all of it, and that's just sexy as sin."

Seeing her shoulders start to relax, Nick pulled her as close to him as possible and thanked God for the woman in his arms.

"I really did buy more than just cookies," she told him as she snuggled in deeper.

"But I love cookies," he responded kissing her hair. "So how about we take them and go to bed?" The smile that she gave him sent heat through every inch of his six-foot-five-inch frame, and as much as he liked cookies, they were going to have to wait.

Chapter 53
Now

It rained overnight and when Charlotte woke-up she saw the hint of a beautiful pink sunrise. Looking at the clock, she saw that it was later than her usual wake-up time, but Nick had kept her up awfully late. With a lazy grin, she looked over at her husband just as he opened his eyes.

"Good morning," she cooed, still on a high from the night before. "I'm going to fix my coffee and take it out on the lanai. Are you interested in joining me?"

Nick yawned and wrapped his arm around her before she could get away. "Do you have early appointments this morning?" he asked, trying to stifle another yawn.

"No, why? Do you have someplace you need to be?"

"Right here with my beautiful wife," he replied, moving his hand from her waist up to her chest. "Lie here with me just a few more minutes, and I promise you won't regret it."

Snuggling back under the covers, Charlotte agreed to five more minutes, but she didn't stop Nick's fingers from the wonderful things they were doing. Trying to suppress the moan that was forming in her throat, Charlotte was just ready to turn over when Nick kissed her neck and got up out of bed.

"Are you going to lie there all day?" he asked her. "You promised me coffee on the lanai."

Men! Charlotte thought to herself. *How would he like it if I got him aroused and then left him high and dry? Well, I'll show him!* Throwing on her robe she gave him a sassy smile and marched into the kitchen to fix coffee.

By the time Nick joined her, she had two mugs of hot coffee and two glasses of grapefruit juice on the table waiting for him to join her. They sat side by side on the rattan loveseat, and Charlotte continued to be the devoted wife even though her body was crying foul.

Nick took a drink of his juice and made a face. "Grapefruit juice?" he asked with a shudder. "I don't like grapefruit juice."

"I'm sorry," she said sincerely. "I didn't even think to ask you, but I can pick up some orange juice before I come home today."

"So, what else did you buy at the store?" he quizzed, "or should I check for myself?"

Nick padded into the kitchen, and Charlotte could hear him opening and closing cabinets before he got to the refrigerator. "So, where's the food? I don't see any meat, or cheese, or chips, or beer.... How do you live like this?"

Very indignantly, Charlotte followed him into the kitchen to defend herself. "I've never had to shop for a man," she said, arms folded across her chest, "and I bought chicken, so I did get meat."

"Honey, chicken is poultry, not meat, but I'll concede on that point. I think I'll do some shopping today while you're working or we're going to have to let Pop feed us again." Nick was smiling but Charlotte wasn't.

"Fine," she said flatly. "You go buy all the man food that you want, but don't expect me to eat it. And be careful. You might run into Peter."

Nick couldn't keep from laughing. He knew that life with Charlotte would never be dull, but he also knew he was going to have to up his game if he was going to keep up with her!

Chapter 54

Now

They drank their coffee is silence, and finally Nick offered to fix some scrambled eggs. He could see that Charlotte was about to protest so he decided it was time to put his foot down.

"I don't care if you eat any or not Charlotte," he told her sternly, "but Babycakes needs breakfast." He waited for a minute for her to argue, but instead she nodded and went into the kitchen to help.

"You know that I really don't know how to cook," she said glumly. "I mean other than simple things. Maybe I need to have Pop give me some lessons."

"I'm sure that he'd be happy to," Nick assured her. "In the meantime, I won't let you starve. I may not have the skills of my dad, but I can do wonders with an egg. Now, how about toast, can you do that?"

Charlotte stuck out her tongue playfully, glad the tension between them had eased. She really didn't know how to shop or cook for a man, but she did know how to make a mean slice of toast. Putting the bread in the toaster, she vowed to call Pop that day and get started on cooking lessons as soon as possible. Even her own mom knew how to cook, and anything Maggie Luce could do, Charlotte could do, too.

After swallowing the last bite of her eggs, Charlotte took Nick's hand and smiled at him. "Do you realize that this is your last morning before you become a college student again?" she asked. "Am I going to have to worry about co-eds throwing themselves at my husband?"

Giving her hand, a squeeze Nick said, "It's only two classes and a certification, Charlotte. I'm not exactly going to be recreating the campus experience. And as for college girls, you have nothing to worry about. I don't ever plan to take off my wedding ring, so they'll all know that I'm taken."

It was on the tip of her tongue to harass him some more about the college girls, but her heart wasn't in it. She loved that he didn't have plans to remove his wedding band, but besides that, she knew cheating just wasn't something Nick Greyson would ever consider.

"I'm not going to take off mine either," she announced, and the subject was dropped.

"So, what are you going to do today?" Charlotte asked as they cleaned up together. "I need to see more of my clients, but before that I want to go through the mail and pay bills. Which reminds me, we should stop by the bank and get you added to my accounts."

"I'm going to Bradenton to get my books, and I'll have lunch with Noah before he heads back out on the water," Nick told her. "I can stop by the bank before I come home, but won't you need to do something first? I remember the hoops I had to jump through to get added to Pop's accounts," he added with a wink.

"Very funny," she said, "but just think, without those hoops, we might not be here today, and personally I'm very happy that we are."

Nick pulled her onto his lap and nuzzled her neck. "Me too," he told her honestly. "Me too."

Chapter 55
Now

Charlotte showered while Nick made his lunch plans with Noah, and then she headed to her closet to find something to wear. If she was going into the bank today, she wanted to look good but in a casual, I didn't put any effort into this look way. Deciding that a pair of trousers and a blouse would give her just what she was looking for, she mulled over several pairs before deciding on some soft, gray skinny pants, and a turquoise striped wrap-top.

Nick could hear the sobs coming from the bedroom the minute he turned the shower off, and without even grabbing a towel, he rushed into the bedroom.

"What's wrong?" he said, taking Charlotte in his arms. "Are you hurt? Is it the baby?" Nick couldn't stop the concerns that were running through his head, but he was not expecting his wife's reply.

"I'm fat!" she wailed.

Nick shook his head in disbelief. "You're pregnant, Charlotte, not fat," he said, trying to appease her. But when she stood up it was all he could do not to laugh.

"Look at me," she demanded. "Even Becca's pants tip won't work!"

Charlotte stood there with her pants barely past her hips, and the blouse gaping over her chest and belly. It was like she went to bed a little pregnant and woke-up a lot pregnant.

"Oh honey," Nick said, rubbing circles up and down her back, "we just need to take you shopping. Don't they make special clothes for pregnant women?"

That only brought out more tears and more sobs. "They're called maternity clothes, Nick," Charlotte said sharply, "but I have all these beautiful things, and I'm not ready to wear a tent."

Nick took a big breath and looked his wife up and down. She obviously couldn't wear what she had on, but surely she could find something in that massive closet of hers not only to fit but to make her feel good about herself again.

Taking her hand, he led her to the closet and started making suggestions, only to have each one turned down. Realizing that anything he said or did at this point was going to be met with a negative reaction, he made a suggestion.

"Why don't I skip lunch with Noah, and we go shopping today instead?" he asked, hoping this was the right thing to say. But Charlotte shook her head.

"There isn't any place on the island to buy maternity clothes," she said, still sniffling. "I need a specialty shop and a woman to shop with; I need Becca!"

Nick's skin had dried off from the shower, but the stress of the situation was causing him to perspire. Trying one more time to get things under control, he said, "You need to find something that you can wear, even if you have to wear the same thing every day, and this weekend we can go to New Smyrna and see Becca." Without giving Charlotte any time to protest he grabbed a pair of yoga pants and a T-shirt from a drawer and told her to put them on.

Amazingly Charlotte did as she was told, and Nick headed back to the bathroom for his second shower of the morning.

Chapter 56
Now

When Nick turned off the shower this time, he noticed that everything was quiet. Not sure if that was good or bad, he rushed out of the bathroom only to find Charlotte on the phone, talking with Becca.

"You need to stop running around naked, Nick," she told him as she hung-up the landline. "What if someone would have been here?"

Nick was on the verge of saying the word he had asked Noah to refrain from, but using all his will power, he abstained. "So, do you have a shopping trip lined up?" he asked as sweetly as possible.

"I do!" Charlotte replied excitedly. "We're going to Becca and Jared's on Saturday morning and you men are going to be on kid duty while we ladies go shop. There's even a new boutique that sells stylish maternity clothes Becca's going to take me to. Isn't that perfect?"

"Perfect," Nick replied, although he really was pleased. He loved the Tyler kids, and he liked Jared, but he hoped more than anything Dr. Tyler could give him a clue on how to live with his pregnant wife.

After finally getting dressed, Nick helped Charlotte straighten up the clothes mess in their bedroom, and he got ready to head to Bradenton to buy the books he needed for his classes.

Charlotte was sitting at the computer working on bills when he stepped up behind her and started massaging her shoulders. "So, are you going to work from home today, or what?" he asked, afraid to bring up how she was dressed.

"I don't know yet," she answered in such a calm manor, you would never have known about her meltdown a short time earlier. "I'll make a few calls and see how things go, but don't worry about me."

"I always worry about you, Charlotte," Nick told her, kissing the top of her head. "It's who I am. But if you don't have to go see any clients, I'd love to have you ride along with me this morning."

"I'm fine, Nick, really," she assured him. "Now get out of here so you don't have to rush. Call me when you're on your way home though, okay?" Charlotte got up and fixed Nick's collar before giving him a chaste kiss on the cheek and handing him his keys.

Nick looked her over for signs of PTSD and slowly headed for the door. "Have a good day," he said cautiously, the whole time wondering which woman he would come home to; the manic clothes maven, or his loving wife.

No sooner was Nick's Jeep down the street than Charlotte called his dad. "I need to learn how to cook," she said, "and I need to know how to cook Nick something special for tonight. Can you help me?"

Chapter 57

Now

"This is Nick's favorite food, and really easy to make," Pop said, showing Charlotte the lasagna recipe. "Don't you remember how I always made it for his birthday?"

Charlotte shuddered. "I remember how good it was, but I guess I forgot that it's Nick's favorite. It looks so complicated though. Isn't there something easier?"

Pop smiled at her. "You said you wanted to make Nick a special dinner, so which is it, special or easy?" he asked. "Maybe I need to ask why you feel the need to fix him something special. You didn't have an argument, did you?"

"No, no argument exactly, but I don't know how to live with a man, Pop. Plus, I kind of threw a hissy-fit this morning over clothes, so I need to do something nice for your son."

He couldn't keep the laughter back when Charlotte said, "hissy-fit."

"I'm not sure I even know what a hissy-fit is, Lottie," he told her, his eyes filled with kindness, "but there's nothing unique about living with a man. I can tell by the way you and Nick look at each other that you have the important parts covered, and trust me, the rest will fall in place."

Charlotte threw her arms around him and said, "I love you, Pop, and I will never be able to thank you enough for the way you made me feel like part of your family even when I really wasn't."

"Now that's not true, Lottie. You became a part of our family years ago. I'm just glad you and Nick had the sense to make it legal. Now start making a list of ingredients you're going to need, because we have shopping to do."

Charlotte started her grocery list, but the thought of going back into Publix had her nervous. What if Peter was there again, or what if one of the clerks had heard their conversation? She was trying to figure out a way out of the whole shopping experience when Pop told her it was time to go.

"We'll buy everything we need and make the lasagna at your house," he said to her. "That way Nick will smell it when he comes in, and he'll know that you were trying to make amends for the ah, hissy-fit."

The way Pop said it gave Charlotte the giggles so that when they left for the store, she felt lighthearted for the first time all day.

Pop showed her where to find the basil and oregano and explained ow they flavored the sauce. When they got to the cheese aisle he said, "I like to use ricotta cheese, even though lots of people use cottage cheese in the cheese layer, and I shred the mozzarella and parmesan so they have the freshest taste."

"While we're buying cheese," Charlotte said, "what kind of cheese does Nick eat? I can't believe I married him and have no real clue what food he really likes."

"Nick isn't picky, Lottie, just buy whatever looks good. Swiss, cheddar, Colby, he'll eat any of them. Since we're here, we might as well stock up. Tell me what you have at home, and we can buy everything else while we're here."

She told him about the grapefruit juice incident at breakfast, and only buying a package of chicken breasts, quickly giving Pop the picture that Charlotte needed a shopping intervention. An hour later, Charlotte had a full shopping cart and a huge weight lifted off her shoulders, knowing that she had finally mastered grocery shopping for a man.

Chapter 58

Now

By the time Nick called to say that he was dropping off Noah and that he'd see her soon, Charlotte had the lasagna and garlic bread prepared and ready to go in the oven along with a big salad ready for homemade dressing. The little table on the lanai was covered in one of Gran's tablecloths and adorned with fresh flowers and candles, and there was even a frosty mug in the freezer, waiting for one of Nick's favorite dark beers.

Charlotte looked over her accomplishment and felt pretty pleased with herself. She'd found a sundress with an empire waist to wear, and that had been a huge confidence booster. With her skin slathered with Victoria Secrets Coconut Body Oil and her hair in long waves around her face, she hoped to erase this morning's disaster from Nick's mind.

When Nick's Jeep pulled into the drive, Charlotte tried to act casual but remembered what he had said the day before about her running into his arms because she had missed him so much. She did just that. Nick was carrying several packages, but he had no hesitation dropping them to scoop up his beautiful wife.

"Hey," she said, looking directly into Nick's eyes. "I'm so glad you're home."

"Me too," he smiled, nuzzling her neck and smoothing back her curls. "I take it you had a good day?"

Charlotte helped Nick pick up his bags and then linked her arm with his. Leading him into the house, she knew the moment he opened the door he could smell the aroma of lasagna, but he looked at her with confusion.

"Did Pop bring us dinner?" he questioned.

"Nope," Charlotte replied with a grin, "but he did teach me some things today, so hopefully, you won't have to starve to death."

Nick looked at the face of the woman he had loved for most of his life and was overcome with emotion. "You learned how to cook for me?" he asked tentatively.

Charlotte nodded and showed him her masterpieces. "I even learned how to shop, so no more empty refrigerator or cupboards. See," she said, opening and closing each one.

"I don't know what to say except thank you, but you didn't have to do all this. I'm not in love with Betty Crocker, Charlotte. I'm in love with you, and I never expected you to change in any way just because we got married." He pulled her close for one of his signature kisses and ran his hand up her smooth, firm thigh.

When she responded by putting her arms around his neck and deepening the kiss, Nick ran his hand further up her dress and moaned at what he found. "Fuck, Charlotte!" he exclaimed. "No panties?"

"I didn't think you wanted that word used around your wife and baby?" she questioned with a sassy smile. "But I thought you might want an appetizer before dinner."

Nick didn't have to be asked twice. He picked her up and carried her into the bedroom, squeezing the round globes of her bottom as he laid her on the bed. "I know the remark about junk in your trunk didn't quite come out right, but you've got a great ass, Charlotte."

She wasn't sure whether to scold him or to laugh. Instead she helped her husband get their clothes off because, come to think of it, she was ready for an appetizer, too.

Chapter 59
Now

The rest of the week went smoothly; Nick had his first day of classes at the State College of Florida on Wednesday, and Charlotte had her doctor's appointment and ultrasound on Thursday. They still agreed that they didn't want to know the sex of the baby, and except for the fact that Charlotte had gained eight pounds in a month, Dr. Stanley was pleased with how well everything was going.

"You played nice in there," Charlotte teased, remembering how Nick had acted at her first OB appointment. "Although, when I told the doctor I was no longer Miss Luce, but Mrs. Greyson, and he called you Special Agent, and you said no, just Nick, I think he got a little confused, don't you? I guess our story is a little out of the ordinary," Charlotte commented.

"There's nothing ordinary about us," Nick agreed, "but that's what keeps things interesting." Giving Charlotte a wink, he held her hand as they walked to the car. Once they were seated, and safely buckled in, he took Charlotte's face in his hands and gently rubbed his thumb over her lips.

"You were well behaved, too," he said with a smile. "When the doctor asked if we had worked out your concerns about sex you only turned a nice shade of pink."

Charlotte opened her mouth to reply but thought better of it. Since the night of the lasagna fest, they seemed to have come to a deeper point in their relationship, and she didn't want anything to spoil that. Using Gran's old adage that you kill more flies with honey than with vinegar, she was attempting to keep her sharp comments to herself. Sometimes it worked, and sometimes it didn't.

"Are you excited about seeing Becca this weekend?" Nick asked on their way home.

"I'm excited to see all of them," she beamed. "I've been a part of the Tyler's lives since the moment Jared and Becca met, and I'm baby Lolly's godmother. To be honest, other than your family, they're the closest thing to family that I have."

"You've got your mom, Charlotte," Nick told her, "and soon you'll have Thomas and his son. They count, don't they?"

Charlotte blew out a big breath before going on. "You're right, I do have my mom, and Thomas is a great guy, but family is more than just blood or a legal document. It's the way you feel when you're with them, and the love that abounds no matter what. I love my mom, and I know that she loves me, but my gran was the only person who ever made me feel that wholeness, until Becca."

Nick's eyes were growing dark as he hesitated to ask her the question that was lying on his heart. "What about me, Charlotte?" he asked, his voice soft and unsecure, "Where do I fit in?"

Taking his hand in hers she answered, "You make me feel like a Princess and your most treasured gift in the world. You're my knight in shining armor, Nick Greyson, and I'll never doubt again that you love me. You and our child are my family, now and forever."

Nick gave her hand a kiss and asked, "Child, not children?"

"One step at a time," Charlotte answered, "one step at a time."

Chapter 60

Now

"Bring it on in, Mrs. Greyson," Jared said to Charlotte, opening his arms for a hug. "Marriage must be just what the doctor ordered," he told her with a wink, "because you look more beautiful than ever."

Charlotte and Nick walked through the door Jared held for them and were immediately surrounded by six little feet and two bigger ones. "Aunt TT," Anna cried, holding on to Charlotte's leg. "I have a new playhouse, and I want you to see it right now."

"It's not just your playhouse, Anna," JD argued, "it belongs to all of us, right Dad?"

Jared tried to get in a response, but before he could, Lolly spoke up. Putting both hands on her chubby little hips, she looked at her brother and sister and said, "Mama said if we don't act nice while Aunt TT and Uncle Nick are here, we won't get ice cream after lunch, and I want ice cream. Are you going to be good or not?"

Charlotte and Nick looked at each other in shock. When had this pint-sized beauty become the queen of the castle, they wondered. But evidently, she had because both Anna and JD said, "Sorry," just as their mother stepped in to take real control, telling them to go play.

"Oh, Lottie," Becca said as she gave her friend a big hug. "You look so good! I can't believe what all has happened since you were here a few months ago. And Nick," she added, turning to hug him as well, "I can't tell you how happy I am that you two finally came to your senses and realized what I knew all along."

Linking arms with her two childhood friends, Becca escorted them to the sun porch while Jared fixed glasses of freshly brewed iced tea. "I don't see a bag," Becca told them. "I thought you were going to spend the night."

Both Charlotte and Nick fidgeted, waiting for the other to speak, when Jared spoke-up for them. "Honey, remember they're really still newlyweds. I'm sure that the quiet and comfort of a motel room is more appealing than having three kids and thin walls to contend with." Giving Nick a nod, Jared continued, "I totally get it."

Charlotte was close with Jared, but the words he spoke caused her cheeks to heat, and she hated that. It wasn't like what he said wasn't right, it was just embarrassing to hear him say it.

Becca smiled at her friends and changed the subject. "I can't wait to take you shopping!" she squealed. "Wait until you see the Baby Bump," Becca told Charlotte. "They have everything from casual wear to designer fashions, and I know you're going to love it. I haven't really needed anything else since...."

"Since you've been knocked-up almost forever," Charlotte finished Becca's thought.

"Not exactly how I was going to put it, but yep, that's why."

Jared put his arm around his very pregnant wife and gave her a hug. "I'm a pediatrician, Lottie," he smiled. "Pregnant women are the backbone of my business, and there's no better advertising than my wife."

They all laughed and discussed Nick's classes and Charlotte's accounting business, and then Becca said it was time to go shopping! Those words were music to Charlotte's ears, and after a quick trip to the bathroom for both the pregnant women, they were on their way.

Chapter 61

Now

Several hours later Charlotte and Becca returned, both with light hearts and even lighter wallets. Becca had been right. Charlotte found everything from jeans to dress pants, professional dresses to designer wear, even some pretty maternity lingerie. She wasn't sure yet about the whole breast-feeding idea, but Becca had encouraged her to buy a couple of stylish nursing bras while they were there.

When the ladies walked through the door of Becca and Jared's home, Nick knew right away that it had been a good day, but something was different about Charlotte. She had given him a big hug when she first walked in, but now he took the time to really look her over. "Is that what you were wearing when you left here?" he quizzed. "I remember you had on the little sundress that you were wearing the other night."

The mention of the other night had Charlotte thinking about the appetizers she Nick had enjoyed just a few nights before, so she missed it when he added, "And now you have on jeans."

She was trying hard not to think about the night she had met Nick at the door without any panties, and instead did a little twirl and said, "Yes, I have on jeans, and they fit!"

Charlotte looked like a kid in a candy store, and Nick was thrilled. He didn't ever want to witness another breakdown over clothes, and if getting into a pair of jeans kept Charlotte happy, he was all for it.

It felt as if they had just arrived when Nick took Charlotte's hand the next day and said they needed to get on the road. The drive from New Smyrna Beach to Anna Maria Island was around four hours, and since Nick hadn't technically been released by his doctors yet, he wanted to be able to take his time.

It had been such a fun weekend, and Charlotte didn't want to leave, but when her old married friend nodded in her direction, Charlotte got the message that Becca was telling her to let Nick make this decision.

There were hugs and kisses to the three Tyler Tykes as Becca called them, and another round of thanks to Jared and Becca for the amazing weekend as Charlotte and Nick headed to the door. They were just about out when Jared touched Charlotte's shoulder and turned her his way.

"The last time you were here I told you that there was a special guy out there for you, and you just needed to believe it. I love it when I'm right," he teased, "but even better than that is knowing that you found him. I really like Nick, Lottie, and I can't tell you how happy I am for both of you."

Charlotte gave Jared a kiss and replied, "And I remember saying that you are one in a million, Dr. Tyler. I meant it then, and I mean it even more now."

Giving Becca a final hug and blowing kisses to the whole Tyler family, Charlotte got in the car with Nick. She looked at the face of her husband, the only man she had ever truly loved and said, "Take me home."

Chapter 62

Now

Charlotte was amazed at how well she and Nick settled in to married life. He went to school one day a week, took a couple of online classes, and started spending time with Coach Donavan and the high school swim teams. She handled the books for her small business clients, worked on her cooking skills with Nick's dad, and spent part of each day emailing, texting, or talking with Becca, Shelly, and Nick's mom. She even committed herself to at least one call or email to her own mom each week, and that seemed to work out well for both of them.

One night while lying in bed after some particularly amorous lovemaking, Charlotte lifted her head from Nick's chest and asked, "How are you going to be when we can't do this anymore, or at least do it like we just did?"

"Why will anything have to change?" he replied.

Charlotte was not all that well versed on pregnancy or childbirth, but Becca had shared enough with her that she knew the day would come when they would have to abstain, even if it wasn't until after Babycakes arrived.

"Well," she started, "at some point, I'll be really big and fat and you might not find that desirable. And even if you do, I may be self-conscious, or not interested, so it kind of worries me. Plus, after the baby is born, I know there's a waiting period, and you don't seem too patient where sex is concerned."

Nick massaged her neck, trying to ease the tension he could feel building in her. "I appreciate that you think I'm some kind of sex God, Charlotte, it's really an ego booster, but Honey, if you remember, I waited for you after I got out of the hospital, and I can wait again no matter how long it is. It isn't just having sex that I want. It's the connection with you, and when the time comes when we can't make love, we'll connect some other way. And by the way, you'll never be big and fat in my eyes."

"You really are a good man, Nicholas Greyson," she said, her face filled with love. "I'm one lucky woman, aren't I?"

"I think we're both pretty lucky," he told her. "Now go to sleep. Tomorrow's a cooking lesson with Pop, and I want you focused."

Every day was something new for Charlotte, and even though she missed her job and particularly her co-workers, she loved the challenges of what she was doing now. All of her small business clients were thriving, and thankfully, none of Tony Neel's illegal activities had done any damage to them. She even took on a new business when her hair stylist, Jen, asked her if she would do the books for Shine Salon.

She spent at least one day a week with Pop, learning new recipes and planning meals for Nick. She loved the special time with her father-in-law and knew that, someday soon, she was going to have to come up with a new excuse for their time together.

"So, Pop," Charlotte said innocently as she rolled out dough for dumplings, "how are things going with my friend, Shelly?"

"I thought I told you that was girl talk, Charlotte, and that you needed to ask her," he replied grumpily.

Charlotte couldn't remember Pop ever calling her anything but Lottie, so she sensed that she had struck a nerve. "I'm not trying to pry," she said guardedly. "Okay, maybe I am, but you and Shelly would be so good together, and I can tell you like each other."

The words, "like each other," brought a smile back to Pop's face. "We're not in junior high, Lottie, but you're right; we do like each other. In fact, I haven't felt this way about a woman since Elizabeth, but there's ten years difference in our ages, and that seems like a lot."

Charlotte started to give him a hug, but remembering the flour covering her hands, she thought better of it. Instead, she stopped what she was doing and looked into his eyes. The same blue eyes as Nick's, the same dark clouds forming, showed he was hurting.

"You may be older than Shelly in years," Charlotte said softly, "but Pop, Shelly is wise beyond her age. She's been through some really hard things, and if she's willing to take a chance, I think you should be, too."

Ignoring the flour covering Charlotte from head to toe, he put his arms around her and lifted her off the floor. "You're right, Lottie," he beamed. "As soon as you finish those dumplings, I'm going to send her a text."

"A text, Pop," Charlotte teased. "Now who's acting like they're in junior high?"

"You're right," he answered. "I'll leave her a voice message."

Charlotte laughed and shook her head, wondering if she hadn't just had her first lesson in parenting, with her as the parent!

Chapter 63
Now

Nick put the last bite of dumplings in his mouth and smiled at his wife. "Delicious," he told her, "every bit as good as Pop's, but how did I rate chicken and dumplings on a Thursday? He only made them on Sunday's."

"Now someone tells me," Charlotte said in exasperation. "I thought it seemed like a lot of effort for a weekday, so I hope you enjoyed them because they won't be on the menu again for a while."

Nick tried not to laugh at her outburst, but it was hard not to. Charlotte had taken to cooking like she did everything else, determined to master it, and she really had. He was just on the verge of telling her how much he appreciated her efforts when her cell phone rang.

Looking at the Caller ID, Charlotte mouthed, "Mom," before answering.

"Mom," she said into the phone, "is everything okay? We don't usually talk on Thursdays."

"It's more than okay, Charlotte!", her mom exclaimed. "Chad is coming next week so Thomas and I can finally get married. You and Nick can still come, can't you?"

Charlotte was trying to make gestures so that Nick would know what was happening in the conversation, but he just sat there with a grin on his face. When Maggie quit talking long enough for Charlotte to get a word in, all she could say is, "Of course we'll be there Mom, but Nick has school, so we won't be able to stay long."

"Just for the weekend, that's all that I ask. Chad will be here through Sunday when he's leaving to go see his mom, and then Thomas and I are leaving for our honeymoon."

Again, Charlotte was trying to find an opening when Maggie shouted out, "We're going to Paris, Lottie! Thomas is taking me to Paris for our honeymoon!"

Charlotte could tell how excited her mother was, so she didn't even correct her when she called her Lottie. She held the phone to her ear and listened to her mom ramble long enough that Nick cleaned up the dishes and the kitchen. Charlotte decided she was getting the best of both worlds; a call with her mom where her life wasn't being scrutinized and no after-dinner clean-up.

Nick was waiting for her in the living room when Charlotte was finally able to end the call, and the first words out of his mouth were, "I take it we're going to Arizona?"

Crawling up in his lap, Charlotte put her arms around him. "You don't mind, do you?" she asked, snuggling in close enough to lay soft kisses on his neck.

"You don't have to bribe me, Charlotte," he told her, realizing he was feeling the effects of her closeness. "I told you before that I'm happy to go to your mom's wedding, and I meant it. After all, she's your mom, and you need to be there."

Charlotte tried to get up, but Nick pulled her back against him. He liked it when she acted soft and girly, and besides, if she moved an inch more, she would feel the erection he was working so hard to get down.

"Thank you, Nick," she said, no longer kissing his neck but blowing in his ear. "I know that my mom can be a handful, but she does love me, and I promised her I would be there."

At this point, Nick would have gone anywhere with her. The friction of Charlotte moving in his lap had finally got the better of him, so he stood up without letting her go. "She's not the only one who can be a handful," he growled, as he carried his giggling wife into their bedroom.

His hands slipping under her shirt, Nick muttered something about having his hands full and started kissing her neck like she did his. Within minutes, their clothes were discarded, and Nick's nibbles were moving south.

"Who needs a honeymoon to Paris?" Charlotte moaned as she grasped at Nick's hair. "I feel like we're on our honeymoon every night of the week." And those were the last coherent words Nick heard.

Chapter 64
Now

Once again, they were at Tampa International Airport, and once again, Charlotte was nervous. "I just really don't like to fly," she admitted to Nick, "but it's the only way to get somewhere quickly. Did you have to fly a lot with the FBI?"

As Nick had predicted, he had been released by his doctors at his last visit, and his termination from the FBI was official. It had been a little harder sending in the resignation letter than he had expected, but whenever he looked at Charlotte, he knew he had made the right decision. "I flew a lot during the whole Stella Harper stalking case but other than that, only a few times a year. I guess flying was never an issue for me."

"Speaking of Stella," Charlotte asked cautiously, "does Noah say anything more about her, or how Adam is doing?"

"I found out from a buddy with the bureau that Adam is still on life support, but that's really all I know. Noah won't even discuss Stella, so I'm trying to stay out of it."

Charlotte took hold of his hand and smiled before saying, "I understand that it's hard being on the outside, Nick. But Noah's a good guy, and I don't think he'd do anything to cause Stella anymore pain."

Nick nodded and replied, "You're right. Now tell me more about your aversion to flying."

"I don't know why it brings me so much anxiety, but it really is outside of my comfort level," Charlotte told him honestly. "Maybe because the last time I flew to Indiana, I was leaving everything I loved on Anna Maria Island."

Nick rubbed her shoulders, trying to get her to relax. "I wish your experiences on a plane had been different," he told her, "but you're headed to Arizona and a celebration this time, and I'm right here."

"I know," Charlotte admitted. "Really, the flights to and from New York were pretty easy. It could be that thinking about my mom's new lifestyle and getting on a plane to go confront it is more than I'm comfortable with."

When it was time to board, Charlotte reminded Nick of the tradition she had before ever stepping foot off the skybridge and onto the plane. "Don't forget to kiss your fingers and touch the plane's logo like this," she reminded him. "Then say arrive alive."

If Nick looked foolish, none of the passengers in line behind him noticed.

For just a weekend Nick thought a carry-on bag would have been enough, but Charlotte was adamant they would need more. "We'll need something to wear tomorrow and Sunday," she told him. "Plus, as my mother's only attendant, I'll need a nice dress, and you'll need a suit."

Nick wasn't about to argue with her, but from what he had seen of Thomas, he had his doubts if even Thomas would be wearing a suit. Charlotte was already nervous about going to visit her mom and getting on a plane. If overpacking and wearing a suit would make her happy, he was willing to man up.

Once safely in their seats, Nick reached over to buckle Charlotte in but stopped when he realized the seatbelt needed to be let out. Afraid that this would set her off even more, he tried to act nonchalant about it, but she caught on right away. "Just what I need," she spewed. "One more reason to feel uncomfortable about this weekend. I swear if my mom says again that my hips have spread, I'll—"

Taking her hands in his, Nick kissed them and smiled at his wife. "Everything about you is perfect, Charlotte," he said quietly, "from your really nice rack to your svelte hips and thighs, you are perfect for me, and I wouldn't change a thing."

After his pep talk, while Charlotte tried to come to terms with him calling her ample chest a rack, she remembered she had told him never to say her lower half was anything other than svelte. He had used that exact word. With a grin on her face, Charlotte sat back in her seat as ready as she'd ever be to face her mom.

I sure hope your husband turns out to be as good to you as mine is to me, Mom, Charlotte thought. *And that you never mention the size of my hips again.*

Chapter 65

Now

The flight to Arizona was less than three hours long, and even though she made Nick hold her hand throughout the entire flight, Charlotte realized when they landed that it hadn't been bad at all. Nick helped her off the plane and was leading her to the baggage claim when he stopped.

"I don't have to worry about running into any of your old boyfriends here, do I?" he asked.

Charlotte couldn't tell if he was teasing her or being serious, so she took a minute to respond. "Well," she replied, "none that I'm aware of."

Nick tried to make a face like he was really angry, but he couldn't hold back his laugh. "Well if we do, don't make eye contact. I'm not FBI anymore so if I hit someone, I'll end up in jail."

The twinkle in his eye was contagious, and soon Charlotte was laughing along with him, forgetting the stress of a visit with her mom.

The Uber driver they hired said he wasn't familiar with the artist colony where Maggie and Thomas lived, but once Charlotte gave him the address, he put it in his GPS, and they were off. For some reason, Charlotte expected to be taken out in the country someplace. She was shocked when the driver pulled up to a very nice gated community just outside of town. Leaning over the front seat, Charlotte told the guard that Charlotte Luce was here to see Maggie Luce.

"I'm sorry ma'am," the guard told her, looking over his clipboard. "I don't have your name down as a guest."

Nick gave her a light tap on her butt and suggested she try using Greyson. *Shit! Shit! Shit!* she thought, before trying Nick's suggestion.

"Uh, try Nick and Charlotte Greyson, to see Maggie Luce," she said, hoping the guard wouldn't notice her embarrassment.

"Yep, right here," he smiled at her. "Maggie told me her daughter and son-in-law were coming from Florida for the wedding, but she didn't tell me you were so gorgeous. I should have known though; all the men follow Maggie around like puppy dogs."

Nick cleared his throat to remind them that he was still there as the guard opened the gate. Giving the Uber driver directions to where Maggie and Thomas lived, the guard gave Charlotte a little wave and stepped back inside his enclosure.

"Hmm," Nick said a little gruffly, "maybe there's something to that pheromone thing after all."

Charlotte had no intention of having this discussion within earshot of the driver, so she turned away and looked over the beautiful rustic cabins of the artist colony. She was just starting to relax and enjoy the view when the driver stopped and said, "This is it."

Charlotte stared at the stately home in front of her and felt her breath taken away. All this time she thought her mom was living in a hovel, and instead, she was living in a mansion? Why hadn't her mother said something? But then again, why hadn't she asked?

Nick was paying the driver and getting the bags when the door to the house was opened by a lovely young woman with rainbow-striped hair and dark brown eyes covered by bright blue glasses.

"Hi," Charlotte said brightly, sticking out her hand, "I'm Charlotte Greyson, here to see my mom, Maggie Luce."

The young woman looked at Charlotte and her face lit up. "Charlotte," she said leaning toward Charlotte's ear, "it's me, Carol."

Chapter 66

Now

Charlotte's mind went blank. She had been the one to send Carol to her mom's, and they even talked about her occasionally using the code name the kitty. Evidently in all the last-minute planning, she had forgotten that Carol would be here. And so would Nick.

Carol pulled Charlotte into the house and threw her arms around her old boss and friend before starting to cry. "It's so good to see you," she sobbed. "You just don't know how much I've missed you or how grateful I am for everything you did for me."

At this point, Charlotte was getting misty-eyed as well, patting Carol's back and trying to comfort her like a small child, when she heard a throat clearing behind her. *Shit! Shit! Shit!* she thought. It was Nick, who had arrested Carol. How was he going to react to seeing her, and more importantly, how was she going to react to seeing him?

Breaking away from Carol, Charlotte looked at Nick and with a tremor in her voice said, "Nick, you remember Carol Neel, my assistant from the bank?"

Charlotte wasn't sure what she expected exactly, but it definitely wasn't what happened next. Carol grabbed Nick around the waist and hugged him; her tears falling harder now. "How can I ever thank you for helping me get out of jail," she cried. "If you hadn't gone to bat for me, I'd still be in that hell hole."

If he hadn't gone to bat for her? What was that all about? *I'm the one who hired the attorney who got her out of jail,* Charlotte said to herself. "Uh, can someone fill me in here?" Charlotte asked, "I'm totally lost."

It was a rare occasion for Nick Greyson to be embarrassed or at least to show that embarrassment, but when Charlotte looked at him, she could see pink on his naturally bronzed cheeks. Carol continued to cry, her arms still wrapped around Nick's waist, when Charlotte's mom walked into the foyer.

"Well," Maggie grinned, "I see we have that out of the way."

"It's good to see you too, Mom," Charlotte said sarcastically. "Now will someone *please* tell me what's going on?"

Carol let go of Nick and did her best to dry her eyes. "You mean you don't know?" she said to Charlotte. "Owen Gardner told me it was only because Nick asked to have the charges against me dropped that the judge agreed to it. I would have gotten out eventually anyway, but probably not until after the trial."

Charlotte looked at her husband in awe and asked, "You did that for Carol, and you never told me? Why?"

Nick was clearly uncomfortable when he answered. "Why didn't I tell you, or why did I do it? I couldn't tell you because it was part of the investigation, and besides that, you weren't speaking to me. But I did it because you were right. I took advantage of our relationship and used Carol as leverage against her brother and that was wrong."

Charlotte felt as if her heart would burst. Nick had tried to rectify arresting Carol and had never once tried to take the credit for it. He could have told her any time after he came out of his coma, but true to his humble nature, he had stayed quiet.

"Nick Greyson," she said, putting her fingers up to his lips, "I've never loved you more than I do right now." Replacing her fingers with her lips, she gave him a kiss that proved just how much.

"Oh, Boss!" Carol exclaimed with glee, "you got one of the gorgeous Greysons, and he's a good one, too." With those words, Nick really did blush, to which the women just laughed.

Maggie hugged her daughter and son-in-law and ushered them into the great room.

"Thomas is finishing up on a sculpture," she told them, "and then he'll be over. Let me take you to your room, and while you get settled, I'll fix us some tea."

155

Behind her mother's back Charlotte mouthed "tea" to Nick, but she followed her mom up a beautiful oak staircase, to a bedroom on the third floor. "Mom, this house is amazing," Charlotte said. "I had no idea that artists lived so well."

"Thomas is one of the leading metal sculptors in the world, Charlotte, and this artist colony belongs to him," Maggie replied. "Didn't I tell you all that when I first started seeing him?"

Charlotte gave her mom a genuine smile and replied, "No, Mom, you didn't, but I know now. You look happy," she said, looking at her mom's radiant face, "I'm glad you found Thomas, and I'm so glad we're here."

Maggie gave Charlotte another hug and patted Nick's arm before heading downstairs, leaving Charlotte and Nick alone.

"If we weren't in my mother's house, and we weren't expected downstairs in a minute for tea, I would show you right now just how much I love you. You never cease to surprise me, Nick," Charlotte said, taking his face in her hands. "Believe it or not, I kind of like your surprises."

Charlotte pressed her body against his and kissed him passionately. She could feel his reaction to her closeness and gave him a sultry laugh. "Hold that thought," she told him, backing away.

Nick groaned but did his best to get himself back in control. "Sometimes I'm not sure if you're an angel or a devil, Charlotte," he chuckled. "But damned if I don't like them both."

Chapter 67
Now

Maggie and Carol were waiting in the great room when Charlotte and Nick walked in, hand in hand. Thankfully the tea turned out to be a delicious, pomegranate iced-tea and not a fussy cup like Charlotte was anticipating. There was also a plate of cookies and a bowl of freshly sliced apricots.

Charlotte reached for a slice of apricot even though she was salivating for one of the yummy looking cookies. She was sure her mother was testing her, but she was pleasantly surprised when Maggie said, "Try a cookie, Charlotte. Carol made them just for you, and they're actually healthy."

Not one to be told twice to have a cookie, Charlotte took one of the delicious looking confections and tried a bite. "Oh my gosh, Carol," she said, her mouth still full. "These are divine! What all is in them?"

Carol was beaming as she went over the ingredients for her concoction. "Flax seeds, chia seeds, walnuts, and organic applesauce and carrots, plus locally stoneground wheat and oats. I added a few golden raisins to this batch, too, but sometimes I use carob chips."

"I have to have this recipe," Charlotte said, putting the last bite in her mouth. "These are some of the best cookies I've ever eaten."

Nick got up the courage to try one of the healthy treats and almost missed what Maggie said to her daughter, "A recipe for who, Charlotte?" she asked with a saucy laugh. "We all know you don't cook."

Before Charlotte could defend herself, Nick laid down his cookie and came to his wife's defense. "Charlotte has actually become a very good cook, Maggie, and I have no doubt that she can make these cookies just as well as Carol."

Charlotte was stunned and looked from her husband to her mother. *Is this really happening?* She thought. Will I come out of this unscathed? To her surprise and delight, her mom just replied, "Good for you, Charlotte. Your gran would be very pleased."

After that they talked about Maggie's wedding the next evening, how Charlotte's new business venture was coming, and a little about Nick leaving the FBI to become a teacher of all things.

"I sure wouldn't have seen that coming," Carol professed, giving Nick the once over. "I mean, who has a teacher that looks like you?"

Knowing Nick was going to be uncomfortable with the way the conversation was heading, Charlotte asked for a tour of the house. Maggie took them from room to room, and each one seemed more beautiful than the last.

Charlotte knew that Thomas was divorced and figured he and his ex-wife had probably bought and decorated the house when they were married. The wonderful antiques, mixed perfectly with some mid-century furnishings, were surely put together by a woman's hand, she thought.

"So, Mom," Charlotte said. "Who decorated the house? It's truly one of the loveliest homes I've ever been in."

"That would be me," came a voice from behind them, and when Charlotte turned around, there stood Thomas. "Coming from you, that's a real compliment, Charlotte. You mom has told me about how much you love quality things, and to be honest, so do I."

Thomas gave her a peck on the cheek, shook Nick's hand, and gave both Carol and her mother a big hug. For a moment the thought crossed Charlotte's mind that the three of them were a little more than friends, but the speculation ended when Thomas looked into Maggie's eyes.

"I can't tell you how much I love your mother, Charlotte," Thomas said with conviction. "Marrying her tomorrow is like a dream come true, and with Carol here, I can take your mom on the honeymoon she deserves and know that someone is here watching over things."

Maggie beamed, and that made Charlotte beam, as well. Her mom was in love with a very nice, and apparently, wealthy man, and for the first time in a long time, Charlotte felt like everything was right with her world. Reaching up to stroke her locket, she mentally spoke to her beloved grandmother.

"Look at us, Gran," she said. "Nick and I are married and expecting a baby, and Mom is getting married for the first time. I know how much she loved my dad, Gran, but Thomas is a good man, and I think you'd like him. We're finally all grown up, and we owe it all to you."

Chapter 68
Then

Lottie woke-up on the morning of her high school graduation giddy with excitement! The day she had been waiting for was finally here, and nothing was going to spoil it. Rolling out of her twin-size bed, she thought again of the life she planned to have after she graduated from IU, and a king size bed was definitely in it. At five feet ten, she was too tall for the little bed she had slept in since leaving her crib. The idea of a bedroom of her own, complete with an ensuite bathroom and a great big bed, was part of her dreams for the future.

Grabbing her robe, she headed out of her room, anxious to have coffee with Gran. Lottie loved that Gran had come for her graduation and was even staying in their little house, and she wanted to spend as much time with her as possible. Feeling confident that her mom wasn't up yet, she stepped out into the hall but stopped when she heard voices.

"Maggie," Lottie heard Gran say, "you know that I've tried to mind my own business where your personal life is concerned, but I'm really worried that the way you live is going to cause a hardship for Lottie."

"The way I live?" Mom questioned. "Is it the way I live or the way I love that you don't like?"

Gran took a breath and tried again. "I don't doubt for a moment that you loved my son, Margaret, but what was your life like before you met him? I told myself I would never ask that question, but with the way I see you cavorting with men when I'm around, it makes it hard for me not to wonder."

Lottie's mother laughed but it wasn't a nice laugh, that's for sure. "I cavort, do I? Well let me assure you that I never cavorted before I met your son. There was never anyone before him, and for the longest time, I never thought there would be anyone after him, but at some point, I realized I needed more than just being Lottie's mother. That may be hard for you to understand, but I was a sixteen-year-old virgin who met a wonderful boy and fell in love. When that boy was taken from me and I found out that I was pregnant, my world fell apart."

Lottie had never seen her mom look so angry, and she had never heard Gran say anything but nice things to her mother. She huddled in the hallway, afraid of what might come next.

"I'm sorry, Maggie," Gran said softly. "I know what you've given up for your daughter, but please remember, that boy was taken away from me, too. I'm grateful for the way you let me into your life, into both of your lives, but I can't help but be concerned for Lottie. She's a young woman now, just about the age you were when she was born, and surely you want her to have some ideals when it comes to love and relationships?"

Mom hung her head, and Gran wrapped her in her arms. "I want Lottie to have choices in her life Maggie, and I know you do, too. She's a brilliant young woman with the world just waiting for her, but she needs to know what her values are and the importance of respecting them."

Mom nodded and swiped at the tears forming in her eyes and said, "I'll talk to her."

Lottie was mortified! She didn't know a lot about boy/girl relationships, but she knew Gran was talking about her having sex, and that was just crazy. She liked Nick Greyson a lot, that was true. Okay, maybe she more than liked him, but Nick didn't think of her that way. Sure, he'd been acting a little different the past few weeks, but he'd never even tried to kiss her, and Lottie was pretty sure that should come first. Besides, watching the way her mom was with men had definitely made her uncomfortable around boys.

Determined not to let the awful start to the morning ruin her day, Lottie breathed deeply and was about to enter the kitchen when she heard her mom say, "Maybe it's time I thought about moving away from Anna Maria Island."

161

Chapter 69
Now

The wedding took place in one of the large artist cabins and was simply beautiful. Maggie wore a short, white lace dress that hugged her voluptuous petite frame and showed off her Betty Gable legs. Much to Nick's surprise, Thomas was wearing a suit.

Chad had arrived just after dinner the evening before, and Charlotte had liked him right away. He was a younger version of Thomas, only with hair cut short military style. For the ceremony he was wearing his Marine Dress blues, which partnered well with Charlotte's pastel ASOS floral print maxi dress with flutter sleeves. It was one of the outfits she had bought with Becca, so thankfully, the tie just under her breasts hid her growing pregnancy.

Gathered together with their family and friends from the artist colony, Maggie and Thomas said their vows in a very conventional ceremony. When the minister was speaking, Charlotte looked over at Nick, and he winked at her. Wasn't it just yesterday that they were the bride and groom?

The dinner reception consisted of Caesar salad, filet mignon topped with cremini mushrooms and béarnaise sauce, and asparagus covered with hollandaise, followed by a traditional three-tiered wedding cake. Charlotte was happy for her mother and also a little perplexed. Where was the gypsy/hippy mom who had raised her?

When the food was cleared away, a band set up, and yep, there was the Maggie Luce Charlotte knew and loved. The first song was a slow one, and Maggie and Thomas danced it alone on the dance floor, but when that song ended and rock and roll began, Maggie danced with men of all ages and sizes, loving the attention she got.

"Doesn't that bother you, Thomas?" Charlotte asked her mother's new husband.

"Nah," he laughed. "That sexy woman was made for men to flirt with. As long as my bed is the only one she gets in, I'm fine with her having a good time."

Charlotte squeezed Thomas' hand, letting him know that she understood. She hoped that her mother understood as well. Thomas was a good guy, and even though she hadn't known him long, she was feeling very protective of her new stepfather.

"May I have this dance, Mrs. Greyson?" Nick asked the next time a slow song came on.

Charlotte felt like a deer caught in headlights when she realized she'd never danced with Nick. Not only that, but the only time she'd ever been in a room with him where there was dancing was at their junior high school sock hops.

"I didn't know you danced," she answered, not really sure what to do.

"Who says that I do?" he teased, but taking her hand, he pulled her out onto the floor. And just like with everything he did, Nick was a terrific dancer.

Charlotte tried her best to follow his moves, and oh yeah, he had moves, when he whispered in her ear, "Try letting me lead."

Chapter 70

Now

The band played their last song, and Thomas took his bride's hand and led her out into the peaceful Arizona night where two horse drawn carriages were waiting. He helped Maggie into the first one, and motioned for Charlotte, Chad, and Nick to get into the second one. Just before they pulled away, Thomas caught a glimpse of Carol standing by the curb and yelled out at her, "Are you coming with us or not?"

Charlotte was overcome with a feeling of peace and love. Snuggled close to Nick, his arms tightly wrapped around her, she knew this was a night she would never forget. But it had been a very long day, and the rocking of the carriage, combined with the warmth and security of Nick beside her lulled her quickly into a deep sleep.

"I hope our baby falls asleep as easily as you do, Charlotte," Nick teased as he gently woke her up. "You missed all the excitement."

Trying to wipe the sleep out of her eyes when all she really wanted to do was close them, Charlotte asked, "I missed what?"

Nick laughed as he told he what all had happened during her nap. "First of all, there were fireworks over the canyon. Big, beautiful fireworks, just like the Fourth of July. But what you'll really be sorry you missed were the fireworks right here, between Carol and Chad. I could feel them all the way over here where I held my sleeping wife."

Charlotte looked across the carriage at her dear friend and new stepbrother and sighed. She loved a good love story, and for Carol's sake, she hoped this one was for real. Charlotte knew how hard it must have been for Carol to leave her brother and her home and move in with strangers, but she had seemed content all weekend. Now when

Charlotte looked at Carol's face, she saw more than contentment. She saw hope.

"Are you going to be able to walk up to bed, Charlotte?" Nick asked. "Because I'm pretty sure I can't carry you up three flights of stairs."

Charlotte was wide awake now and made a face at Nick's comment. "And here I thought I married a *He-Man*," she giggled. "Instead, I got an ordinary man."

"I'll show you ordinary," Nick growled, picking her up and heading for the door. But when he got there and found it closed, he realized that he couldn't continue to carry Charlotte and get the door opened. Setting her gently on her feet, Nick said, "You're right, just ordinary."

They were still laughing when they finally reached the third floor and their bedroom, and both plopped down on the bed.

"This was a good day wasn't it?" Nick asked her, moving a curl off her forehead.

"It was a great day," she replied, "and you know what? I think I finally have a family after all."

When Nick climbed into bed a short time later, Charlotte was curled on her side, looking out the window at the moonlight. He pulled her closer to him and gently rubbed her very visible baby bump.

"How did Babycakes like the festivities?" Nick asked as he stroked his wife's body.

"Just fine," Charlotte responded. "But we're in my mom's house, Nick" she said, trying to grab hold of his roaming fingers. "You know that I'm not comfortable making love with you in someone else's home."

"Who said anything about making love?" he whispered, tenderly kissing her neck. "We are married, Charlotte, and I think it's okay if we fool around a little before we go to sleep. Just think of it as connecting."

And what a connection it was.

Chapter 71

Now

Charlotte and Nick had a three thirty flight back to Tampa, and Maggie and Thomas were leaving for Paris at five, so once again they made plans to ride together to the airport. Because of the late night, everyone had slept in, so instead of breakfast, they had brunch.

Carol was in the kitchen whipping up some kind of sweet concoction, humming and smiling, when Charlotte came in to get coffee. Charlotte just watched her for a few minutes, recognizing the slept with look in Carol's eyes, and she wondered if she was the only person in the world who was intimidated to have sex when others were close by.

When Carol looked up and saw Charlotte standing there, she blushed and said, "Good morning."

Just then the rest of the family wandered in looking for coffee and food, and Charlotte realized they all had that same sexy smile as Carol did, well except for Nick. Putting her arms around him and kissing his face she said softly into his ear, "I'll make it up to you when we get home."

Nick gave her a squeeze before replying, "I never had a doubt." When Thomas offered him a mug of coffee, Nick calmly accepted it as if he and Charlotte were discussing the weather.

"It was so good to see you," Charlotte told Carol just before getting in the car to leave for the airport. "I miss you and our days at Olde Florida, but maybe it all worked out for the best. Nick and I are finally together and happy, and you seem to have found peace and a love interest of your own."

Carol looked at the woman who had sacrificed her own life so that she could know freedom, and she couldn't help the tears from forming. "No one in my whole life has ever done for me what you did, Charlotte, and I promise you that I'll never forget it. And as for Chad, who knows, maybe someday you and I will be more than just friends."

The practical side of Charlotte wanted to tell Carol to slow down, but the romantic side could tell that Carol was right. Whatever had happened with Chad the night before was more than just a wedding hook-up, and Charlotte was looking forward to seeing where it went.

There were hugs to Chad and Carol, and then the two couples got in the car and headed out. It was a gorgeous afternoon for a drive, and Charlotte enjoyed the breathtaking Arizona scenery while Nick talked with Thomas and Maggie about their trip to Paris. It was almost two hours from the artist colony to the airport, but in no time at all, they were there.

"Charlotte," Maggie said, holding on tightly to her only child. "I'm proud of the woman you are. You've made me want to be a better mother and a good wife, and I don't ever want you to forget how much I love you."

"I won't," Charlotte said, trying not to cry. "And I love you, too. We kind of we grew up together, didn't we, but we turned out pretty good. I think the world of Thomas, and I want you to be happy. You deserve that Mom, you deserve to be loved."

Maggie gave Nick a hug, and he and Thomas shook hands before Thomas stepped up to Charlotte. "I promise I'll take good care of her," he said, his eyes filled with love.

Charlotte nodded and looked straight into his eyes. "My mom deserves happiness more than anyone I know, and I think you're just the man to give it to her. She's a little eccentric from time to time, but that's part of her charm. Now go, and let my mom take Paris by storm, but bring her home safely. My baby is looking forward to meeting its grandmother."

Chapter 72
Now

It was after seven thirty in the evening by the time Charlotte and Nick landed back in Tampa and collected their bags. The peaceful feeling Charlotte had experienced at her mom's wedding had stayed with her. Despite still having to go through her preflight ritual, she was very relaxed on the trip from Arizona.

"You look exhausted, Charlotte," Nick said as they headed to the parking garage. "Let's get a room for the night and go home in the morning so you can get a good night's sleep."

"I am tired," she admitted, "but I'd really like to sleep in our own bed tonight. The one at mom's house was okay but not the same."

Nick agreed, and finding his Jeep, he put the bags in the back while Charlotte buckled herself in. "I never really thought about this before," she said, "but what happens if my belly gets too big to fit in the seatbelt?"

"That's a question for another woman," Nick said with a grin. "I haven't a clue."

Sunday night traffic was thankfully light, and before long, Nick pulled into the driveway of Charlotte's little pink cottage. It was his home, too, and he was fine with that, but in his mind, it would always be hers. "We're here," Nick told her because, of course, she had fallen asleep. "I'm trying hard not to get a complex, but you seem to have a difficult time keeping your eyes open when we're together in a moving vehicle. Do I need to work on my conversational skills?"

"Poor Baby," she joked, "let's unload and get inside; I believe I made you a promise this morning."

"Yes ma'am!" Nick responded, grabbing the bags. "I like it when you make good on your promises."

Charlotte put her hands on her hips and questioned, "And when haven't I made good on a promise?"

Groaning, Nick said, "Never, you always make good on them, that's why I like it. Now please, open the door."

Charlotte gave him a look, like she was considering opening the door but not quite sure. When Nick growled, "Charlotte," she opened it right away.

"I thought you would lose that gruff G-Man voice when you left the FBI, but I've got to say, it's kind of sexy." Charlotte flipped her hair and closed and locked the front door behind her.

Heading toward the bedroom, she said, "Maybe we should play *The Untouchables*. You can be Eliot Ness, and I'll be a gun moll you're trying to get information out of after you arrest her gangster boyfriend."

Nick had to grab his side he was laughing so hard. "First of all," he asked her, "how do you even know about Eliot Ness or *The Untouchables*, and secondly, you'd really be in to role play?"

"I don't know," Charlotte sulked. "I mean I know about Eliot Ness from college, but the role play part just came out. Didn't you like it?"

"Oh, Charlotte," Nick said taking her face in his hands. "You are a constant source of wonder to me, and if role play arouses you, I'll give it a whirl, but to be honest, all I really need is you."

Breathing a sigh of relief, Charlotte answered. "I'm really glad, because I don't have the right clothes to play a gun moll."

Chapter 73

Now

The following Wednesday Nick came home from class to find Charlotte mixing a meatloaf, an apple pie cooling on the counter. "To what do I owe this burst of domesticity?" he asked curiously.

Her hand still in the bowl of meat, Charlotte explained that Pop was coming for dinner, and that when the pie cooled, she was going to take a piece to her friend, Mrs. Danvers. "Besides," she admitted, "I don't have anything to do all day except cook."

Nick walked around besides her and saw how sad she looked. "What do you mean you don't have anything to do except cook? What about your small business clients, don't you do things for them?"

Charlotte patted the meatloaf into a pan and washed her hands. "They don't really need a lot," she told him. "Now that I know Tony Neel's illegal activities didn't affect them, it won't take me more than one day a week to do what they need."

Nick felt like a heel. Here he was changing careers and finally realizing his dream of coaching young swimmers, and Charlotte's career had ended. Because of him. "Come here," he said gently, pulling her warm body against his. "Maybe it's time you looked for another job, something that you'd love like you did banking."

Charlotte shook her head. "I can't look for a job when I'm pregnant," she said. "It just wouldn't be fair. I've been on the management end of women having babies, and as happy as I was for them, it was hard on everyone else."

"I'm pretty sure it's illegal to discriminate against hiring a pregnant woman or not allowing her time off when the baby's born," Nick reminded her. "I would think you would support those laws."

"I do support them, Nick, I'm just saying that I won't do that to a company. Part of being a strong woman is knowing what's best for you and going back into the workforce right now wouldn't be best for me. But," she said with a grin, "I do have an idea."

A piece of pie in one hand, Charlotte held on to Nick with the other as they walked the beach to Mrs. D's house. "So," she said, looking out over the Gulf of Mexico, "what would you say to me opening my own accounting office?"

Nick stopped long enough to look over her face before he answered. "Honey, if that will make you happy, I'm all for it, but how is that different? You'll still need time off when the baby comes."

"I know that, Nick, but I could set things up to work from home for now, and maybe find a brick and mortar location later. I'd probably have to be recertified as a CPA, but it would give me something to do besides cook and take care of you."

The dark clouds forming in Nick's eyes let Charlotte know that she had said the wrong thing. *Shit! Shit! Shit!* she thought. *I've got to learn to filter.*

"I didn't mean that the way it sounded, Nick," Charlotte said. "I love taking care of you, and I really like to cook, but I always wanted to work, I always expected to work, it's just that…"

"It's just that you lost your job because I arrested Carol, right? I made a bad call, and it cost you your career. Just say it, Charlotte," he demanded, "just say that I fucked up your life."

Nick took off down the beach, leaving Charlotte in tears, holding a piece of warm apple pie. "You used that word again," she called after him, but if he heard her, Nick didn't acknowledge it.

Chapter 74

Now

When you have a fight with your husband on a public beach, and you're holding a piece of warm pie in your hand, there's only one thing to do, right? You eat it! And that's just what Charlotte did.

Slowly walking home in case Nick came back to apologize, Charlotte had the pie unwrapped and a third of it in her mouth before she was even aware of what she was doing. "Old habits die hard, I guess, Babycakes," she said to her unborn child. "Eating like this is what I did as a kid when Ashley Marshall made fun of me or when I was mooning over your daddy." Then taking one more bite, Charlotte wrapped up the remainder of the pie and threw it in the nearest dumpster.

Remembering that the real purpose of this walk was a trip to Mrs. Danvers' house, Charlotte vacillated between going home for a fresh slice of pie or visiting her friend empty handed. She knew Mrs. D would love the visit with or without the pie, so she turned and headed back down the beach, hoping against hope that Nick turned around as well.

Charlotte knocked on her friend's door several times, but there was no answer. Starting to worry a little bit, she decided to walk around to the back to see if she could peek through the kitchen window. Just as she was cupping her hands to peer inside, a voice called out from the next cottage over.

"If you're looking for Edna, she's not home," the voice said. "Roma picked her up for some appointment in Sarasota."

Charlotte thanked the well-kept older man who stood in his doorway looking at her, and a big smile came across her face. *Why Mrs. D,* she thought, *you've got an admirer.*

By the time she returned home, Charlotte had calmed down, but Nick was nowhere to be found. It was time to put the meatloaf and baked potatoes in the oven if they were going to be ready for dinner, but all she could think about was Nick and their argument. Pop was due around six thirty, and with a heavy heart she put the food in to cook and went in to take a shower.

Charlotte decided that she wanted to look her best when Nick came home because surely, he would. They were married for heaven sakes and had a baby on the way! Nick Greyson was not the kind of man to walk away from his family over one little fight, was he? She wrestled with her thoughts as she smoothed her skin with his favorite Victoria's Secret coconut oil and brushed her wavy locks until they hung softly around her shoulders. She even debated on wearing the sundress, yes, that sundress, that had worked so well before, but she decided it was not Pop appropriate.

Instead she put on a pair of soft gray yoga pants that clung snuggly to her curves and an oversized white tunic trimmed in blue. Applying a coat of mascara and swiping her lips with EOS Coconut Crème lip balm, Charlotte was confident Nick would be on the lanai drinking a beer when she stepped out. But he wasn't.

Sitting down on the big wicker loveseat because her legs were starting to shake, Charlotte reached for her locket, closed her eyes, and talked to Gran.

"Oh Gran," she cried, "me and my big mouth. I'm just not good at this relationship stuff, but I've really been trying. I know I hurt Nick's feelings, but I didn't mean to. I wish you were here to guide me; I even wish Mom was here to guide me but she's still in Paris with a husband who hasn't abandoned her. Help me know what to do Gran, please," Charlotte begged. "Give me a sign that everything is going to be okay. I need to know that Nick still loves me."

"He does," she heard Nick say when she opened her eyes, and there he was standing at the doorway, Pop right behind him.

173

"Where have you been?" she sobbed, jumping into his waiting arms. "I've been so worried, so scared."

Nick held her and stroked her back, letting her get the tears out before speaking. "I walked to the marina," he finally told her. "I needed to cool off and I needed advice, and well, Pop is the best person I know when it comes to advice."

"I'm so sorry, Nick," Charlotte told him, oblivious to her father-in-law's presence. "I do love taking care of you, and I love having you take care of me, it's just—"

"That you miss your job," he said, finishing her sentence.

"I do miss it, Nick, I'm trying to be truthful with you, but I don't miss it half as much as I would miss you."

As he lowered his face to hers, Nick gave her a kiss that drove the doubt out of her mind and put all kinds of sexy thoughts in it. Remembering that they weren't alone, Charlotte untangled herself from Nick's arms and tried not to look at Pop.

Just as she was moving toward the kitchen to put the finishing touches on dinner, she felt a soft flutter down low in her belly. Automatically her hands reached for her stomach, causing the color to drain from Nick's face.

"Are you okay, Lottie?" he asked. "Is our baby okay?"

With a smile from ear to ear she replied, "I think I just felt our baby move Nick. Gran sent me a sign. We're going to be fine."

Chapter 75

Now

All through dinner Charlotte kept waiting for another flutter, but it just didn't happen. The three of them tried to have a normal conversation, but between Nick and Charlotte's spat on the beach, and Babycake's first kicks, it was really hard. Pop could tell that the young couple needed some alone time, so as soon as he had finished eating, he said he needed to get back to the marina.

With the kitchen cleaned up and the dishwasher running, Nick sat down on the couch and pulled Charlotte onto his lap. "I'm really sorry I lashed out at you today," he told her. "After seeing Carol, it really hit me how much my actions have changed both of your lives, and I kind of lost control when you were talking about your job. You know it wasn't you I was mad at but me."

"I know, Nick, but maybe it's a good thing that it all came out, because now we can truly move forward. Plus," she added, "I realized while I was walking home that I don't want to be a CPA or start an accounting firm. I just want the life we have together now."

Nick tried to interrupt, but Charlotte put her finger to his lips and kept him from talking. "I will want to go back to a real job someday," she told him, "but for now I want to be your wife and Babycake's mom. It's not what I ever expected to want, but I do, so please don't try to change my mind."

Nick pushed her hair behind her ears and caressed the face that was so precious to him. "Promise me you'll let me know if you change your mind," he said. "I don't have to be your whole world, Charlotte, I just want to be in it."

"I don't know what to tell you, Coach Greyson," she grinned. "You've pretty much been my whole world since we were kids. I just didn't know how to deal with it then, but I sure do now."

Pressing her lips to his, Charlotte kissed him with all the heat and passion she felt inside. Nick responded, and it didn't take long before they were sprawled out on the couch, making out like teenagers.

"You know we can take this to the bedroom," he said, his voice deep and filled with desire.

"I know," Charlotte said with a soft chuckle, "but I missed out on this when we were in high school, at least with you."

Nick sat up, pulling her with him. "And who were you groping on your mom's sofa? I know a lot of guys wanted to go out with you, but I didn't think you had any interest in them."

"There was no one," Charlotte told him with mischief in her eyes, "but I had you going there for a minute, didn't I?"

"Not funny, Charlotte," he told her, "not funny at all."

"Well since I've been so naughty maybe I should go to bed without my dessert." Of course, what Nick didn't know was that she had pretty much had her dessert before dinner while she was walking on the beach.

"I'm not that hard-hearted," he told her, helping her to her feet. "Let's have some pie and then we'll go to bed."

Charlotte cut the pie and poured them each a glass of milk. "You never did tell me about your visit to Mrs. Danvers' house," Nick said to her. "Did she like the pie?"

Shit! Shit! Shit! she thought. Evidently Nick's FBI thought process was still in play, or she looked guilty. How else could you explain him bringing up the pie for Mrs. Danvers just as she was thinking about it?

Chapter 76
Now

By morning everything was back to normal and life was good. Nick was studying for his first midterm, and Charlotte decided to take advantage of the beautiful autumn day by going for a walk on the beach. She still owed a visit to Mrs. Danvers, so she put on her tennis shoes and warmed up, thinking she might even do a little running while she was out.

Just as she was headed in to tell Nick she was leaving, he stepped into the kitchen. "You going back to see Mrs. Danvers, today?" he questioned. "Maybe you should take her another piece of pie?"

Nick had a smirk on his face that Charlotte wanted to slap right off! He obviously knew that she had eaten Mrs. D's pie, so why didn't he just come out and say it? Trying to get him to admit that he was purposely goading her, Charlotte tried another tactic.

"I'm not sure where I'm going," Charlotte said with a fake smile on her face, "but I'm not sure that Mrs. D should have any more pie. Roma really watches what she eats."

"Uh-huh," Nick said, looking right at her.

"Okay, okay," she yelled, "I ate the pie before I even got to Mrs. Danvers' house. I ate it, and I'm not sorry!" Charlotte put her hands on her hips and dared him to try to shame her.

"Baby," Nick said like a sexy country western singer, "I don't care how much pie you eat; I don't care how many cookies you eat, but I don't understand the secrecy." He walked toward her like a cat stalking his prey, and Charlotte got goosebumps.

"How did you know?" she demanded.

"Because Pop and I stopped by the drugstore yesterday on our way here and ran into Mrs. Danvers and her daughter. I asked about your visit, and she said they had been gone all day and hadn't seen you."

"I wish you would have told me this last night," Charlotte said.

"And I wish you would have told me the truth," Nick responded. "So, let me make this clear. I don't care what you eat, or how much you eat, as long as you take care of yourself. But I don't ever want you to think you have to hide your food intake from me, because I'm truly a judgement free zone."

Charlotte was embarrassed and relieved all at the same time. "No more food secrets, Nick, I promise."

"That sounds like there may be other secrets," he questioned, cocking his eyebrow.

"Not necessarily," she said with a grin, "but a girl has to keep her options open."

Chapter 77

Now

Now that the truth was out, Charlotte took a minute to cut a piece of pie for Mrs. D. If she had been with Roma the day before, she would surely be alone today and up for some contraband. When she knocked on the door of her friend's cottage, Charlotte was pleased to find that she was home but not alone.

Sitting on what Mrs. Danvers called the settee, was the gentleman from next door who had spoken to Charlotte the day before. And as comfortable as he looked, she was pretty sure this wasn't his first visit.

"Charlotte dear, come in," Mrs. D said, opening the door. "Richard from next door stopped by to make sure my doctor's appointment went well yesterday," Mrs. Danvers said, her cheeks showing a little color.

"I actually came by yesterday, and he told me you were out with Roma," Charlotte told her friend. "I hope everything is okay?"

"It was just a routine visit to my ophthalmologist," Mrs. Danvers assured her. "My eyesight isn't getting better but it's not getting worse, and that's the good thing. Now come in and sit down and tell me what's new with you."

Being a romantic at heart, Charlotte wasn't about to get in the way of Mrs. D's courtship, so she politely declined. "I've taken up cooking," she said with pride, "and I wanted you to taste my first pie." Handing the package to Mrs. Danvers, Charlotte added, "I would have brought two pieces if I had known you have company, but maybe you can share it?"

Mrs. Danvers gave Charlotte a hug and nodded. "Please bring that handsome husband with you the next time. His father told me all about your impromptu wedding, but I want all the details from you. Men always leave out the good parts."

Charlotte smiled and promised to return soon with Nick in tow. "Should I call before we come?" she teased. "You know, in case you have company?"

This time Mrs. Danvers really did blush, but she pretended like Charlotte was reading the situation wrong. "You young people," she protested, "always on the lookout for love."

Charlotte gave her another hug and whispered in her dear friend's ear, "I think Leo would approve," and she walked out the door.

The stroll on the beach gave Charlotte lots of time to think. Deciding what she needed to do was add a few more small business clients to the ones she already had, she started a mental list of who might be a good candidate. In fact, she was so deep in thought that she jumped when she felt the flutter in her stomach.

"Hi Babycakes," she said softly as she touched her rounding belly. "I wish I knew what was going on in there. Your daddy is going to be so happy when he can feel you move, and just so you know, we're both excited to meet you. We love you, Little Bean, you don't ever have to doubt that."

Feeling on top of the world, Charlotte picked up her pace and headed for home to share the news with Nick, and of course, so she could call Becca! Who better to talk with about baby stuff than an experienced, almost four-time mom?

Chapter 78

Now

Charlotte added three more small business clients to her list, Nick Aced his midterm, and Babycakes was stirring up lots of flutters. To celebrate, she and Nick decided to go out for dinner. She hadn't really dressed up since her mother's wedding, and Charlotte wanted to go all out, knock 'em dead, well as least as much as she could considering there was half a basketball protruding from her midsection!

After a relaxing in a bath, she looked over her repertoire of body care items, and decided to go with Josie Maran's Juicy Peach whipped argan oil body butter. Peaches had been out of season for some time, but the smell of the rich fragrant emollient had her salivating. *If only I could drink*, she thought, *I'd have a Peach Daiquiri tonight*. Alcohol was out of the question, of course, but maybe the restaurant could make her one without?

It had been so humid the last part of summer that trying to straighten her hair had been a waste of time, but with the cooler fall temperatures, Charlotte decided to give it a try. Body smooth and soft, hair straight and silky, the only thing left was deciding what to wear.

Nick had been sent to the guest bathroom to get ready so that Charlotte could make an entrance, but he was starting to get antsy. "Hey," he said knocking on the door, "when are you going to let me in?"

"I'm not," Charlotte responded. "Grab a beer or glass of tea and go wait for me on the lanai."

Charlotte was pretty sure she heard him swear, and she laughed, especially when she could tell he was holding back from using that word.

Charlotte looked through her meager rack of maternity outfits, well meager by her standards, and pulled out a deep periwinkle wrap dress, knowing it would be perfect. Somehow, she was able to encase the girls in a satin ecru bra, and even though the matching panties didn't quite cover her stomach, they worked well enough. Wondering what Nick would say if she didn't wear any panties, Charlotte started to laugh and thought better of it. They were finally going to have that dinner at Mar Vista out on Long Boat Key, and it was a long way from home if he got carried away.

A slight dust of bronzing powder across her cheeks and nose, two coats of black mascara, and a swipe of Josie Maran Lip Sting plumping butter, and Charlotte was ready. She grabbed her Louis Vuitton mini pouchette and was headed to the door when she remembered perfume. Not having time to really coordinate her fragrances, she opted instead for a quick mist of tropical body spray and taking a final look in the mirror, she was ready.

Nick was on the lanai, drinking a beer when she walked in. The grumpy look on his face was quickly replaced with a big smile when he finally saw his wife.

"You look amazing," he told her, getting up so he could put his arms around her. "Every man in the restaurant is going to wish you were with him tonight, but you're all mine."

The high-heeled ankle boots that Charlotte wore added a good three inches to her height, so reaching up for a kiss was easier than usual. "I take it you like?" she asked, twirling around in front of him.

"I like it so much," Nick responded huskily, "that I'd be willing to stay home and order pizza. Even that vegetarian crap that you like."

"Nothing doing," Charlotte grinned. "You said we were going out to celebrate, and I want my celebration dinner."

Putting his keys in his pocket, Nick grabbed Charlotte's hand and escorted her to the door. "We'll go to dinner like I said, but the celebration is going to happen right here. That is, if I can wait that long."

Charlotte gave him a saucy grin, and Nick returned it with a wink. *If he can wait that long? What about me?*

182

Chapter 79

Now

Charlotte's days soon became repetitious, but for someone like her, who liked organization and symmetry, it was perfect. She was getting up early again, and after a healthy breakfast with Nick, she would head to the beach for a walk. Some days he joined her, and some days she went alone, but for the first time in months, she was back in her zone.

Thanksgiving had been held at Stavros in Tarpon Springs, with Dimitri and Maya preparing all the food. Elizabeth and Gus had Skyped before dinner, and with both the Greyson and Mara's families there, the meal had been a mixture of traditional American and Greek delicacies. Charlotte had eaten her fill, but now that she was exercising again, food didn't have the hold on her that it had just a few weeks before.

A week after the holiday, Charlotte was walking the beach and enjoying the crisp air blowing out over the turquoise water of the Gulf of Mexico. All of a sudden, she realized that December was upon them. She and Nick hadn't even discussed Christmas, but she thought maybe it was time to get him that big California king bed he wanted. Suddenly, her cell phone rang. Seeing the caller ID read Jared Tyler, she answered with a smile.

"Good morning," she said happily into the phone. "To what do I owe this early morning call?"

"Becca's water broke, Lottie," Jared said nervously. "We're getting ready to leave for the hospital, but she wanted you to know."

"Oh my gosh, Jared!" Charlotte exclaimed. "Her due date isn't for three more weeks."

"You and I might know that but evidently Baby Tyler does not," he chuckled. "Anyway, I'll call you as soon as there's news."

"News?" she questioned. "As soon as I can round up Nick, we'll be there. You don't have babies without me!"

"Thank God," Jared said, letting out the breath he'd been holding. "Becca said to tell you it wasn't necessary for you to come, but I know she really wants you there. We both want you there."

Just then Charlotte heard a loud moan in the background, so she said her goodbyes and quickly dialed Nick. Thankfully he was helping his dad at the marina today and able to take off.

"I need to go home and change, and then I'll pick you up," she told her husband. "We'll probably want to stay overnight, so I'll throw a few things in a bag for you, okay?" Nick agreed, and Charlotte jogged home, both praying for Becca and the baby and holding her swaying belly.

Nick and Pop were waiting outside for her when Charlotte pulled up. She jumped out and gave her father-in-law a kiss and settled herself in the passenger seat. "You're going to let me drive your baby?" Nick asked. "We can take the Jeep, you know."

"It's fine," she said quickly. "I'm too nervous to drive, and I'm already buckled in. Now come on, this is baby number four, so it might arrive before we make it over the bridge!"

Nick had to put the seat way back to get his frame behind the wheel, but as soon as he was settled, they were off. He reached over and took Charlotte's hand, rubbing his thumb over her fingers to calm her down.

As soon as he could see her breathing had returned to normal, he asked, "Have Becca and Jared picked out names for this child?"

"Becca likes to actually see the baby before saddling it with a name," she told him. "I think they have a few in mind, but knowing Becca, she may come up with something totally different at the last minute."

"And what about us, Charlotte?" Nick questioned. "When will we start thinking of a name for our baby?"

Our baby? Charlotte thought, her heart beginning to pound. This was just too much pressure!

"How about we get through the birth of Becca and Jared's baby, and then we can talk about names for ours?"

Nick nodded, and Charlotte closed her eyes, hoping that she would follow her normal pattern and fall asleep, but it just didn't happen. Instead for the next few hours, names danced in her head like sugar plums, and all she could think was *Shit! Shit! Shit! Naming a child is a huge responsibility.*

Chapter 80
Now

Charlotte was right about how quickly Baby Tyler would be born. Only an hour into their trip, she received a text that read, "baby is perfect, can't wait to meet Aunt TT," but that was all. In true Becca fashion, she wasn't giving any hints about her newest addition, even to her best friend!

Charlotte knocked on the door before walking in the hospital room with Nick. She remembered from Becca's three other births what an intimate scene it was between Jared and Becca and their newborn, and she didn't want to make anyone feel uncomfortable.

Jared came to the door and led Charlotte and Nick to his wife's bedside. He was absolutely beaming, and Becca had a glow about her that said, "I'm the luckiest woman in the world."

Holding out her hand to her friends, Becca said softly to the bundle sleeping in her arms, "This is your Aunt TT and your Uncle Nick," she cooed. "You're going to love them a lot."

Charlotte could feel the tears in her eyes, and when she looked at Nick, he had them too. "So, the white blanket doesn't give me a clue, do I have a niece or a nephew?" she asked.

Becca smiled, and Jared spoke for both of them. "Please meet Bradley Jackson Tyler," he said with pride. "JD is excited to finally have a brother, but Anna and Lolly haven't weighed in yet. I think they'll warm up to him, though. Don't you?"

Becca handed the sleeping baby to Charlotte, and as she did, he opened his eyes. "He's so beautiful," she said, the tears finally running down her cheeks, "but then all of your babies have been." Running her finger gently over his face, Charlotte laughed when he rooted in her direction.

Nick hadn't said a word yet, but watching his wife gently talking to the newborn, he asked about the name. "Charlotte told me that you like to wait until your baby is born to name them, but how do you know what fits?"

"Well," Becca told him, "usually I can tell just by looking at them. I know it sounds strange, but it's worked so far. This little guy looks a lot like the pictures of my brother Brad when he was born, and well we couldn't name him after my brother and not include Jared's, so that's where Bradley Jackson came in. We're going to call him Jack for short."

"I know that Lolly is named after Charlotte, but they don't look anything alike. What made you chose her name?" Nick inquired.

"To be honest, we named her Charlotte because when she cried, she turned bright red like Lottie's hair use to be.

"Very funny," Charlotte teased, even though she had been so thrilled to have a namesake that she hadn't cared why they had chosen her name.

"And Anna?" Nick continued. "Who is she named for?"

"Why, Anna Maria Island, silly. The place where I met my closest friend. Besides, the first time I looked at her little face I felt like I was home, so Anna Maria Tyler she is!"

Charlotte handed the now fussy baby back to his mother and took Nick's hand. "We're going to let you feed this guy and get some rest," she said, "but we'll be back again later. Are the kids at home where we can see them?"

"My mom was here earlier, but she's there with them now," Jared spoke up. "I know they'd love to see you."

Charlotte bent down to give Becca a goodbye hug, and Becca whispered in her ear, "You're next, Sweetie, are you ready to be a mommy?"

Was she ready? Charlotte had her doubts, but right now they had things to do, and she pushed them as far down as they would go.

Chapter 81
Now

As they were leaving the hospital, Charlotte asked if they could do a little shopping before heading over to see the three older Tyler kids. "They have the most wonderful children's store on Flagler Avenue, and it's kind of a tradition that I buy something for the new baby to wear home from the hospital."

Nick agreed, and Charlotte directed him to one of her favorite shopping areas in the world. "I'll tell you what," she grinned. "Let's stop at Breakers for lunch first, and then you won't be grumpy while I shop. They have every kind of burger you could ask for, and we can look out over the ocean while we eat."

"You had me at lunch," Nick winked, "but in case you've forgotten, I'm a pretty darn good shopper. For a guy."

"Yes, you are," Charlotte smiled, looking down at her beautiful diamond wedding band.

Lunch was just as good as Charlotte had promised, even though Nick decided to forgo the IPA that the waitress tempted him with. Charlotte thought the young woman was trying to tempt him with more than a beer, but bless his heart, Nick didn't seem to notice.

Their stomachs full, Nick and Charlotte held hands as they walked down the street to the Angels By the Sea boutique. Charlotte was like a kid in a candy shop as she oohed and aahed over the tiny little outfits before finally settling on one for Baby Jack. Walking toward the cash register, she saw Nick sitting in a chair, a bag in each arm.

"What did you buy?" she asked him.

"Just some things," he answered, holding tightly to his purchases. "I'll show you later."

Before leaving the shopping area, Charlotte insisted on taking Nick to Silly Willies to get some treats for his nieces' new puppy, Socs. "Christmas will be here in a few weeks," she told him excitedly, "and we can put them in his stocking."

"A Christmas stocking for a dog?" Nick questioned, shaking his head. "I don't see Maya putting up a stocking for a pet," he insisted, but Charlotte knew better.

"You're forgetting the charm of your nieces if you think that pup won't have a stocking. In fact, let's just get him one while we're here."

And so, they walked to the pet store where they did indeed purchase Socs a Christmas stocking and treats to fill it, and they ended up at Beachside Candy Co. where they bought people treats for the three Tyler children and Nick's two nieces.

Charlotte wrapped her hands around Nick's arm as they headed back to the car. "You know," she told him, "New Smyrna Beach is probably my second favorite place in the world. If it wasn't for our life in Anna Maria, I could easily live here."

Nick's hands were laden with packages, but he stopped walking so he could look at his wife. "I love what we have on the island," he told her, "but my life is wherever you are. Whether it's here or AMI or even Arizona, I'll be happy as long as we're together."

Charlotte reached up for her locket without even thinking and silently asked her gran, "What did I ever do to deserve this man?"

Chapter 82

Now

On the drive home from New Smyrna, Charlotte relived the past two days in her mind. Baby Jack had been born, they had spent some fun time with JD, Anna, and Lolly, and Nick had bought things for the baby. Their baby.

When they had finally gotten back to the hotel the night before, Charlotte had pestered him until he broke down and showed her his purchases. And OH! what purchases they were! A plush gray quilted blanket with light blue satin trim had Charlotte close to tears and that was before she saw the stuffed manatee that played "My Bonnie Lies Over the Ocean," the one song she had learned how to play on Gran's old piano. There was also a mobile of colorful fish, just what every well-equipped, Florida baby room needed.

The bucket seats made it impossible for her to rest her head on Nick's shoulder, but that's exactly what she wanted to do. Instead she rubbed his neck and watched him as he drove.

"I love everything you bought," she told him again. "Our baby's room is going to be amazing. I do have to ask though; did you get the blanket with blue because you're hoping for a boy?"

Nick squirmed just a little but told her honestly. "I just liked it. I wasn't thinking boy or girl, just that it's my favorite color. Does that make a difference?"

"Not at all," she told him. "I was just curious, because you know before long, we're going to have to seriously think about turning the guest room into a nursery."

"I like the sound of that," Nick replied. "Maybe we can work on that over my Christmas break?"

"Speaking of Christmas," she grinned, "I thought we might stop at Mattress Express on the way home and pick out that California king that you've been wanting."

Nick's face lit up. "Seriously?" he asked. "Because I'm ready for a bed where my feet won't hang off the edge, and one that's just ours with no ghosts of lover's past." Nick looked at Charlotte to see if he had touched a nerve, but when she nodded, he breathed a sigh of relief.

Who would have thought a bed could make someone so happy, but thinking back to sleeping in a twin size for most of her childhood, Charlotte understood. "How about we make this our Christmas present to each other," she suggested.

Nick shook his head. "This is our first Christmas together, Charlotte, and a bed isn't very romantic. I want to get you something special."

"What's more romantic than the place where romance happens?" she asked him. "I can think of some very romantic ways to use a new bed." She gave him a very sultry look, and Nick knew he was about to cave.

"Okay," he finally said. "We'll buy a new bed that both of us like, plus new sheets and blankets and all that other fancy stuff you like. Deal?"

"Deal," she said, and she laid her head back on the headrest and closed her eyes. She was going to need a nap if she was going mattress shopping, and pretty quickly, she was sound asleep.

Chapter 83
Now

Charlotte had been right, mattress shopping with Nick was exhausting but also a lot of fun. He insisted that they lay down on every option and even spooned her to check the comfort level. After moving from one bed to another, pretending they were sleeping or watching TV, Nick finally proclaimed a winner.

The bed had to be ordered and wouldn't be delivered until the next week, so Charlotte begged off shopping for linens, telling Nick she wanted to surprise him. "The things you had at the condo are nice," she told him, "but a little neutral for my taste. I want to get us something rich and luxurious for our new bed, something that makes you never want to leave it."

Nick's voice was low when he told her, "It's having you in it that makes me not want to leave, but if you want fancy, I'm okay with it. Although, I think rich and luxurious are just other words for expensive." Nick gave her a subtle wink, and hand in hand, they completed the paperwork and paid for their new bed.

Just as they were getting in the car, Nick's cell phone rang. "Hey, Pop, what's up?" he asked his dad. Then, "Sounds good, but let me ask Charlotte."

"Pop made white chili for dinner and Noah's home. Do you want to join them?"

Charlotte nodded, tired from a long two days and thrilled not to have to cook. She always loved spending time with Nick's dad, and for some reason Noah had stopped his constant flirting, which made being around him enjoyable, as well. Nick accepted the invitation and said they would be there in about forty-five minutes.

The marina had been a safe haven for Charlotte growing up, and she felt that same peace when she went there now. With the exception of the twelve years that she and Nick didn't speak to each other, she spent as much time there as anyplace else on the island.

Pop was slicing homemade bread when they walked in, and Charlotte immediately gave him a hug. As always, she offered to help, but he shooed her out of the kitchen and insisted she put her feet up.

It was too cold to sit on the deck this time of year, but Charlotte loved looking out at the crystal blue Gulf of Mexico through the big glass sliding door. Nick went in search of his brother, so she had a few minutes alone to think back over the past two days.

Becca and Jared were naturals at having babies, but they were both health care professionals. How would she and Nick deal with the issues of labor and delivery, not to mention being fulltime care givers to a newborn? She was trying to talk herself out of a panic attack when Nick came into the room and put his hands on her shoulders.

"What's going on in that beautiful head of yours?" he asked as he started to slowly massage the knots he felt. "You seem pretty tense."

Charlotte didn't want him to know she had doubts about their parenting skills, well mostly her parenting skills, so she smiled and said she was fine.

Nick came around the chair and squatted on his heels in front of her. "Charlotte," he said with authority, "we're not playing this game. Tell me what's wrong."

"Are you ever afraid?" she asked, her voice anything but strong.

"I'm afraid of a lot of things but mostly just failing you in some way. What is it you're afraid of?" Nick asked her.

"Becca and Jared are so good at having babies and raising kids, but how do we know we will be? Even your dad knows more about being a wife and a mom than I do, so what does that say about me?"

Nick looked into her troubled green eyes and brushed a loose curl from her face. "Honey," he began slowly, "I don't think anyone really knows how to be a parent until they are one. Kids don't come with instruction books, although it's a hell of an idea; that's why you rely on friends and family for support."

Charlotte started to object, and Nick put his finger to her lips. "I know you think Pop is the end-all when it comes to parenting and running a home, but he's only that way because he had to be. He and Mom didn't have any idea how to care for babies when Maya was born, and you should hear the stories of some of the mishaps they had in the beginning. They learned how to be parents, and I promise you Charlotte, we will, too."

When Pop came in to tell them it was time to eat, Nick helped her up and asked," Are you going to be okay?"

Charlotte put her arms around him and nodded into his shoulder. "As long as you're right there with me, I think I can be."

Nick tilted her face toward his and answered, "There isn't any place in the world that I'd rather be."

Chapter 84
Then

By the time they were in high school, Becca had made it known to everyone who would listen that she intended to enter a convent after earning her nursing degree. Lottie didn't understand it at all, but Becca was her oldest friend, and she kept her mouth shut so she wouldn't hurt her friend's feelings.

Despite not being interested in boys like most of the girls their age, Becca was always interested in talking about them with Lottie. "Do you think you and Nick will get married some day?" Becca asked one afternoon as they finished their cones at Two Scoops.

"Why are you asking me that?" Lottie answered. "You know Nick and I are just good friends."

"Who are you kidding, Lottie?" Becca teased. "You love Nick Greyson and you know it."

Lottie blushed a deep shade of red as she noticed the girls at the next table watching them. "Keep your voice down, Becca," she begged. "Ashley has spies everywhere."

Ashley of course was Ashley Marshall, the prettiest and most popular girl in school and the one person who did her best to make Lottie's life a daily living hell. She had never gotten over Nick choosing Lottie instead of her when he had come back to AMI in the fifth grade, and Lottie knew the only relief from the endless taunting would be when she left for Indiana and IU.

"Sorry," Becca whispered, throwing her napkin in the trash. "I'm ready to go anyway."

"How many babies do you want to have when you get married?" Becca asked her friend.

"What?" Lottie exclaimed. "What's going on with you today, Bec? For someone who's decided not to get married and have kids, you sure are interested in them."

Becca dragged her feet over the sandy road before answering. "Just because I want to go out in the world and help people doesn't mean I don't think about getting married or having a family. I like boys as much as any girl, but I believe I'm being called to something higher."

Lottie tried to comfort her friend the best way she knew how. With honesty. "I'm going to tell you the truth Becca," Lottie started. "I'm not sure I even want to have kids. I see what having me did to my mom, and anyway, babies scare me."

"Oh Lottie, you silly goose," Becca laughed. "When the time is right, you'll feel differently. Babies only scare you because you've never been around them. I'm sure there are ladies in our church who would love to find a babysitter, maybe you need to do that instead of moping around on the nights Nick and Noah sneak off together."

"I do not mope, Rebecca Rose Huddleston, and I do not want to babysit! Maybe I'll change my mind someday, but right now, all I know is that I don't want to end up like my mother, saddled with a kid I didn't want and wasn't ready for."

Becca looked like she was about to cry, which made Lottie feel terrible. "I'm sorry Becca," Lottie said. "I don't know where that came from. You know I would never hurt you for the world, but your life and my life are different, and we want different things."

Becca swiped at her eyes and nodded in agreement. "I'm sorry, too, Lottie," she said. "I just always thought we'd get married and raise our kids together right here on the island, but it doesn't sound like that's going to happen for either of us. I want to be a nun and serve God, I really do, but part of me wants a normal life, too."

"You've got years before you have to make a commitment to the church, Becca, so why not just wait and see what happens? And who knows, someday maybe we'll both fall in love and want to get married and have kids, but that's a long way off."

"Except you are already in love," Becca laughed, running down the street. "You're in love with Nick Greyson, whether you admit it or not."

Chapter 85

Now

When they got home, Charlotte got ready for bed, but instead of taking her into his arms like every other night, Nick tucked her in.

"Are you upset with me, Nick?" she asked him, trying to get out from beneath the covers.

"Why would you think I'm upset?" he responded, trying to get her to lay back down.

"Because of this?" she said, gesturing to the bed. "You're treating me like a two-year-old, or are you practicing for fatherhood?"

"Charlotte," Nick said, running his hand through his hair, "you've had two big days and one emotional meltdown. I think you'll feel better after a good night's sleep, don't you?"

"I'll feel better if my husband treats me like a woman," she said with a sexy grin.

Nick gave her a gentle kiss, but not what she was hoping for. "Well, it's a start," she smiled. "Now why don't you get naked and join me in bed?"

"While I would love nothing more," he said with a sigh, "The thing is, I have a paper due tomorrow, and I have to finish it tonight."

Charlotte felt miserable. "Why didn't you tell me, Nick?" she asked. "I could have gone to New Smyrna alone; Becca would have understood and so would I."

"I was right where I wanted to be," he responded, "and you going alone was never an option."

"But we wouldn't have had to stay so long or gone bed shopping. We could have come home before it got so late," Charlotte added.

"Please believe me when I tell you I knew what I was doing. I loved our time in New Smyrna, and I loved shopping for a bed with you. Even though right now all I really want to do is climb in that bed and make sweet love to you, I have to finish my paper."

"Maybe I should get up and help you," Charlotte pouted. "I am pretty smart you know."

"I do know that," Nick answered with a wink. "I wasn't the valedictorian of our class, and I didn't earn the distinctions in college that you did, but I can write a paper on my own. If you really want to help me, you'll go to sleep, and maybe we can work on the naked part later."

"You've turned me into such a slut, Nick Greyson," Charlotte told him. "I hope you're happy."

Nick put his finger to her lips and said, "That's my wife you're talking about, and I prefer to say she's wanton. And you know what?" he said with a chuckle. "I am happy. I'm very happy."

And this time when he tucked the covers around her, Charlotte stayed put, and soon she was fast asleep.

Several hours later Charlotte woke up as Nick crawled into bed next to her. He curled up against her back as he did every night, his arm around her waist, his hand protectively covering their unborn child. As she lay there, somewhere between dreamland and reality, she could feel the hard length of her husband pressing against her backside.

"Did you get your paper finished?" she asked, wiping the sleep from her eyes.

"All done," Nick replied, nuzzling her neck and moving in even closer.

Charlotte knew she was in control here. Should she close her eyes and drift back into sleep or turn toward her husband and show him just how wanton she was?

Rolling over on her back, Charlotte stroked the anaconda until Nick started to moan. She started laying kisses down the planes of his sculpted chest, following the trail of soft dark hair on his belly and telling him, "You deserve a reward for working so hard."

But before she could make it to her final destination Nick was between her thighs saying in a very husky voice, "We both deserve a reward."

And boy did they get one!

Chapter 86

Now

Early the next week while Nick was helping at the marina, Charlotte got a call saying the new bed was in and ready to be delivered. She planned for it to arrive on Wednesday while Nick was in class so she could surprise him. After a call to the Salvation Army to have them pick up their old bed plus some of the things from Nick's condo that he didn't need, she headed off to Bradenton and Bed Bath & Beyond for new linens.

Shopping for bedding was just one rung below shopping for clothes, and Charlotte was having a ball. She finally decided on a dusky blue and ivory quilted comforter set, done in a shell motif that she thought was appropriate for their cottage on the beach. Add two sets of eight-hundred thread count sheets, one in the blue and one in the ivory colors that matched the comforter, and she was done!

The shopping had put her in such a good mood that she decided to make Nick a special dinner and see if Pop wanted to join them. She hid her new purchase in the trunk of her car and drove back to the island. With the radio up, she listened to her favorite new country song as she drove along the beach to the marina.

With no one to talk to, Charlotte instinctively touched her locket and had a few words with her gran. She used to worry that maybe it was a little weird that she continued to have conversations with her dead grandmother, but after a while, she didn't care anymore. She loved her gran, and she missed her desperately; what did it matter if talking to her brought Charlotte comfort? And besides, sometimes Gran answered back.

Pulling into the marina, Charlotte could see a very large boat was docked and that Nick and Pop were talking to someone standing beside it. Not wanting to get in the way of business, she went in the front door and shrieked. There sitting on the couch, looking out at the men, was her dear friend, Shelly.

"Oh my gosh," Charlotte exclaimed, giving Shelly a hug. "I didn't know you were going to be here today. You should have let me know."

Shelly turned a little pink before answering. "Well, I didn't exactly know myself," she stammered. "Nicholas brought me here yesterday, and we were going to enjoy being outdoors because it had turned so warm, and one thing led to another, and it got too late to drive me home. Luckily, I have a few days off, but as soon as he's done with his customer, I'm sure he'll be taking me back to Tampa."

Shelly was doing her best not to look Charlotte in the eye, but Charlotte jumped right in and asked the question she was dying for an answer to. "So, you and my father-in-law, you're going to give this thing a chance?"

"We're taking things slowly, Charlotte. We both have scars to deal with," Shelly told her friend.

"But you stayed here overnight, that sounds like more than slowly if you ask me," Charlotte grinned.

"We didn't sleep together, if that's what you're implying," Shelly said a little indignantly. "I slept in Maya's room, and thankfully, she's about my size because these are her clothes I'm wearing."

Shit! Shit! Shit! Charlotte thought. *Now I've offended her!*

"I'm sorry Shelly," Charlotte said, trying to back pedal on her words. "I'm just so happy to see you and Pop together that I might have gotten a little carried away. Forgive me?"

Shelly smiled. "There's nothing to forgive, Charlotte," she said softly. "The truth is, we came very close to making love, but thankfully, we both came to our senses in time. Sam is the only man I've ever been with, and that was twenty-five years ago. I've waited all this time thinking that I'd never fall in love again, so the last thing I want to do is make a mistake."

Charlotte put her arms around Shelly and held her for a moment. Shelly Bert was used to taking care of others, and it felt good for Charlotte to be able to take care of her.

"You told me about Sam, but I didn't realize there hadn't been anyone else," Charlotte admitted to her friend.

Shelly looked at Charlotte before answering. "Casual sex is just not for me. I told you about my family and about their convictions, and even after all these years, they mean something to me. I'm not saying I would have to wait for marriage, but it's going to have to be pretty darn close."

Charlotte nodded, but inside her stomach was churning. She had encouraged both Pop and Shelly to give a relationship a chance, but what if one of them ended up getting hurt? She cared too much about these people to watch that happen to either of them.

Just then, Nick and Pop came in from outside. Nick instinctively gave Charlotte a kiss, but instead of enjoying it she couldn't take her eyes off Pop and Shelly. But when Pop took Shelly's hand and kissed it, Charlotte smiled and took a deep breath. Pop was a true gentleman, and he wouldn't push Shelly into anything she didn't want, and that gave Charlotte peace.

"I came to invite Pop for dinner," she told Nick, "but I didn't know he had a guest. I'm going to stop at Publix, so what would you like for dinner."

"Steak!" Nick and Pop said at the same time.

Charlotte looked at her friend and the two men, unsure of how to respond.

"If Shelly is willing to put up with my company for another night," he said looking up at her, "I'll grill steaks for all of us right here."

Charlotte held her breath and grabbed Nick's hand as she waited for her friend to answer.

"Okay," Shelly said shyly, "I'd love to."

Chapter 87

Now

On Bed Day, as Charlotte had been secretly calling the day their new bed was arriving, she was so excited that she knew Nick was suspicious. He was going to the high school today to work with Coach Donavan. As soon as he was done eating breakfast, she rushed him out the door.

"If I didn't know better," he told her with a smirky grin, "I'd think you were trying to get rid of me. I didn't use to have a jealous nature until I married my sexy wife; is there anything you want to tell me?"

"Nick, please," Charlotte scoffed. "I'm five months pregnant; who would be interested in me?"

"Not exactly the comforting answer I was hoping for, but I'll go with it," he told her. "And just for the record, you're even sexier now than you were on our wedding day, and that's saying a lot."

Charlotte softened and pulled him back inside the door. "Come here, Big Boy," she grinned, and she gave him a long, slow kiss. "If I'm sexier now, it's only because you make me feel that way," she whispered in his ear. "Now go before you're late, and the coach makes you swim laps."

"It would be worth it for another kiss like that," Nick told her. "I'm pretty sure I'm going to welcome the cold water of the pool anyway."

Charlotte watched him pull away and then started to prepare for Bed Day.

The old bed was stripped down to the mattress, and the sheets were immediately thrown in the washer. Charlotte hoped to have all the old bedding clean and ready to donate along with the old bed.

Boxes of Nick's kitchenware that Shelly hadn't needed were pulled from the garage along with two boxes of clothes he no longer wore. Charlotte knew she should go through her things as well, but getting rid of clothes was hard for her. She did find a couple of outfits that Peter had suggested she buy, along with the practically brand-new black teddy that she stuck in one of the boxes, hiding it underneath one of Nick's suits!

The final load of wash was just being pulled from the dryer when the Salvation Army truck pulled up. Looking at her cell, Charlotte saw that it was just noon, and everything was going as planned. All the old bedding had been washed, and so had the new things she had purchased the week before. Now all that was needed was to move out the old and make room for the new.

The movers were working on the bed when her phone rang. Nick! she said under her breath as she answered the phone. "Hey!" she greeted him "You never call me when you're with Coach, what's up?"

"Maybe that's a question for you," he said a little sharply. "I called to make sure everything is okay but… what's that noise in the background? Is someone there?"

Charlotte wasn't good at lying, so she sputtered out a half truth. "It's actually the Salvation Army," she told him. "I'm having them take some of the boxes out of the garage. I hope you don't mind?"

"It's great," Nick responded, and Charlotte could hear the relief in his voice. "I'll be home around four o'clock. Do you need me to pick up anything for dinner?"

Charlotte tried to mentally tally the hours needed to complete her surprise and decided having Nick stop at the store would just buy her some more time.

"How about getting one of those rotisserie chickens you like so much? I've got everything here to make a salad, and I can warm you up some leftover mac and cheese to go with it." Charlotte hoped that she sounded sincere. She did have the stuff for salad, but she had planned on ordering Chinese so they could enjoy their new bed without any interruptions. The chicken would keep until tomorrow.

"You're sure everything is okay?" Nick asked once more, and as soon as Charlotte assured him that it was, he told her he loved her and ended the call.

Chapter 88

Now

"Charlotte, are you here?" Nick called when he walked into the quiet cottage. There were no lights on inside, but her car was in the drive which caused Nick's FBI training to kick into gear. The problem was, he needed to search the house, and he no longer had a weapon to lead with. Once more yelling out his wife's name, Nick was getting ready to dial 911 when she answered.

"I'm in here, Nick," she called out, "and I'm fine so put down the phone."

Still not convinced, Nick walked into the bedroom, ready to hit send, if something was out of place. But the only thing he saw took his breath away.

Stretched out on the bed, on their new California king, was his beautiful wife, her hair falling in cascades of silk over her creamy bare shoulders, her thighs slightly parted with one knee bent, giving him access to all of her delicious, ripe body.

When he didn't speak right away, Charlotte's modesty took over, and she tried to turn away. But Nick wasn't having it.

"Don't" he said in his deep FBI voice. "Don't move an inch."

Charlotte was breathing deeply by now and could feel the color on her cheeks. She hoped that Nick would like her surprise, but in her mind, she hadn't been left on display so long. Feeling extremely vulnerable while Nick's gaze raked over her, she was just about to speak when he finally did.

"You are the sexiest, most unbelievably gorgeous woman there ever was. There are no words to tell you what I'm feeling right now, but fuck Charlotte, what you do to me."

Smiling she reached up and pulled him down to her. "So, you like our new bed?" she purred.

"I like everything about it," he groaned, trying to get out of his clothes.

Charlotte helped him get out of his pants, kissing her way up his body as she did so. She loved his strong muscular legs and his flat stomach covered in dark hair and the place in between that brought her such pleasure.

When she thought she had teased him enough, she smiled up at his beautiful face, and seeing the arousal in his eyes said, "You said that word again, Nick. What am I going to do with you?"

Without even stopping to answer, he flipped her over and found her center. It didn't take long for either one of them, and as Nick pulled her body on top of his, he said, "Give me few minutes, and I'll show you." And did he ever.

Chapter 89

Now

Christmas morning was crisp and cool for Florida, and Charlotte relished snuggling down into the covers next to Nick. Despite her ever-growing belly, she was still able to get close enough to feel his warmth, and she smiled as she counted her blessings.

Almost as if he had eyes in the back of his head, Nick seemed to sense that she was awake and turned over to greet her. "Merry Christmas, Mrs. Greyson," he said, his voice still thick with sleep. "I loved sleeping on our Christmas present last night," he added, "and I loved your Christmas Eve gift even more."

Charlotte squirmed as he ran his hand under her night shirt, but when he stopped, she didn't know if she was disappointed or relieved. They were having Christmas dinner with Nick's family at the marina at one o'clock, which left time for some Christmas morning activities, but she had a special breakfast planned, and it needed to get into the oven.

"I'm going to get you some juice and coffee," she told him as she slipped out of bed. "You stay right there. I'll be right back."

A few minutes later, the special breakfast in the oven, Charlotte returned with a mug of hot coffee and a glass of cranberry juice for Nick. He eyed the glass suspiciously which made her laugh.

"It's cranberry juice, Nick," she laughed. "It's always been a Christmas tradition for Mom and me. Just try it, it's good."

Nick wrinkled his nose but took a little sip of the ruby red drink. "Mmm," he said, taking a bigger drink, "it is good."

After downing the juice, he took the mug from Charlotte and tried to coerce her into getting back in bed. "No dice," she smirked. "I want to see what Santa brought me."

They had agreed when the expensive bed was purchased that they wouldn't spend any money on each other this year, but after some pouting and whining on Charlotte's part, Nick had given in and they had decided on one present each. The caveat was that the gift couldn't come from a store or be purchased online, and it had to have special meaning to both the giver and the receiver.

"Can I at least shower and get dressed first?" he tormented Charlotte, knowing that patience wasn't her strong suit.

"Your childhood was as close to normal as anyone I know," she told him, hands on her hips. "Why is it that even my mom understood the need to get up and do Christmas in our pjs? Some years we stayed in them all day long."

Nick chuckled and pulled her down beside him on the bed. "I'm good with that if you are," he smirked, "but you do remember that I don't wear pajamas, don't you?"

Charlotte's face turned a little pink, but she held her ground. "Then put on a pair of sweatpants because Christmas officially starts in ten minutes!"

When Nick joined Charlotte on the lanai, the lights on their little Christmas tree were sparkling, and Charlotte was curled up in front of it, enjoying a mug of dark coffee with Peppermint Mocha cream. She patted for Nick to sit down beside her, and he lowered his long frame onto the floor.

"This is the best Christmas morning I've ever had," she told him with tears in her eyes. "A year ago, I spent Christmas with... well anyway, this one is the best by far, even without a bunch of presents and you without pajamas."

Nick was pretty certain with whom his wife had spent the last Christmas, but he decided it didn't matter anymore. Charlotte was with him. They were married and going to have a baby, and he agreed, it was the best Christmas morning ever.

"Now," she told him, "you sit right there while I bring out your Christmas present."

Nick knew that her gift to him would be something she had baked, but he was good with that. He loved goodies of all kinds and was enjoying being Charlotte's guinea pig while she perfected her baking skills. What he wasn't prepared for was the plate of gooey, nutty, caramelly goodness that she sat down in front of him.

"Sticky buns?" he questioned. "You made my mom's sticky bun recipe?" As a boy, the one home-baked thing Nick could remember his mom making was sticky buns for Christmas morning. The fact that Charlotte had found this out and made them for him, had him pushing back his own Christmas emotions.

"I can't think of anything I would have liked more," he told her, as he softly kissed her lips, "but I'm afraid my present is going to seem pretty anticlimactic after this."

"You've already given me the best gift imaginable," she told him, stroking her belly, "but come on now. I'm ready to unwrap something."

Nick handed Charlotte a small box that he had obviously wrapped himself. She hesitated at first, afraid that he had bought her some kind of extravagant jewelry despite the rules, but when she opened it, her face sparkled like the Christmas tree.

"Your class ring, Nick!" Charlotte squealed. "Do you have any idea how long I've coveted this thing?" Nick took the ring from her hands and slipped it on the middle finger of her left hand. It was way too big, but he loved how excited it made her, and he only wished he would have given it to her fifteen years ago.

Charlotte moved the ring around in the light, much like she had her engagement ring when he'd given it to her, and gave him a big thank you kiss.

"When we were in high school, I used to dream about wearing this ring," she told him, "although I never really thought that dream would come true. Even when I hoped you were going to ask for more than friendship at the Sendoff, I never would have expected this."

"I wish I could go back and erase the pain I caused you when we were kids," Nick said, gently cupping her chin "All I can do is promise to do better in the future."

"It's okay, Nick," Charlotte replied, kissing the hands that were caressing her cheeks. "We'll never know how our future would have turned out if things had happened differently back then, but I love how it's turning out now."

Nick repaid her forgiving spirit with one of his signature raw kisses, but he didn't try to push for more. He knew this Christmas morning was a memory they would never forget, and he wanted it to be extra special for both of them.

When Charlotte finally broke away, she filled a plate of the still warm sticky buns for Nick and said, "Eat." The moans he made as he savored the first bite made Charlotte giggle, but she was thrilled that he liked her gift.

When Nick had eaten his fill, and the coffee mugs were refilled, Charlotte pulled a package out of a drawer and said to him, "You have one more present to open."

Nick face look confused as he reminded her of their one gift rule. "But this one's not from me, see?" Charlotte said pointing to the tag.

She watched him melt as Nick looked at the tag that read, "To Daddy, From Babycakes."

Nick's hands were shaking as he carefully unwrapped the package, and when he opened the box, Charlotte watched in wonder as tears rolled down his cheeks.

"It's our baby," he said, gingerly touching the picture in front of him.

"I had a 3-D ultrasound as a surprise," she told him. "I made the technician promise not to give it to me if it showed the baby's sex. I guess Baby Greyson is onboard with keeping it a surprise because that part of the body doesn't show."

"I'm overwhelmed," Nick said, choking back tears. "You are the most amazing and thoughtful person I've ever known, Charlotte Greyson, and I love you so much. I just wish I had the words to tell you."

This time when he kissed her, Charlotte gave him the encouragement he needed, and they made love on the floor under the twinkling Christmas lights as Nick showed her just how strong his love was.

Chapter 90

Now

Christmas at the marina was just as magical as Charlotte remembered, only now she was a true part of the Greyson family. Pop had told her more than once that he always thought of her as a daughter, but now she actually felt like one.

Dinner was a big affair with more food than a family their size could eat, and Charlotte was stuffed when she finally backed away from her plate. She loved watching Nick with his dad and siblings, and for a few minutes, she sat there in awe, knowing that this was what she wanted for her child.

In fact, she was so deep in thought that she almost missed it when the twins asked her to go sit by the Christmas tree with them. "We can't open presents until everyone is done eating," said Steffi.

"As soon as someone puts their fork down, we have to bring them in here," added Nikki.

Charlotte laughed at the two little geniuses before her and agreed that she would help move things along. When Nick heard his wife's laugh, he winked and got up from the table to join her. It didn't take long after that for the entire family to be corralled into the living room, waiting for presents to be handed out.

The girls got the toys they had wanted, Maya and Dimi were given tickets to a five-day cruise, complete with babysitting service and arrangements with Dimi's family to run Stavros in their absence. There was a beautiful gold bracelet for Shelly, a new wakeboard for Noah, and finally it was Nick and Charlotte's turn.

It had been agreed that the only presents being given this year were from Pop to his family. He had asked that any money they wanted to spend on him be donated to the local food pantry, and his children complied with his wishes.

So now, he told Nick and Charlotte to close their eyes, and when he said to open them, before them stood a beautiful wooden rocking cradle, complete with everything a cradle needed, except of course the baby.

Charlotte was speechless and didn't even try to push back the tears that were running down her cheeks. Nick took her hand, and it was apparent that he was just as emotional but trying to man up.

"I don't know what to say," Nick finally spoke. "You made this for us Pop?"

Pop smiled and answered, "Actually Noah and I made the cradle together, and Maya and Shelly took care of the rest. We wanted you and your baby to have something from all of us. Your mother wanted to be a part of things, too," Pop said, pulling a large box out from behind the recliner. "This is from her and Gus."

Inside the box was a delicate handmade quilt in shades of cream and aqua. "Did Elizabeth make this herself?" Charlotte asked, her lip quivering?

"She did," Pop replied. "When Nick was a baby. I didn't even know she still had it. Being part of this was important to her, but her hands are too stiff now for quilting.

Nick got up and hugged his dad and brother while Charlotte started with the women. By the time they had all hugged and thank you had been said a dozen times and a call was made to New York, everyone was definitely feeling the joy of Christmas.

Chapter 91
Now

Nick was deeply involved with his job as a teacher and coach by the time spring rolled around, and Charlotte was counting down the days until Babycakes' debut. The nursery had been painted a soft aqua, to go with the quilt Nick's mom had made, and was ready for a baby, whether it be boy or girl. A crib with the mobile Nick had purchased in New Smyrna attached and a dressing table with storage for clothes along with a matching rocker filled the room, and Charlotte loved it. Most mornings after Nick left for work, she would sit in the chair, rocking and dreaming about holding her baby in her arms.

It was in this chair one sunny April morning when Charlotte first felt a little cramping in her side. As a first-time mom, she didn't even consider she might be in labor, but she hadn't slept well the night before and even felt a little queasy. She decided something she'd eaten hadn't agreed with her. Not wanting to worry an already nervous dad-to-be, Charlotte kept quiet and did not share her symptoms with Nick.

Foregoing a second cup of coffee, she took a few sips of Coke, hoping that it would calm her jittery tummy, and headed to the shower. The hot water felt wonderful, so she lathered head to toe in her Philosophy Lemon Custard shower/shampoo combination. Just as she was about to wrap up in a towel, a cramp the size of Texas seized her, and Charlotte started to panic.

Shit! Shit! Shit! She thought. What was wrong with her? Babycakes wasn't due for another week, but she'd never experienced anything like this before. Finally, she was able to get out of the shower, wrap up her hair, and put on a thick robe before lying down on the bed and calling Becca.

"Hey Lottie!" Becca answered, always a ray of sunshine in anybody's bad day. "How's my most favorite pregnant woman in the world?"

Charlotte could hear baby Jack gurgling in the background as she told her friend how she was feeling. "Do you think I have food poisoning, Bec?" Charlotte asked. "I've never felt anything like this is my life."

"Sweetie," Becca said calmly, "I think what you're experiencing are labor pains. They may just be Braxton Hicks at this point, but you should probably call your doctor, just in case."

Charlotte was about to respond when another hard cramp hit her. "It feels like period cramps on steroids, Becca, please tell me that's not how labor is going to be."

"Charlotte," Becca said firmly, "you need to call Nick. If I was closer, I could be more help, but what you're describing is more than Braxton Hicks. Do you want me to have my mom come over?"

Charlotte was an emotional mess, but what she wanted was her mom, and she knew that couldn't happen. "No," she finally answered. "I'm going to call Nick and see if he can skip swim practice today."

Nick arrived home in record time and found his wife curled on their bed, her hair still wet, and swaddled in her robe.

"Oh Baby," he said sitting down beside her and gently rubbing her back. "I'm going to call Dr. Stanley, and then I'll dry your hair and help you get dressed."

Charlotte nodded as another pain ripped through her. "Nick!" she called, and the feeling subsided, "hurry."

Chapter 92
Now

Thirty-six excruciating hours later, Charlotte was finally allowed to push. Her body was exhausted but that didn't stop the pains that felt as if they were tearing her apart.

"You can do this, Charlotte," Nick encouraged her. "I know it hurts, but the pains will stop once the baby's born, right, Dr. Stanley?"

The young doctor nodded and gave Charlotte some encouragement of his own. "You've been waiting a long time to meet your baby, Charlotte. Aren't you ready to find out if it's a boy or a girl?"

Charlotte grasped Nick's hand and squeezed for dear life the next time a contraction hit her. "Good girl," Nick whispered, but inside he was scared to death.

"One more big push should do it, Charlotte," Dr. Stanley said. "Come on push right now."

And the next thing she heard was music to her hears.

"Congratulations, Mr. and Mrs. Greyson, you have a daughter."

The nurse laid the baby on Charlotte's chest, and she and Nick cried right along with the now squalling little girl.

"Is she okay," Charlotte asked. "She looks, fine doesn't she?"

Dr. Stanley asked Nick if he wanted to cut the cord, and once he did, the baby was whisked away. "She's perfect," Dr. Stanley told Charlotte, "and she's a big girl."

The nurse weighed and measured the little bundle before returning her to her parents and proudly announced," Ten pounds four ounces, twenty-three and a half inches long. She beats the record of any birth I've been involved in."

"Charlotte, Nick, you introduce yourselves to your daughter while we finish up here. I need to deliver the placenta, and it's being a little stubborn."

"I love you so much, Lottie," Nick said through his tears. "You made me the happiest man in the world when you married me, but this, this little girl is a gift from Heaven."

All of a sudden Charlotte felt hands kneading her stomach and her baby being lifted from her arms. "Hey," she said, "You'd sure be good at making bread, but why are you taking my baby?"

Nick heard the doctor say, "We need a type and cross on Mom and have the lab ready with two units of blood. Stat." And his world came unglued.

"What's going on?" he asked, but no one answered.

Finally, a nurse put her arm around him and said, "Come on Dad, you need to move to the waiting room."

"Like hell," Nick exploded, grabbing on to Charlotte's hand. "What's going on with my wife?"

Dr. Stanley nodded his consent for Nick to stay and told him what he asked to hear. "Charlotte's hemorrhaging, and we have to get the bleeding stopped. I've given her a coagulant, and we have her on an IV drip, but if we don't get this under control, I may have to do an emergency hysterectomy."

When Charlotte heard those words, she started to hyperventilate, and it took everything Nick had to calm her down. Just when he thought she was relaxing, he realized that her face was a ghostly white and her eyes were rolling back in her head.

"Charlotte, look at me," he commanded. "We have a daughter, Honey, a beautiful daughter who needs her mommy, so you open your eyes and look at me."

Charlotte did her best to obey, oblivious to what was going on around her, but finally the loss of blood was stronger than Nick's words.

"I love you, Nick," she whispered, as she tried to smile.

"You promised that you'd never run away from us again, Lottie. You promised, and I'm holding you to that. Do you hear me? You promised," Nick wept as he cradled his wife's head. "You promised."

Chapter 93

Now

Beep. Beep. Beep. Where was that noise coming from? Trying to come out of the dark, all she could think was, *I'm in Nick's hospital room.* The incessant beeping continued as Charlotte opened her eyes, trying to focus on the room around her.

Instinctively her hands moved to her stomach, and she moaned when she found it flat. Hearing her anguish, Nick was up and immediately at her side.

"Nick," she said, her voice raspy and dry, "my baby, where's my baby?"

Nick looked toward the heavens and gave a silent prayer of thanks. "She's right here, Sweetheart," he told her, "sleeping like an angel."

Charlotte tried to prop herself up but immediately laid back down as the room begin to swim.

"Take a drink of water," Nick encouraged, putting the straw to her parched lips. "The doctor said you need plenty of fluids."

Charlotte drank as much as she could and let Nick lay her back on the pillow. Her mind was starting to clear as she looked at the bassinet holding her sleeping daughter. "Can you move her closer so I can see her better?" she asked.

Nick rolled the bassinet as close to the bed as possible and placed Charlotte's hand on their sleeping daughter's head. "She's beautiful, Charlotte," he said, tears once again streaming down his face. "She's beautiful, just like you."

Charlotte gently caressed the baby's head and asked the question that was burning a hole in her heart. "And will we be able to have more babies, Nick?"

Leaning over to kiss her face, Nick looked into Charlotte's eyes and said, "Yes, Lottie, we can have more babies. You were right about that handsome young doctor. He's the best, and I'm forever in his debt."

Just then the nurse came in and was pleasantly surprised to see Charlotte awake and talking. "You gave us all quite a scare, Miss Charlotte," she smiled, "but between Dr. Stanley and this husband of yours, you're going to be just fine. Now, I need to get you cleaned up, Dad, you need to step outside and give all the people waiting out there the good news."

Nick kissed Charlotte's hand and leaned down and kissed his daughter's head before moving toward the door.

"Does this young lady have a name?" the kind nurse asked. But both Charlotte and Nick shook their heads.

Once the nurse had cleaned her up and assured Charlotte that she could still breastfeed the baby even though they were giving her bottles now, Charlotte closed her eyes. Before she fell asleep, she said out loud, "I have a daughter, Gran. Nick and I have a daughter."

Chapter 94

Now

Charlotte slept through the night, not even waking up when a nurse came to check on her. The sun was coming in through the window when she opened her eyes and saw Nick asleep in the chair, his arm reaching over the bassinet, their daughter's hand wrapped around his little finger.

"Good morning," she said softly, hoping only to wake Nick. "I have a feeling I'm more rested than you are," she teased him.

As gently as possible, Nick pried his little finger from his daughter's hand and sat down by his wife. "You're quite a trooper, Mrs. Greyson," he told her, "and quite popular, too. The waiting room is filled with people wanting to see you, and they won't leave until they do."

"People are here to see me?" she asked. "Who?"

"Well, Becca and Jared of course, and Pop and Shelly and Maya and Noah, and your mom, Charlotte, your mom is here." Nick looked at her face, pale from loss of blood but still radiant with love.

"I hope Becca will forgive me," Charlotte told him. "I really want to see my mom first. I guess it takes having a baby of your own before you truly respect what a mother goes through. But before you let her come in, we need to name this little girl."

Becca's theory didn't work on Baby Girl Greyson, but it didn't take long for them to arrive at a name. Then Nick helped her sit up long enough to wash her face and brush her teeth in the bedside basin. He brushed her hair into soft waves around her face. The nurse came in and took care of Charlotte's hygiene issues while Nick went out to talk with the waiting room crowd.

"Before you face the world, would you like to hold your baby?" the nurse asked. Charlotte nodded, ready to get her arms around the little person she helped make.

"Have you ever seen such a beautiful baby?" Charlotte asked the nurse as she gently rocked the sleeping infant.

"I never have," the nurse said with a wink, "and she's such a good sleeper, too."

As if on cue the baby started to wiggle and soon was face to face with her mom. Charlotte cooed to her and reminded her of who she was, and as she looked up, her own mother was standing in the doorway.

"Oh, Lottie," Maggie sobbed. "I should have been here with you."

"No one knew this was going to happen, Mom," Charlotte told her, "but you're here now, and there's someone who wants to meet you."

Maggie looked down at the face of her granddaughter as Nick walked around to the other side of the bed. Both of them were filled with so much love for the woman holding the babe in her arms, that it was impossible to believe there was a time when none of them ever thought this moment could happen.

Holding their daughter in one arm, Charlotte took Nick's hand and introduced her mother to their child. "Mom," she said, her face glowing with joy, "I'd like you to meet your granddaughter, Quinn Margaret-Elise Greyson."

Maggie was speechless for a moment, and when she spoke, her voice quivered. "After your dad," she cried, reaching out to stroke the sleeping baby.

"And you and Gran," Charlotte smiled. "Quinn was Nick's idea, so even though he couldn't be physically present, her grandfather would always be a part of her life, and Margaret-Elise is to honor the two women who shaped mine"

Maggie was crying as she reached for the baby. "Come here to your Gran, Quinn," she said, taking the baby from Charlotte's arms, "and let me tell you all about your namesake."

Chapter 95

Now

Because of her ordeal in delivery, Charlotte was kept in the hospital a couple of days more than normal. She insisted she was fine, but Dr. Stanley made certain she could get up and down on her own as well as walk unassisted before he would release her.

Federal medical leave time wasn't in effect for Nick yet because he hadn't been at his job at least a year, but the school did grant him two weeks off since actual swim meets weren't scheduled yet. Charlotte agreed that she would let him take her and Quinn to the marina to stay with Pop while he was at school if her red blood count wasn't up by the time his leave was over.

Maggie wanted to stay, but since they had turned the guestroom into the nursery, she had no place to sleep. She proposed that she sleep in with Charlotte and Nick sleep on the couch, but he had nixed that pretty quickly. When Charlotte left the hospital, Maggie went back to Arizona. Becca's mom was more than willing to come over a few days a week and stay until Charlotte got her strength back, so when she finally got to leave the hospital, there was at least a plan in place.

Thankfully, Quinn took to breastfeeding without any problems, and Charlotte found that nursing her and rocking her daughter were some of her favorite times of day. She missed sleeping with Nick in their own bed while she was in the hospital, so putting Quinn in her cradle and climbing in with Nick was another favorite. Having him hold her was a luxury she didn't want ever to do without again.

The two weeks went by quickly, and all of a sudden, it was Sunday night, and Nick was going back to work the next day. They were lying in bed watching Quinn sleep when he pulled her into his arms. "I don't want to leave you," he told her, "but if we want to stay on the island, I need this job."

Charlotte understood and agreed, but she did tell him what was in her heart.

"I don't want you to leave us either, Nick, but women have been having babies since the beginning of time, and they managed. I'd venture to say that most of them didn't have a husband who was so willing to help either, so in that respect I'm blessed."

He continued to stroke her back, and just as she was about to drift off, Quinn let out a wail. Nick got out of bed and talked to his crying daughter while he changed her, and Charlotte sat up and opened herself to the hungry baby. Her milk had started to let down the moment the crying had started, and all Nick had to do was hand Quinn to her mother, and she immediately latched on.

"I'm glad these things finally have a purpose," Charlotte laughed as Quinn suckled vigorously.

"They've always had a purpose, Charlotte," Nick replied with a smirk, "just maybe not one as altruistic as feeding a hungry child."

"Do men ever stop thinking about sex?" she retaliated.

"I'm hoping that you haven't quit thinking about it either," he told her. "I was terribly fond of that wanton woman sleeping next to me every night."

"I haven't quit thinking about it, trust me, but my belly looks like a waterbed and my boobs drip like an old faucet. By the time your daughter quits using them like an open buffet, they'll probably be dragging the ground." Charlotte looked right at him, almost as if she was daring him to agree, but he just smiled and shook his head.

"When the time is right and when you're ready, I'll want you despite everything you just said. Probably even more knowing what you've gone through to have our child. I love you, Charlotte," Nick went on, "not the picture-perfect body you worked so hard for."

So, what could she say to that except, "It's a darn good thing."

Chapter 96

Now

All the years of healthy eating and exercise paid off as Charlotte bounced back much quicker than anyone expected. She slept when Quinn slept, and found pretty quickly that she was good at motherhood. Pop and Mrs. Huddleston both checked in on her the first few weeks, even bringing homecooked meals, but by the time her daughter celebrated her one-month birthday, Charlotte was back to her old self.

"I can't believe that Quinn's a month old already," Nick said that night as they lay in bed. "She's going to grow up so fast, and I can't stand thinking about it."

Charlotte looked at her husband, and her heart went out to him. Already, Quinn had him wrapped around her little finger, but Charlotte understood because she felt the same way.

"I know, Nick," Charlotte tried to pacify him. "She's just one month old. Let's not rush things, okay? What you need is something to focus on besides our daughter."

"Yeah," he said, "and what would that be?"

"Me," she replied with a smile. "My checkup went well with Dr. Stanley, and I'm ready to start connecting. I bought you a present."

Reaching into the night table, Charlotte handed Nick a box.

"Condoms?" he said with a groan, looking at the box that read extra-large lubricated and ribbed for her pleasure. "I thought being married meant the end of those things?"

Charlotte grinned and gave him a little kiss. "I don't want to put any hormones in my system that might transfer to Quinn, so Dr. Stanley said this was the best way."

Nick nodded as he moved closer to her and pulled her into his arms. "Are you sure about this?" he questioned, remembering that just a few weeks ago, he thought he was going to lose her. "I don't mean the condoms, I can live with that, but about being ready for sex?"

"One hundred percent," Charlotte smiled, "but we may need to take things slow. I pushed out a ten-pound baby so I'm not sure how things will be down there, but I'm ready to find out."

Nick couldn't help but chuckle. "You sure know how to bring in the romance, Charlotte. I'll say that for you, but I'll be gentle, and you can tell me if you're uncomfortable or need to stop, okay?"

She answered him by slipping her hand inside the shorts he had started wearing to bed once Quinn was born. He hadn't needed any prompting, but Charlotte continued to stroke him while he kissed his way from her neck to her chest.

"Am I allowed to touch you here?" he asked when he reached her very swollen breasts.

"Please," Charlotte almost begged, "but if you get a little squirt, just ignore it."

It wasn't the hot passion that they had the first time they made love, but it was loving and tender and satisfying. Afterwards, Charlotte lay on Nick's chest and made circles in the hair on his belly.

"Are you disappointed," she asked him.

"Never," Nick answered, running his fingers through her hair. "You are still the most amazingly sexy woman I've ever met, and nothing will change that. Now, you'd better try to get some sleep before the princess wakes up. She may not take kindly to the fact that I touched her chuckwagon, so I'd expect her to be hungrier than normal."

Charlotte closed her eyes and quickly drifted off to sleep. In fact, she slept so soundly that she didn't hear Quinn cry or feel Nick leave the bed to get her. When she did open her eyes, the first sound she heard was Nick singing to Quinn, the song Pop used to sing to him.

"Lawnmower, lawnmower, lawnmower,
Lawnmower, lawnmower, Lou…,
Lawnmower, lawnmower, lawnmower,

Lawnmower, lawnmower, Lou…,
Lawnmower, lawnmower, lawnmower,
Lawnmower, lawnmower, Lou…,
Lawnmower, lawnmower, lawnmower,
Oh, how I love you."

Charlotte smiled. How could you not love a man like that?

Chapter 97

Now

Quinn was three months old on the Sunday afternoon when Nick got up to answer the knocking on the door. He stood there for a moment not saying anything, but a familiar voice from outside made Charlotte look up.

"I'm Martin Riggs of Olde Florida Bank," said the voice. "This is Brad Huddleston. We'd like to see Charlotte if she's available."

Shit! Shit! Shit! thought Charlotte. This couldn't be good. She hadn't seen Martin or Brad in a year, and now they were here knocking on her door… and on a Sunday!

Still holding her sleeping baby, Charlotte said to Nick, "It's fine, let them come in."

"You look well, Charlotte," Martin told her first thing. "Motherhood agrees with you."

Charlotte nodded, deciding that whatever news they came to share, she wasn't going to make it easy on them. They fired her for heavens sakes! And even though everything had worked out, it still hurt to think that because she supported Carol, the bank had let her go.

Charlotte watched Brad squirm a little and knew this was hard on him. As Becca's big brother, he had watched her grow up, and then he had hired her at the bank. He had also been the one to tell her the bank was terminating her, and Charlotte still hurt from that decision. But as much as she wanted to tune them out, she had always had good manners, so she introduced them to Nick and offered them a seat.

"All the employees of Olde Florida wanted to do something for you, Charlotte," Brad stammered. "We didn't know what you might need. So, instead we started a savings account for Quinn. Becca gave me the information she had, but I'll need you to complete this paperwork if you would."

Charlotte looked at the document and her eyes about popped out of her head. "Ten thousand dollars, Brad? I didn't have that many friends at the bank."

Martin Riggs cleared his throat, and Charlotte realized that he had involved some of the bank's upper echelon to arrive at that figure.

"This is very kind of you gentlemen, but totally unnecessary." She showed the document to Nick, knowing that he was having a hard time keeping his cool.

"Please accept it, Charlotte," Brad spoke up. "Think of it as a start on Quinn's college savings."

Charlotte looked at Nick and when he nodded his agreement, she replied to her visitors. "Thank you. On Quinn's behalf, Nick and I accept your generous gift. But surely you didn't come all this way on a Sunday afternoon to bring paperwork that could have been sent in the mail?"

"I'm not going to beat around the bush anymore, Charlotte," Martin said, getting up from his chair. "We want you back. Olde Florida made a colossal mistake when they let you go, and we want to rectify it now."

You could have heard a pin drop in the room after Martin Riggs' confession. Charlotte was too dumbstruck to talk, and Nick looked as if he wanted to punch something or someone.

Finally, she spoke. "I don't understand, Martin," she told him. "The bank said I was a liability, and now, a year later they want to say 'Oops,' and expect I'll drop everything and come running back?"

"No, that's not what anyone is saying. But I will tell you this," Martin addressed Charlotte. "You were the best damn thing that happened to Olde Florida in a long time, and I messed up big time by not seeing your perspective with Carol. We've had three commercial bankers in the Anna Maria office since you left, and not one of them did the job you did. Two left for other financial institutions, and one transferred within the company, but we could put ten people in that office, and it still wouldn't work."

Martin walked over closer to Charlotte before making his final plea. "The employees, the customers, the community, they're all loyal to you, and unless you come back, I'm afraid that office won't survive. They need you Charlotte, and I need you too, so all I ask is that you think about it."

Charlotte shook her head. The words Martin said were all she had dreamed of hearing, but that was before Quinn. She had a new purpose and a new vision now, and she wouldn't turn her back on it because Olde Florida was finally willing to admit its mistake.

Putting Quinn in Nick's arms, Charlotte gathered all her courage to tell them, "Thanks, but no thanks," when Nick spoke up.

"She'll think about it."

Chapter 98
Now

Charlotte was seething as Nick escorted Martin and Brad out of the house, yet she had no idea what to do. Was she mad at Nick for telling Martin she would consider going back to work, or was she mad at Martin for even offering? If Quinn hadn't been sleeping, she would have screamed to let off her pent-up frustration.

When Nick came back into the room, he walked straight to her, but when he tried to put his arms around her, Charlotte pushed him away.

"Do you want to tell me what's going on with you, Charlotte?" Nick quizzed. "Am I the bad guy here?"

"I don't know what you are, but I don't appreciate you putting words in my mouth or making decisions for me," she spat. "You know as well as I do that I can't leave Quinn, so why not just let me cut my ties with Olde Florida and be done with them?"

"Because that's not what you want," Nick responded softly. "They hurt you when they let you go. I understand that, but I also know that you loved the job, and deep down, you want to go back. All I said was you'd think about it, not that you would accept."

Charlotte didn't want to cry but postpartum hormones were raging inside of her, and she couldn't push them down. "How can you know what I want, Nick?" she continued to argue. "You were only part of my life at the bank for a few weeks, so don't tell me you know me better than I know myself. I wouldn't have lost my job in the first place if it wasn't for the way you treated Carol. Even you've admitted that was a mistake so don't try to tell me what I want."

Nicks eyes turned dark, as close to navy as possible, and Charlotte knew she'd gone too far. She hadn't meant to bring up Carol again.

She'd been over that hurt for months, but her life was here now, with him and their child, wasn't it?

"Nick," she said walking toward him. "I didn't mean...."

Before she could finish her sentence, Quinn began to cry, so instead of trying to soothe her husband, she went straight to her daughter.

That night, for the first night since their marriage, they didn't talk and cuddle in bed, didn't even say "I love you," or kiss each other goodnight. Both stayed on their own sides, as close to the edge as possible.

Chapter 99

Now

Gran always said things looked brighter in the morning, and she was right. Charlotte hadn't slept much the night before, and she doubted if Nick had either, but when she woke up, they were both in the middle of their big bed. Nick's front to her back, just like normal.

Charlotte tried to turn over gently, hoping Nick would stay asleep, but as soon as she did, she realized that his blue eyes were staring right at her. Without saying a word, she reached up and ran her fingers over the dark stubble on his chin, trying to come up with the right words to say. She knew that Quinn would wake up any minute, and she wanted to talk with him first.

"I was out of line last night, Nick," Charlotte started. "Having Martin and Brad come by yesterday was such a shock and then for Martin to offer me my job back, I guess I went a little crazy."

"Just a little," he teased, pulling her closer. "I wasn't trying to speak for you Charlotte, I was buying you some time to really think things over, but I'm sorry if you thought otherwise."

"The thing is, sometimes when I'm nursing Quinn, I start to wonder what's going on at the bank, and then I look at her beautiful face, and I'm ashamed of myself. She's smiling now, and she wiggles when she hears my voice. How could I go back to work and miss a minute of that?"

"Do you think it's not hard for me to leave every morning, knowing that I'm missing moments with her that I'll never get back? I know it would be difficult, but we can make it work if you want it to. But, you're right, it is your decision."

"Speaking of her beautiful face," Charlotte told him, "I think Miss Quinn is waking up. I'll get her changed and bring her in here to feed her, okay? I think she likes starting her mornings out with her daddy."

"And her daddy doesn't like the way we ended things last night. I don't ever want to go to bed angry like that again," Nick said to her. "Promise me that we won't."

"I promise," Charlotte said with a soft kiss, "and I also promise never to bring up the situation with Carol again. That's over and done with, and it wasn't fair for me to throw it in your face."

Quinn had a dry diaper and a smile on her face when Charlotte took her in to Nick. He kissed her and blew raspberries on her tummy while Charlotte opened her gown and got ready to nurse. It was obvious that the baby was hungry because once Charlotte's nipple found her mouth, she chowed down. Every so often, she looked at her daddy just to make sure he was still there.

"Do you think her eyes will stay blue?" Nick asked as he watched his girls together.

"I'm not sure," Charlotte replied honestly "She looks just like you, so I would think so."

"And here I was, going to say she looked just like you," Nick smiled.

"Her eyes are blue, and her hair is dark," Charlotte said. "I'm thinking this is a Greyson baby all the way. And think about it, do you really want two women with redheaded tempers in the house?"

Nick pretended to be horrified when he replied, "I do not." Secretly though, he would have loved his daughter to be a replica of the woman he adored. He gave them both a kiss and headed to the shower, thankful that the morning turned out much better than he had expected.

Chapter 100

Now

A week later Charlotte called Becca's brother and asked for a phone conference with him and Martin Riggs to discuss the possibility of her returning to Olde Florida Bank. She and Nick had talked about it at length, and in the end, he had been right. She missed her job and wanted another opportunity with it.

"Charlotte, I'm so glad you called," Martin told her. "I want to make this right, for you and for the company."

"I haven't agreed to come back," she told the men firmly, "I just want to hear your offer, and then Nick and I will talk it over and I'll get back with you."

"I have to say," Martin told her, "I'm happy that Nick recovered from his injuries and that the two of you worked out your differences. Family is what life is all about, Charlotte, but I still think you can balance being a wife and mother with being a market president for Olde Florida."

And there it was, what she was hoping to hear. "So, I'd return in my old position?" she questioned, wanting to make sure there was no confusion.

"The only thing that would change is your salary," Brad chimed in, "because we owe you a big raise."

Charlotte wasn't sure how to broach the subject of time to either leave to feed Quinn or have a private area for pumping breastmilk, so she was glad when Brad brought it up for her.

"It's the law, Charlotte, that we provide a private area and time for nursing mothers to take care of things, so please don't let that affect your decision," Brad told her. "Olde Florida respects a mother's rights."

They talked for about twenty minutes more, and Charlotte told them she would have a decision by the end of the week. When they hung up, her heart was light and free, and she knew she wanted to take the job if only she could bring herself to leave her little girl.

After dinner that night, with Quinn fed and fast asleep in her crib, Nick sat Charlotte down and asked about the call.

"So, when do you start?" he smiled, knowing what his wife wanted, even if she wouldn't admit it.

"I didn't accept yet, Nick," she said, twirling a long curl around her fingers. "I told them we would discuss their offer and make a decision together."

"I appreciate that, I really do, but I support whatever you decide. If you want this, Charlotte, you need to at least give it a try," he said, trying to calm her fears. "There's nothing that says this job is forever or that you can't leave it if it isn't what you're hoping for."

Charlotte nodded and let him pull her into his lap. "The only demand I have is that I don't lose that wanton woman who's finally come back to me. Don't get me wrong, I like the sweet stuff occasionally, but I really love it when the vixen in you comes out."

"Demand?" she grinned. "Let's change that word to concession."

"So, you're taking the job then, right?" Nick asked.

"If we can work out day care or a sitter for Quinn, then yes, I want to at least give it a try."

"The school year ends next week, so I'll be able to be with her most of the summer. But I think I have it covered for times when I can't." Nick told her, with a sly smile. "I wasn't supposed to tell you, but your mom and Thomas have bought a house on the island so they can be closer to you and Quinn. They're moving here from Arizona."

"They're going to leave the artist colony and move here? What about Carol and their work?" Charlotte asked.

"Apparently, Chad asked Carol to move with him to his new assignment in Hawaii, and she said yes. As far as their work, your mom said they could do that anywhere if they have enough room. The house they've purchased is huge. So," Nick said, "how do you feel about that?"

"My mom was never very maternal, Nick," Charlotte reasoned. "What makes you think she would want to help out with Quinn so I can go back to work?"

"Because I asked her, that's why," Nick said with frustration. "People change, Charlotte. Your mom is older now and maybe she wants a chance to give Quinn what she didn't give you. But it's your call. They're moving here regardless, but if you don't want them helping with Quinn so you can go back to work, we'll find someone else."

Charlotte thought for about two seconds before answering. "I'm going to go call my mom, and if I like what she has to say, I'll call Brad in the morning."

Before getting off Nick's lap she gave him a long, deep kiss and said, "Thank you for being such an understanding husband. Now give me ten minutes to talk with my mother and then meet me in the bedroom. That's where I left my inner vixen."

Chapter 101
NOW

Two weeks later, the morning bright and sunny on Anna Maria Island, Charlotte knew her day of reckoning was here. She had put off trying on any of her work clothes, hoping she could lose a few pounds, but after only two outfits, she realized she was fighting a hopeless battle.

Nick brought Quinn into the bedroom to see what mommy was up to only to wish that he hadn't. Charlotte was lying on the bed, trying to zip up a pair of pants, and even he could tell it wasn't going to work. Dresses and skirts were scattered on the floor, and when Quinn started jabbering, Charlotte looked up, mortified for Nick to see her like this.

"Houston, we have a problem," she said, trying to keep the panic out of her voice. "In two days, I have to walk into the bank looking like the polished, professional market president I once was, and nothing I have will fit my fat ass or my humongous boobs. Seriously, Nick, nothing."

Holding his happy child in front of him so that Charlotte couldn't see the laugh that was trying to escape, he sat down on the bed and tried to comfort her.

"The last time we had a catastrophe like this, you went shopping with Becca. But since we don't have time for a trip to New Smyrna, how about a trip to the outlet mall instead?" Nick asked her. "I know you like all those expensive, high end stores, but surely there's something at Ellenton you'd like?"

Charlotte sat up, causing what little bit of the zipped-up pants she was wearing to totally rip. "See," she said grumpily, "this is what you and your super sperm did to me."

Quinn must have noticed a change in her mother's voice, because she immediately burst into tears, which made Charlotte feel awful.

"Come here beautiful," she soothed her fussing daughter. "I love Daddy's super sperm. Well, I love what came from it, anyway. So, stop crying and Daddy will take us shopping, and we can buy all kinds of pretties!"

Nick shook his head when he realized his four-month-old daughter had gone from crying to laughing in less than a minute.

"Un-fricking believable," he laughed. "It was bad enough I have to live with one shopaholic diva, and now I have two?"

"Not have to, Nick," Charlotte corrected "You're privileged to. You get to live with two shopaholic divas. Now if you'll get the princess into some clean clothes, I'll change, and we can go." She leaned up and kissed his cheek, but when he turned to go, she swatted his rear.

"You'll find that shopping makes me frisky," she said with a wink, and then started looking through her closet for something "shopping appropriate."

Chapter 102

Now

It was early enough in the morning that the Ellenton Outlet Mall wasn't overly busy, so Nick hoped they could go in a couple of stores, get what Charlotte needed, and go home. Wrong! Charlotte wanted to go into every fancy named store, and within an hour he couldn't tell you if he was in Ann Taylor or the Saks Fifth Avenue Outlet.

Quinn was being good as gold, strapped in her baby carrier on Nick's chest. He offered to take her on a walk to give Charlotte time to actually shop. They arranged a time and place to meet, and he took off.

When he walked by The Children's Place, Nick couldn't help but be drawn to all the pretty things for little girls in the window. Finding the door, he entered in to a world of tiny clothes that he didn't even know existed. Right away a young associate stepped in to help him, because who wouldn't want to help a tall, sexy man, especially one holding a baby?

Not quite sure what to do with the attention the young woman was giving to him and Quinn, Nick mentioned his wife was outside, but she didn't seem to hear him. He was just about to mention Charlotte again when he looked out the window, and there she stood. But it wasn't seeing Charlotte that concerned him, but the woman with blonde curls standing in front of her had Nick's blood pressure spiraling out of control.

Throwing the items that were in his hands to the sales associate he said, "I've got to go," and he rushed out of the store just in time to see Charlotte put her arms around the one person in the world he figured she hated, her long-time nemesis, and the person most responsible for their twelve lost years; Ashley Marshall.

Nick stopped in his tracks, not at all sure what to do. The last time he had seen Ashley, she had been half naked on her knees in front of him, and he cringed as he remembered that night. She had overheard him talking to Noah about a special surprise he had for Charlotte and had intervened by making it look like she and Nick were getting ready for some extracurricular fun. When Charlotte, still going by her childhood nickname of Lottie had walked in, Ashley had taunted her by saying, "Get lost, Lottie Loser."

But now here was his wife, his soulmate, and the one true love of his life, hugging Ashley like she was a long-lost friend. Nick cleared his throat to let them know he was there. "Charlotte?" he asked guardedly.

"Nick," Charlotte said sweetly, "you remember Ashley Marshall, don't you?"

Nick looked at his wife and then looked at the blonde, wondering if he was on some kind of hidden camera show. "Uh, sure," he said without commitment. "How are you, Ashley?"

He noticed how red her face had become, obviously remembering the Senior Sendoff horror, but it also looked like she'd been crying. He was trying to think of something polite to say when Ashley spoke up.

"Nick," she said, almost in a whisper, "I was just telling Charlotte how sorry I was about everything that happened when we were in school. I was a different person then, but I've changed a lot, and I'm so very sorry. I was always jealous of Lottie, her grades, how pretty she was, just about everything. I thought if I could take you away from her, I'd feel better about myself. But you were too loyal for any of my tricks, and nothing I did ruined your friendship, until the Sendoff."

For the twelve years he and Lottie were apart, Nick had thought a lot about what he would say to Ashley if he ever saw her again, but the words that came out of his mouth were not at all what he expected. "It was a longtime ago, Ashley," he told her. "Charlotte and I have everything we ever dreamed of, so if she can forgive you, I guess I can too."

Charlotte reached up and pulled her now sleeping baby from the carrier on Nick's chest and introduced her to Ashley. "And this is

Quinn," she said, not able to hold back a huge smile, "the joy of our life."

"She's beautiful," Ashley said, reaching out to touch the bundle in Charlotte's arms. "Congratulations, I'm so glad everything worked out for you."

There didn't seem to be anything left to say. Ashley told them goodbye and walked away. Nick put his arm around his wife, and with their baby between them, held her close.

"I don't know what all happened there, but I've got to tell you I'm pretty much in awe right now," Nick said. "Ashley sure looks the same, but her spirit is definitely different."

"Things changed for her after graduation, Nick. Her parents moved away, went bankrupt, and lost everything. She had to drop out of college, and the only job she could get was as a waitress. At the restaurant one night she served a pastor, and it changed her. She turned her life over to God and ended up marrying the pastor. The Ashley we knew doesn't exist anymore, but there's a new, happier Ashley in her place." Charlotte stopped long enough for Nick to assimilate all the information she had given him.

"Ashley and her husband are in the mission field now, and she's doing her best to ask forgiveness of anyone she's wronged. Our lives didn't turn out like we hoped when we were young, but neither did Ashley's. The thing is, I think we're all pretty lucky that they turned out better."

"We're more than lucky, Lottie," he told her, kissing her head. "We're blessed. But tell me, how did you get all of that in the few minutes you were out here?"

"We're women, Sweetheart," she told him with a smile.

Chapter 103

Now

Nick woke-up about four o'clock on Monday morning, and the first thing he noticed was that Charlotte wasn't beside him in bed. He didn't hear Quinn crying, so he tiptoed into her room to make sure she was okay. And there he found his wife, rocking their sleeping child, trying to sing her the Lawnmower song while tears streamed down her face.

"Honey," he said, kneeling down in front of the chair, "is Quinn okay?"

Charlotte nodded and tried to wipe her nose with the sleeve of her robe.

"Are you okay?" he asked quietly, even though he knew the answer to his question.

"How am I going to leave her, Nick?" she sobbed. "What's she going to think when she wakes up from her nap and realizes I'm not here. How's she going to feel when you stick that rubber nipple in her mouth when she expects it to be me? You think I'm so strong, but I'm not."

Nick wanted to put Quinn back in her crib so he could hold and comfort his wife, but something told him it was not a smart idea. Instead he wrapped his long arms around both of them and just held them that way. Finally, Charlotte laid her head on his shoulder, and he could feel her start to relax.

"I can't understand exactly how a mother feels leaving her child for the first time," he said cautiously, "but I can promise you that while Quinn and I will miss you, we'll be fine. I'll have lunch ready around eleven o'clock so you can come home and eat, and Quinn can nurse. When I have to give her a bottle, I'll put your IU sleep shirt beside her so she can smell her mommy and taste her, even if the receptacle feels different."

That made Charlotte smile, so she got up, put Quinn back in her bed, and took Nick by the hand.

"Where are we going?" he asked.

"I need to work through my grief," she said with a grin, and Nick got her drift pretty quickly.

By seven, Charlotte was showered, her hair in a professional bun on top of her head, sitting in her robe nursing her sweet baby girl. When Quinn was content, she fell away from Charlotte's breast, and Nick took her from her mother's arms so he could burp her.

Charlotte finished getting ready and put on the new light blue Banana Republic suit she had purchased in Nick's honor. With her tan Louboutin heels and new Coach purse, she looked and felt once again like a market president of Olde Florida Bank.

The last thing she did was put on her locket from Gran while lifting up a prayer that Gran would watch over Nick and Quinn and would give her the strength to make it through the day.

After hugging and kissing Nick and Quinn goodbye, Charlotte stepped out the door of her little pink cottage into the warm Florida sunshine and said, "I'm Charlotte Luce-Greyson, first female market president of Olde Florida Bank, and the youngest in the bank's one hundred-year history, and I can do this." And of course, she did.

The End

Note from the author

Dearest Readers,

This book is dedicated to you. I can't thank you enough for all of the wonderful words of encouragement you've shared with me, and it's because of them, and you, that I keep writing.

I hope Nick and Charlotte's stories have touched your heart as much as they have mine. Writing the AMI Series has been one of the biggest joys of my life and being able to share them with you is just icing on the cake!

Charlotte found her Happy Ending, and her fairytale came true, so while there may be another book in the series someday, it will not be centered around her. She and Nick may make an appearance, but expect another heroine and hero to emerge.

Thank you so much for taking this journey with me, and as always, I ask that you leave a review on Amazon and Goodreads. I can only perfect my craft by knowing your thoughts.

Wishing all of you the Happy Ending that Charlotte found,

As Always…

Dana L

The song Lawnmower, that Nick sings to Quinn in chapter 96 is one that my dad made up and sang to my brother, Tom, when he was a baby. My dad was an engineer and loved all things mechanical, so naturally a lawnmower was right up his alley.

When I was born, the song was brought out of storage, and it became a tradition with my girls as well. Last week when my two-year-old granddaughter was visiting, she sang it to me while playing my grandmother's piano, and I knew it had to be sung to Baby Quinn. My dad didn't live to see my dream of becoming a published author come true, but I know he would be proud of me and pleased that his legacy lives on.

Follow Dana to hear the latest.

Website: DanaLBrownBooks.com

Facebook: @DanaLBrownAuthor

Twitter: @DanaLBrownBooks

Instagram: @dana_brown_author

Email:info@danalbrownbooks.com

Amazon Author page:amazon.com/author/danalbrown